"Okay, Dr. Hartman, let's get to work," Hope said briskly.

With her fingertips she wiped moisture from the corners of her eyes.

Charles leaned back in his chair as if to distance himself from her. "Get to work on what?" he asked cautiously.

She gave him her sweetest smile. "Our friendship. It's clear that you need me, Charlie, and I've decided to take the job." She offered her right hand so he could shake it.

He turned his head and looked at her sideways. "Not a good idea," he warned, ignoring her hand.

She leaned forward, taunting him, her eyes boring into his. "Scared?"

His head jerked slightly and he gave her a thin-lipped smile. "Of a Girl Scout? Hardly."

She again extended her hand and this time it was clasped briefly. As he started to withdraw, Hope impulsively tightened her grip. "You won't regret it, Charlie."

Books by Brenda Coulter

Love Inspired

Finding Hope #216

BRENDA COULTER

Married at nineteen to a ridiculously patient man, Brenda Coulter worked for two banks and two oil companies before impulsively ditching the office routine to study astronomy at Ohio State University. Just over a year later she had an even better idea, so she became a mother and turned full-time homemaker.

Her two teenage boys were still works-in-progress as the year 2000 drew to a close, and it was then that Brenda stumbled across her first inspirational romance novel. Instantly captivated by the idea of a love-conquers-all story with a golden thread of faith woven through the plot, she decided to try her hand at writing one.

Now she finds enormous satisfaction in writing for several hours each day, in part because fictional characters are so much easier to reason with than teenage boys.

Besides, her husband is becoming a very good cook.

FINDING HOPE

BRENDA COULTER

Love Inspired.

Published by Steeple Hill Books™

STEEPLE HILL BOOKS

Steeple
Hill™

ISBN 0-373-87223-2

FINDING HOPE

Copyright © 2003 by Brenda Coulter

This edition published by arrangement with Steeple Hill Books.

® and TM are trademarks of Steeple Hill Books, used under license. Trademarks indicated with ® are registered in the United States Patent and Trademark Office, the Canadian Trade Marks Office and in other countries.

Visit us at www.steeplehill.com

Printed in U.S.A.

You will seek me and find me when you seek me with all your heart.

—*Jeremiah* 29:13

To Mikel,
who has always deserved better
but still won't admit it;

and to Tristan and Ian,
who have emptied our bank account
and filled our hearts.

Chapter One

"Oh, now, that's just perfect!"

Behind the wheel of his silver Mercedes, Dr. Charles Hartman swore viciously. Then he flung open his door and leaped out to confront the driver of the older-model Ford that had just run into him. "Are you out of your mind?" he bellowed.

Although the hospital parking lot was nowhere near full, this idiot had come screeching around the corner on two wheels, making a beeline for the space right next to him, just as though there weren't a hundred others to choose from. Charles was backing out at the time, and his Mercedes had been smacked neatly on the left taillight.

Now his jaw clenched in exasperation as the driver of the Ford, a young woman, hurtled towards him. A slender but sturdy-looking female in faded jeans and a turquoise T-shirt, her long almost-black hair was caught up in a bouncy ponytail. In the brilliant midday sun her dark blue eyes sparkled with tears.

That she was crying did nothing at all to lessen

Charles's rage. Sheer exhaustion was effectively dousing that fire. He meant to stay furious, but when he turned to slam his car door, a shooting pain in his lower back caused his shoulders to sag. He sighed and the anger leaked out of him like air from a punctured tire.

The past twenty-four hours at the hospital had been grueling. Two of the lives he'd battled for had been wrenched from his grasp. It was now barely one o'clock in the afternoon, but all he wanted was for this day to be over. If he could reengage his weary brain long enough to string together a few coherent sentences, he'd give this careless kid a stern lecture and be on his way.

"I'm so awfully sorry!" the girl wailed. "It was completely my fault. Here—take this," she said cryptically, thrusting a small object at him. "I have to go!"

His hands came up reflexively, trapping a thin leather wallet against his chest. His eyebrows drew together and his mouth fell open as he gazed at the lunatic girl.

Charles was virtually never at a loss for words, especially acerbic ones, but just now he was too fatigued to come up with any of the caustic remarks he was known for. His tired mind worked to understand what the young woman expected him to do with her wallet.

She was babbling as she backed away from him. "Put it under the front seat and lock my car, okay? I'm so sorry! I'll pay for it, I promise. But I really have to go now!"

Still openmouthed, he watched dumbly as she pivoted on the balls of her feet and sprinted away from him. The girl had some speed, he noted absently, but then she was all legs. Her dark ponytail bobbed wildly as she dashed across the street, charged up the steps and crashed through Lakeside Hospital's main entrance, heading straight for the information desk.

Charles stared at the wallet in his hands. What was he

supposed to do with it? Did she expect him to copy the information on her driver's license and report the accident? He had neither the time nor the patience for that.

Curious, he opened the wallet. According to her license she was twenty-three-year-old Hope Evans. No middle name. Five feet, five inches. Brown hair and blue eyes.

A stickler for accuracy, he'd have said dark chestnut hair and sapphire eyes. Not that it mattered, of course; she'd have to be a good ten years older and in a much higher tax bracket before he'd have looked at her with anything approaching masculine interest.

It was a nicer picture than what was usually found on a driver's license. She was smiling. And while she wasn't what he would have called beautiful, there was a definite sweetness to her face. Not that "sweetness" was a quality that had ever appealed to him.

In addition to the license, her wallet contained a credit card, a University of Chicago student ID and two one-dollar bills. Nothing else.

He inspected her car, but apart from an almost microscopic dent and a dab of his own car's silver paint, the Ford was undamaged.

Charles leaned against his own car and closed his eyes. With his thumb and index finger he pinched the bridge of his nose. He was almost grateful for the steady throbbing of his head because it helped take his mind off the stabbing pain in his back.

He opened his eyes, thoughtfully tapping his chin with the wallet. Directly in his line of sight was the parking attendant's booth, on the side of which the lot's hourly fees were clearly posted. A practical man, Charles wondered how the girl expected to pay for parking here.

He reached for his own wallet. A quick look inside revealed that, like the girl, he was down to his last two bills. His were in a more convenient denomination, however: he had two fifties. He removed one and folded it around her one-dollar bills.

She had asked him to leave the wallet in her car, but he couldn't bring himself to do that. This was Chicago, and not the very best neighborhood, either. Heaving a mighty sigh, he turned back towards the hospital. Maybe somebody at the information desk would remember which patient she had asked for.

He dragged himself across the street and up the steps, resenting with every footfall the young gazelle who had lightly leaped up this same hill just a minute ago.

Well, *she* wasn't thirty-five. And it was a safe bet that she hadn't been on her feet all night long and all morning, too, doing back-to-back surgeries on three people who had been in the wrong place at the wrong time. Neither had she watched helplessly as the life ebbed out of a gunshot police officer and then just a couple of hours later, a teenage pedestrian hit by a speeding motorist.

Charles sighed again. It galled him that some lives just couldn't be saved, not even by a genius like himself.

He gave an involuntary grunt as he fought a gusting early-May wind for the right to pull open one of the tall glass doors of the hospital's main entrance. He thought grimly that somebody in building support should be informed that the doors were far too heavy for old people, sick people and bone-weary trauma surgeons to manage. He made a mental note to use the handicapped entrance the next time he was this tired.

The elderly volunteer at the information desk didn't remember which patient the ponytailed menace had asked for, but the room number stuck in her mind because it happened to be the last four digits of her daughter's telephone number. She was eager to discuss this remarkable coincidence with Charles, but he thanked her gruffly and headed up to room 6120.

Twice he was waylaid by colleagues who didn't sufficiently grasp the concept of being "off duty." It was some fifteen minutes before he poked his head into the room where the girl was visiting an old man.

"Excuse me—Ms. Evans? May I speak with you?"

She looked puzzled but she nodded politely. He backed out of the doorway and waited in the hall.

She followed immediately. "Yes?"

It was apparent she had forgotten his face. Without a word, he presented her wallet.

She flushed. "Oh, it's you! I'm so sorry about your car. It was all my fault, completely my fault."

"I agree," he said dryly, wondering how many more times she was planning to say that. "But it's not important. Forget about it." He turned away.

"But it *is* important!" she called after him. He didn't look back, but she followed him, chattering maddeningly. "Please wait—I feel just awful. I was in a terrible hurry, so I didn't take time to look, but I know there was some damage. I felt a nasty crunch and I definitely heard some smashing and splintering and…"

Here she paused to take a breath, and the resulting two seconds of silence were deeply treasured by Charles. He kept walking, but she stuck to him like sun-warmed bubblegum to the sole of a shoe. "I've done it before," she confessed, "so I know exactly what those sounds mean."

He stopped suddenly, and he heard a syncopated shuffle that told him she'd almost run into the back of him. He turned, fixing her with an incredulous stare. It was a chilling look that could send the toughest ER nurse scurrying for cover, but for some reason it didn't faze this college girl. Although he had her wide-eyed attention, she wasn't exactly cowering before him.

He must be losing his touch. He tried again, this time employing the deadly quiet voice that could reduce thick-skinned surgery residents to quivering blobs of jelly. "You make a *habit* of this?"

Her heart-shaped face registered surprise at his sharpness, but after regarding him for a couple of seconds her features relaxed and she broke into an impish grin. "Last time I got a Jaguar," she said proudly. "You're a Mercedes, aren't you? I have an unerring eye for quality, don't you think?"

Her screwball humor knocked him off balance. He felt his lips twitch but he was careful not to smile. "What did you do to the Jag?" he asked before he could stop himself.

Her grin faded. "Well, I took out a headlight, although I'm not certain it was entirely my fault. But the driver was an attorney with an amazing vocabulary and he ripped me up pretty thoroughly with a lot of words that made me blush." Smiling again, she slid her wallet into the back pocket of her jeans, the masculine gesture oddly accentuating the sweet femininity she exuded. "You're much nicer than he was."

It wasn't often that people accused Charles of being nice. It wasn't true and it annoyed him. Most people tagged him as impatient or abrasive. Those were pretty fair assessments, he had to admit. But this irritating girl was smiling brightly, silently insisting that he was a nice guy, a regular sweetheart.

He wasn't.

He didn't return the smile. "Excuse me," he said abruptly, showing her his back again.

"Please wait!" she begged. She was beside him instantly, detaining him with a hand on his forearm. "I was flippant with you just now, but I'm really sorry about what I did to your car. It's just that I was distracted. My adopted grandfather's here, and I've been out of town for three days, so I just found out he had another heart attack.

I was in a rush to see him and I think I was crying a little, and—well, I was careless and I hit you, but now you know why I had to run off. Gramps is better now. I was just talking with him. Anyway, thank you for bringing my wallet. May I know your name?''

"Dr. Hartman," he said shortly. He was desperate to get away from this chatterbox. "It's okay about the car." He looked pointedly at the hand on his arm and it was immediately withdrawn. He gave her a curt nod and walked away, rolling his eyes and grunting impatiently as she called, "Thank you, Dr. Hartman. I'll remember you in my prayers!"

He was halfway to the elevator lobby when Dr. West, the hospital's chief of surgery, approached him. "Hartman! They said you were gone already. Can you spare a minute?"

He couldn't, but he did. In fact he spared almost five of them. When he was finally free to make another bid for the elevators he noticed Hope Evans in front of the coffee machine. As she reached for the wallet in her back pocket he averted his eyes and quickened his pace, desperate to escape.

But she had spotted him. "Goodbye, Dr. Hartman!" she trilled. "Have a lovely day!"

Too late for that. Ignoring her, he kept walking. He had almost gained the polished-steel sanctuary of an elevator when he heard her double-time footsteps behind him. A tidal wave of annoyance washed over him as she called his name. He stopped, but he didn't turn. His head rolled back in a slow-motion whiplash and he stared hopelessly at the white-tiled ceiling.

When she caught up to him she spoke softly, wonderingly. "Why did you put a fifty-dollar bill in my wallet?"

Dr. Hartman always resented being caught in the act of anything foolish people might mistake for kindness.

He regarded her through narrowed eyes. "I happened to notice you didn't have enough to pay for parking," he said roughly.

Her long ponytail swung from side to side as she gave her head a vigorous shake. "It was very kind of you, but I can't take it. Especially since I hit your car."

He ignored the bill she held out to him. "How were you planning to pay for it, then?" He had no idea why he asked; he was certainly in no mood to chat with this ditzy female.

Bright spots of color appeared on her cheeks, making her look like a painted china doll. Her milky complexion and her remarkable blue eyes, framed by delicate brows and fringed with long black lashes, enhanced the effect. "I was going to ask if I could pay them tomorrow," she said, obviously embarrassed by the admission. "Today I'll get a paycheck and—"

"Well, it's no business of mine," he interrupted, ruthlessly denying the sympathy her grave expression was kindling in him. "Just take the money. It's nothing to me." He would have turned away but something in her face stopped him.

"Please, Dr. Hartman." Her tone was soft, sweetly insistent. "It's something to *me*."

Aggravated by the way her dewy eyes and gentle voice were getting to him, Charles sternly reminded himself that Hope Evans was the reason he was not in bed, asleep, at this very moment. In an instant the tattered remains of his compassion shriveled up and blew away like dead leaves on a busy Chicago street corner.

"I'll admit I could use some help today," she said. "But please—will you allow me to pay you back?"

"Yes, of course," he lied. He shifted his weight to one foot and pressed a hand against the small of his back, arching against another spasm of pain.

He saw a look of concern flit across the girl's face, but she caught her bottom lip between her teeth and made no unwelcome inquiries as to his health. She tucked an escaped strand of hair behind her ear. "I'll return your money tomorrow. Okay?"

"Fine," he said, moving away from her and stepping onto an empty elevator.

"But how will I find you?" she persisted.

If he was lucky, she wouldn't. Ever again. "You can leave it for me at that desk," he said, nodding towards a nurses' station. He pressed a button and watched with intense satisfaction as the elevator doors closed between Hope Evans and himself.

The elevator didn't appear to be moving, so he touched the button again. As he leaned his forehead against the panel and allowed his heavy eyelids to droop, the elevator lurched violently, throwing him off balance and slamming his cheek against the cold steel edge of the door opening.

Squeezing his eyes shut, he screamed a curse as an electric current of pain ripped through his face.

When the bell announced his arrival at the ground floor, Charles reached for the keys in his pants pocket. As the door opened, he squared his shoulders and lifted his chin. Then he stepped off the elevator and slowly made his way to the handicapped exit.

Charles opened one eye and peered at his bedside clock. He'd been asleep for almost three hours. He fumbled for the ringing telephone and pulled it to his ear. Dipping into the dangerously low reserves of his energy supply, he was able to manage a fairly impressive snarl. "What *is* it?"

The small portion of his brain that was currently online calculated that, at this point, barring an extreme emergency at the hospital, any person with the slightest instinct for self-preservation would hang up and pray that Dr. Hartman didn't have caller ID.

This individual possessed no such instinct.

"Afternoon, Trey," the caller boomed. "Are you up?"

Even in his groggy state Charles could not have failed to recognize that voice, a rich baritone remarkably similar to his own. "No, Tom," the doctor growled, "I'm sound asleep. And if you're very, very lucky, in a few hours I'll wake up convinced that I merely dreamed this call."

Apparently aware that his call was about to be terminated, Thomas Hartman spoke rapidly. "I can get away from the office in another hour. Let's play squash."

"No."

"C'mon, Trey. We haven't played since last Monday. You want me to get soft?"

"I want you to get *lost*," Charles said. He hung up the telephone, switched off the ringer and closed his eyes.

An hour later he was awakened by the insistent chiming of his doorbell. Outraged, Charles whipped back the sheets and threw his long legs over the side of his bed. He knew very well who was leaning on the button, so he didn't bother to pull on his pants before he strode angrily to the door of his apartment and yanked it open. His strength spent, he allowed his weary body to sag against the doorframe. "Tom, do you *want* to die?" he asked tiredly.

"Not smart to threaten a lawyer," Tom responded. He flattened his palm against his brother's bare chest and shoved him out of the doorway. "Get your gear," he said, stepping into the apartment and pulling the door shut. "We've got a court in twenty minutes." With his thumb he pointed over his shoulder. "By the way, do you know you have a broken taillight?"

Charles had forgotten about Hope Evans until that moment. Now he felt a surge of irritation as he remembered her effusive gratitude and her unrelenting perkiness. He shuddered. "A girl hit me," he said.

Tom studied the bruise on his brother's cheek. "What on earth did you do to her?" he asked, quietly astonished.

"The girl didn't do this," Charles snapped. With his two middle fingers he gingerly explored his cheekbone, wincing at the sharp pain. "She hit my car."

"Oh." Tom seemed a little disappointed by the answer. "Then who hit *you?*"

"An elevator."

Tom eyed him skeptically. "Have you been drinking, Trey?"

Charles ignored the question because it was a stupid one. His brother knew very well that he'd given up drinking years ago when he'd started his surgical residency. A man who was continually sleep-deprived didn't need alcohol fogging his brain.

He yawned and stretched. At least his back felt better now. He padded across the wide hardwood floor in the direction of his kitchen.

"Okay, fine," said Tom, tagging along. "You can explain it to me later. Now get your stuff, will you? I have a feeling I'm going to annihilate you, finally, and I'm eager to get on with it. C'mon—I'll buy you a steak after."

Charles opened his sparkling-clean and nearly empty refrigerator to remove two small bottles of vegetable juice. He passed one to Tom and uncapped the other for himself. "All right," he said.

Suddenly the idea of wielding a racquet and sharing an enclosed court with his brother and a fast-moving rubber ball was beginning to appeal to him. Unlike the refined game of tennis, squash could get rough; especially the way Charles played it when he needed to work off some tension. And judging by the way he felt right now, today's match was likely to set new records for incivility.

Late the next morning Charles reached over a chest-high counter at Lakeside Hospital's sixth-floor nurses' station and picked up a telephone. As he tersely answered questions put to him by the caller, a nurse presented him with two phone messages. Then she lifted a large tin box from the desk and placed it on the counter before him.

He handed her the telephone and she hung it up. "This is mine?" he asked, frowning at the square, emerald-colored tin.

It was. When he pried off the lid and lifted a paper doily, his jaw dropped in amazement. Assaulted by the unmistakable scent of molasses, he stared for a long moment before he gave his head a brisk shake and replaced the lid on the tin. He then turned his attention to the messages.

Three nurses drew near and looked on with interest. He ignored them, as he always did. The rapt attention of women was no novelty to him.

His shaving mirror told him no lies. He was moderately good-looking in a rugged sort of way. Not handsome. Just over six feet tall, he had light brown hair and alert hazel eyes that were usually narrowed in some cynical contemplation. He didn't smile much, he knew. Even when he did, it was little more than a sardonic upturning of one corner of his mouth—usually the right side, although he was flexible.

But he didn't have to be handsome or charming, he thought bitterly. He could look like Notre Dame's hunchback and act like the Wicked Witch of the West's favorite brother and women would still throw themselves at him because in the end it was all about money. Specifically "old" money.

He dated frequently, but he scrupulously avoided young women and those of the middle class. Since no woman could be interested in him apart from his money, he opted to stick with the ones who were sophisticated enough not to make it so tiresomely obvious.

The nurses were circling now, showing a little more boldness than usual, but the frustratingly fascinating Dr. Hartman pretended not to notice.

He opened the box again and inhaled the deep, spicy-sweet aroma of molasses. He selected one picture-perfect oatmeal cookie and gazed reverently at it. Plump and golden brown, it was thickly studded with raisins and walnuts and—here was the stroke of brilliance, Charles thought—it was flecked with tantalizing bits of orange peel.

Silently passing the open tin to one of the nurses, he bit into his cookie. It was impossibly delicious. Coffee, he thought urgently. The phone calls could wait.

He detached the small white envelope that was taped to the lid of the tin. As he opened it and removed a neatly folded sheet of paper, something else slipped out.

Confusion gave way to annoyance as he watched a fifty-dollar bill flutter to the floor. He bent to retrieve it, stuffed it in the chest pocket of his white lab coat and scowled as he read the message.

> Dr. Hartman,
> You were wonderful about the car, but what really touched me was your concern about how I was going to pay for parking. May God reward you for your kindness.
> Sincerely,
> Hope Evans

He crumpled the note and carelessly pitched it at a wastepaper basket. It troubled him not at all that he missed.

When the greedy nurses finally surrendered the tin, Charles took another cookie and replaced the lid. He chewed slowly, fully aware that subtle magic was being worked on him. He snorted in contempt, loathing himself as he yielded.

He loved oatmeal cookies and these were by far the best he'd ever eaten. Hope Evans might be oppressively sweet, but she was also a culinary genius, and if he ever saw her again he wouldn't hesitate to tell her so.

Charles didn't smile often, but he was doing it now, with *both* sides of his mouth. He tried not to do it, because he was irked by the way the girl went on and on about his "kindness." But he just couldn't help himself.

Chapter Two

"Hello, handsome. Are you behaving yourself today?"

Careful of the oxygen and IV tubes that snaked everywhere, Hope leaned over the hospital bed to bestow a tender kiss on the old man's cool, papery forehead. When he smiled and held out a feeble hand, she scooted a chair closer to the bed and sat down. Capturing his icy hand in both of hers, she rubbed it briskly, as if by warming the one extremity she might restore health and strength to the rest of his worn-out body.

Nearly six feet tall in his younger days, John Seltzer looked small and fragile in the white expanse of the bed. He'd lost his appetite a couple of weeks ago and now he appeared to be shrinking, evaporating before Hope's eyes.

He gently reproached her. "Weren't you supposed to be at school this morning, sweetie-pie?"

She gave his hand a reassuring squeeze. "I'm on top of it, Gramps. I'll finish my course work in just three more weeks, then I'll have the whole summer to finish my thesis. I'll be able to turn that in during the fall quarter, so please don't worry. I'll make you proud."

"You always do, Hope." Faded blue eyes regarded her with obvious affection. "I couldn't be any prouder of you."

She swallowed hard and looked away from him. She might have quit school by now if it hadn't been for Gramps.

Sometimes she forgot the old man was actually no relation to her. A longtime friend of her parents, John Seltzer was a retired missionary who had come home from Africa five years ago, his health broken.

At that time, Hope's parents, both teachers, had been seeking a new challenge. Hearing God's call, they sold their small farm and purchased a two-bedroom house in a nice suburb of Chicago. Then just after Hope's high school graduation, they left to take their friend's place at a school in Africa.

They planned to return to Chicago one day, but for now Hope lived alone in their little house. Gramps resided just across the street, and Hope believed the Lord had positioned him there to comfort and guide her, especially during that first scary, lonely year on her own.

She managed a sunny smile for her friend. "Everything's fine at your place," she assured him. "I caught your paperboy this morning and asked him to stop delivering for a while."

Gramps withdrew his bony hand from hers and patted her arm. "Thank you, sweetie-pie. You run along now."

She pulled her feet up and sat cross-legged in the armless chair. "No, I want to talk, unless you're too tired."

The wrinkles in his forehead deepened. "Is something worrying you, Hope?"

"Just you," she answered truthfully. "I hate seeing you in that bed. But I have some good news." She raised her eyebrows and tilted her head back, encouraging him to guess.

His weary eyes lit up. "Have you picked up another translating job?"

Hope beamed at him, grateful that he always took pleasure in her little accomplishments. "It's a software manual. English to French, German and Spanish. It's a big job, Gramps. I'll be able to pay off the last of my undergraduate loans."

"That's my girl," he said warmly. "Smart as a whip. I don't know how you manage to keep all those languages straight."

"Well, it's a real trick to give a strictly accurate and grammatical translation when the speaker never pauses to let you catch up," she admitted. "But I can do it, Gramps—my brain actually *works* that way. I'm just beginning to understand what an incredible gift God has given me."

Foreign missionaries and international students had been frequent guests in the Evanses' home, so Hope had become interested in languages at an early age. She'd learned Spanish in elementary school, French in middle school and German in high school. Remarkably bright, she had a flair for grammar and a gift for accents. She'd picked up two more languages in college.

Her parents had given their fifth child and only daughter enough money to see her through her freshman year. Since then, she'd been able to support herself by translating documents. Working hard, Hope had ripped through college, earning her bachelor's degree in just three years. Now wrapping up work on her master's, she dreamed of traveling the world as a simultaneous interpreter.

She had accomplished a lot, but without God's gifts

and her parents' careful nurturing, she would not now be in this position to pursue her dream.

"I'm thankful for everything God has given me. My sharp mind and most of all, Mom and Dad." She gave Gramps an impulsive hug. "And you, of course. You've done more for me than you'll ever know," she said softly.

"You really are a sweetie," he said, patting her arm. "It's been a privilege to watch you spread your wings, but I'll miss my little bird when she flies away."

"I'll always return to my nest," Hope promised. "The assignments will be short-term, you know. A weeklong conference here and a three-day seminar there. Still, I imagine I'll get homesick for you."

With that thought, sadness settled around Hope like a dreary morning mist. Gramps wouldn't be around much longer, whether she stayed in Chicago or not.

To hide her melancholy she busied herself straightening his bedcovers, then took a plastic pitcher across the hall to refill it with fresh water and ice.

When she returned to his room, they talked for several minutes and then Hope encouraged him to sleep a little. She promised to return in an hour or two.

She saw the objection flicker across his face even before he opened his mouth. "No, sweetie. You don't have to—"

"I'm going to hang around for a while," she said firmly, silencing his protest. "I'm hoping your doctor will wander in before too long. There's a nice visitors' lounge just down the hall, and I've brought some work to do. So I'll see you later."

Hope sank into a comfortable wingback chair in a remote corner of the spacious lounge. Grateful to be alone in the restful greens and beiges of the room, she slipped off her penny loafers and pulled her long legs into the chair with her.

A soft sigh escaped her as she rubbed moisture from her eyes. Yes, she was sensitive. Her brothers had always teased her about her overactive tear ducts. But she had good reason to be worried about Gramps. His weak heart had just about reached the end of the road.

She wrapped her arms around one knee, drawing it to her chest. In her agitation, her body rocked slightly as she whispered a desperate prayer. "Please don't take him yet," she begged. "I know it's selfish, but he's taught me so much and I just can't do without him. Oh, please— not just yet...."

She untangled her arms and legs and got to her feet. A cup of coffee would clear her head; then she would review some of her notes while Gramps slept. She pushed her bare feet into her loafers and headed for the coffee machine just across the hall.

Approaching with quarters in hand, she groaned in dismay when one slipped from her grasp, bounced twice on the well-polished floor and rolled in a wide half circle before disappearing under the machine.

Delving into her pocket for more change, Hope became aware that someone was standing immediately behind her. "Why does the coin *always* go under the machine?" she grumbled companionably. "Do they put suction devices down there, or what?"

"I've often wondered." The deep voice floated over her head as Hope pulled her fist out of her pocket and opened it. Seeing only a useless assortment of pennies, nickels and dimes in her palm, she heaved a dramatic sigh.

"Please allow me." A masculine hand, large and long-fingered yet surprisingly graceful, fed coins to the machine.

Hope's gaze traveled up the sleeve of a white lab coat, past broad shoulders around which a stethoscope was slung, pausing to rest for the briefest moment on a shapely but unsmiling mouth before finally meeting a pair of sober hazel eyes that she recognized. "Dr. Hartman! Thank you so much."

"Not at all." Today his manner was polite if not actually friendly. "Thank you for the cookies," he said. He stepped back and showed her the green tin he held under his left arm. "Oatmeal happens to be my favorite and these are remarkably good."

She gave him a warm smile. Yesterday his harsh words had scraped her like sandpaper, but he'd been incredibly generous, for all that. He was a puzzle, this poker-faced doctor with the sharp tongue and the soft heart.

He chewed his lower lip and stared at her for several seconds, apparently considering something. "I'm taking a short break," he said at last. "Would you care to join me?"

He was just being polite, Hope realized. Trying to make up for yesterday. She ought to have let him off the hook, but the moody doctor fascinated her. She accepted his offer.

"Let's go over there," he suggested, nodding to indicate a small seating area at one end of the corridor. He handed her the cookie tin. "I'll bring the coffee. What do you take?"

"Black with one sugar, please." She turned away as he pressed the buttons on the machine.

What on earth am I doing? Hope wondered as she walked to the end of the hall. She wasn't at all interested in men and she never went on dates. So why had she just agreed to have coffee with this stranger, a man who apparently never smiled, someone who almost certainly had been hoping she'd refuse him?

She could almost hear her mother's voice. *Sweetheart, that impulsive nature of yours is going to get you into trouble.*

But it was only coffee, right? How much trouble could she get into over coffee?

After considering a comfortable-looking sofa and the two armchairs adjacent to it, Hope opted for the little bistro table and chairs because they were situated directly under a live, potted tree and in front of a sunny window. She placed the cookie tin on the table and sat, nervously tapping both feet as she looked out the window and waited.

A sturdy paper cup full of steaming coffee was set before her with a quiet, liquidy *thunk.* Smiling her thanks, she looked up as Dr. Hartman took the chair opposite her. When he turned his head briefly, she saw a purple bruise on his right cheek.

"I did that to you?" she gasped. "Oh, I'm sorry!"

"No," he said shortly. "I got knocked against the door in that ancient elevator, that's all."

That cleared up a mystery for Hope. "So *that's* what it was." She nodded sagely, then answered the question she saw in his eyes. "I was standing in front of the elevator when you got on it and after the door closed I heard something awful."

"Yes, that would have been my face shattering," he said ruefully.

She hesitated. "Um, what I heard was more like yelling."

"Ah," he said knowingly. "I imagine I said something terribly shocking?"

She nodded, trying not to smile.

Dr. Hartman opened his mouth to speak again, but his lips clamped shut as his pager signaled him. He removed the device from his coat pocket and glanced at the message. "In your dreams," he muttered. He replaced the pager and returned his attention to Hope. "Was it as bad as what the attorney in the Jag yelled at you?"

Remembering, she shuddered. "Not even close. But what you said was quite audible. An old lady who had just come around the corner gave me a look of stern disapproval."

He drummed his fingertips on the edge of the table. "Why?"

Hope lifted a shoulder and dropped it again. "Beats me. I guess I look like someone who would shout really bad words in a deep, manly voice."

He made an amused noise in his throat. "Not much, you don't." His eyes, frankly appraising, never left her face as he swallowed some coffee and set down his cup. "You look like a Girl Scout," he concluded.

His fingers were drumming again, all ten of them, and Hope guessed he already had a pretty good caffeine buzz going. She watched for a moment before realizing his quick, light movements were not random ones. "What are you playing?" she asked suddenly.

His hands stilled. "Chopin," he replied in obvious disgust. "A piece I don't even like." Leaning back in his chair, he shoved his misbehaving hands into his pockets for a time-out.

"Ever think about switching to decaf?"

"Nearly every day," he said. "How's your grandfather?"

Hope gathered her long, loose hair and flipped it behind her shoulders. "I'm worried about him, to tell you the truth. He's only sixty-seven, but his dear heart just won't go on much longer, and I'm going to miss him so much. He's not really my grandfather, just a sweet old man who's been friendly with my parents for years. They're missionaries, in Africa, and I'm pretty much alone here except for—'' She stopped abruptly. "Sorry. You didn't ask for my life story, did you?''

Ignoring the question, Dr. Hartman opened the tin and offered her a cookie. When she politely declined, he shook his head. "I just can't believe how good these are,'' he said with feeling. He bit into one with obvious relish.

Hope leaned her elbows on the table, holding her coffee cup in both hands. She blew across the surface of the hot liquid before taking a cautious sip. "So, what kind of doctor are you?'' she asked.

He smiled, tight-lipped. "I'm a surgeon. Trauma.''

Hope was interested. "You put people back together after nasty car wrecks and things like that,'' she stated.

He glanced at his watch. "I've never heard it put quite that way, but that's pretty much what I do.''

"Oh, I know what you do. You bark orders and everyone jumps and then you say arrogantly heroic things like, 'Nobody dies tonight! Not on *my* shift!'''

His startled expression tickled her. "You've said it,'' she crowed. "Haven't you?''

"You must watch an awful lot of television,'' he answered evasively. He finished his cookie and reached for another.

"You're an adrenaline junkie. You make rapid-fire decisions and you're never wrong. You don't have any patience with people who are tentative and you're not terribly forgiving of mistakes. You work too much and you don't get enough sleep and you drink way too much coffee.''

He eyed her warily. "Where did you pick all that up?''

"I just spent three days with a good friend who is an ER nurse in Cleveland. She has lots of stories about ER physicians and trauma surgeons.''

"I'll bet." His flat tone said clearly that he wasn't interested in hearing any of the stories.

Hope was talking too much. She always did. Her brothers had told her so often enough. She looked out the window and waited for Dr. Hartman to say something.

He didn't. He, too, stared out the window.

Sneaking a look at his profile, Hope was struck by the way the brilliant sunlight bounced off the subtle waves of his honey-brown hair. At the zoo she'd seen lions with coats of that color, not quite golden, and she had wondered if their fur was as silky as it appeared. It was odd how dangerous things were so often beautiful.

Dr. Hartman interrupted her daydream. "I should get back to work," he said.

"I've really enjoyed our talk," Hope said honestly, "but I know you're busy. Thanks for the coffee, Dr. Hartman."

He swirled the coffee in his cup, watching the spinning liquid in apparent fascination. "Do you suppose you could call me Charles?" he asked absently.

She ran her middle finger around the rim of her own cup and considered that. The man was not going to win any prizes for his sparkling personality, but she liked him. "Tell you what," she offered, "I'll call you Charlie."

He nearly choked on his coffee. *"Charlie?"*

She nodded firmly. "Sure. Didn't they call you that when you were a boy?"

"No, they called me Trey."

Hope wrinkled her nose. "You mean like the playing card? The one that comes after the ace and the deuce?"

"Exactly."

"So what are you," she asked provocatively, "the offspring of riverboat gamblers?"

His mouth twitched. "Not exactly." He swallowed the last of his coffee. "I'm Charles Winston Hartman III," he said. "My grandfather is called Charles and my father goes by Winston. I suppose they called me Trey to avoid confusion."

Hope tossed her head. "They might have considered that little snag before they gave you a name that was already in use by two men," she opined. "I take it you don't come from a long line of original thinkers?"

One side of his mouth turned up, an almost-smile. "Actually, we're all doctors."

"What? Not all *three* of you?"

"I'm afraid so," he said. "Dr. Charles Winston Hartman, in triplicate. It's awful, isn't it?"

She laughed, but the latest edition of Dr. Charles Winston Hartman barely cracked a smile. Goodness, but the man was strung tight.

Hope twirled a lock of hair around her finger. "Well, I think Charlie is a good name for you," she said boldly. "It makes you seem more—" She broke off.

"More what?"

"N-nothing." She stumbled over her words. "I'm sorry." She really ought to bite her impertinent tongue, she thought distractedly. When would she learn to think first?

His eyes nailed her. "I can take it. More what?"

He wasn't going to like this. She nibbled her bottom lip for a moment before she answered. "More… approachable?"

He cocked an eyebrow at her.

"Well, you pretend not to care," Hope said defensively, "but you really are a Charlie at heart. I can tell."

That obviously annoyed him. "You're trying to tell me that a…Charlie…is a nice guy?"

Hope almost laughed at the way his upper lip curled

in distaste as he pronounced the nickname. She sipped her coffee, watching him over her cup. His gruff demeanor didn't fool her for a second. He was a Charlie, all right.

"I'm not a nice guy, Hope." His tone was quietly menacing. He snapped the lid on the square tin and stood up. "But thank you for the cookies."

Hope wondered why the man was so determined to hide his kind heart. She had seen it and she had an inexplicable need to tell him so. She watched him take four long strides away from her before she put down her cup and called, "Charlie?"

He turned.

She elevated her eyebrows and tried to look innocent.

He stared for a moment, answering her broad smile with a scowl. She expected him to turn on his heel, but he surprised her by coming back to the table. Cradling the cookie tin in one arm, he put his free hand on the table and leaned forwards, looking straight into her eyes. "Have dinner with me tonight."

"Why?" The thoughtless question leaped out of her mouth before she could stop it. Deeply ashamed, she lowered her eyes, intending to avoid his unnerving gaze by staring into her coffee cup. But he was there, too—his face was clearly reflected in the dark liquid.

His answer was delayed by several heartbeats. "Because," he said finally, "you interest me."

Hope groaned inwardly. "I don't mean to. I wasn't flirting—honest."

"No, I didn't think you were," he replied imperturbably.

Somewhat relieved, Hope spoke to the face in her coffee cup. "Thank you, Dr. Hartman, but I don't go out with men."

"Don't you? Why not?"

She forced herself to look up. "Because I plan never to marry."

His hazel eyes glinted with amusement. "Let me assure you, Hope, the only thing I am *proposing* is dinner and conversation."

"I'm sorry. I never go on dates." But for the first time she found herself tempted to make an exception.

"Goodbye, then," he said abruptly. He snatched his empty cup off the table, crushing it in his hand as he walked away.

Hope couldn't get Dr. Hartman out of her mind. She wished she hadn't turned down his invitation. Her "no" had been automatic, a reflex.

She would never marry. She had reasons, good ones, and they began and ended with a handsome college student named Trevor Daniels. But now for the first time in almost seven years, she felt a twinge of regret.

Although she went to the hospital every day to visit Gramps, nearly a week passed before she saw Charles again. One morning she glimpsed him in the hall just as the door of her elevator closed. She frantically pressed the "open" button, but it was too late. She got off at the earliest opportunity and hurried back up to the sixth floor.

She'd missed him, of course. She stood in the middle of the hall and stared at the ceiling, completely at a loss to understand why she suddenly felt so depressed.

"Is something wrong?" a nurse asked.

"I'm all right, thank you," Hope replied without a particle of conviction.

"I've seen you in here a lot," the nurse commented. "You're with Mr. Seltzer, aren't you?" Hope nodded and the woman went on. "He's doing better. Try not to worry." She lightly touched Hope's shoulder before continuing on her way.

Hope's dreary mood lifted as she watched the nurse go. There were a lot of nice people in the world, she reflected. It was silly of her to be chasing after a charm-school reject like Dr. Charles Hartman. She made up her mind to forget him.

She had just pressed the button to summon another elevator when she saw him come out of a room not twenty feet away. The resolution of a moment ago was instantly forgotten. "Dr. Hartman!" she called eagerly.

He stopped, but he didn't turn. He didn't look up from the clipboard he was writing on, but from the angle of his head she understood that he was listening, waiting.

"Charlie?"

She read his annoyance in the slight jerk of his head, the stiffening of his back. He turned, frowning. A second later he recognized her and his expression softened.

"Hello, Hope." He didn't smile, but his eyebrows lifted slightly and he looked almost friendly. He replaced his ballpoint pen in the chest pocket of his white coat and waited for her to speak.

She was direct. She didn't know any other way. "Charlie, I've thought about it and I want to go to dinner with you."

He regarded her thoughtfully. "Thanks," he said quietly, then he gave his head a brief shake. "But I don't think so."

Surprised and embarrassed, Hope lowered her gaze. "I understand. I'm sorry to have troubled you."

She was aware that his head dipped slightly as he attempted to engage her averted eyes. Not succeeding, he studied her face for a moment before he spoke. "No, I don't believe you *do* understand."

She looked up. "Of course I do. I don't interest you anymore." She gave him a rueful grin. "It's okay, Dr.

Hartman. I'm not going to throw myself off a bridge or anything like that.''

The firm line of his mouth bent a little, but it straightened almost immediately. ''As a matter of fact, you interest me very much. But I think a friendship with you would take more energy than I'm willing to expend. I suppose that hurts your feelings?''

She told him the truth. ''No. I'm just disappointed, that's all.''

''Are you? Why?''

She shrugged. ''I don't think that can matter to you. And I don't want to keep you from your work.''

She saw his smile the instant before he smothered it. ''You're smooth, aren't you, Hope?''

Smooth? Her mouth fell open and she shook her head slowly. If he thought she was unruffled, then he was way past mistaken and halfway to shockingly ignorant.

''So you want to go to dinner with me?'' He hugged the clipboard and waited.

Hope's eyebrows drew together. Hadn't they already established that? She blinked at him. ''Is that a renewed invitation or mere idle curiosity?''

His mouth twitched again. He was definitely amused.

Hope didn't try to hide her frustration. ''Look, Dr. Hartman, I have accepted your rejection. Shouldn't you be getting back to your work?''

He ignored the question and asked one of his own. ''How about seven-thirty tonight?''

Her breath caught in her throat. Was he actually smiling?

''Are you free?'' he persisted. He *was* smiling.

Openmouthed, Hope stared, uncharacteristically speechless.

''Just nod your head,'' he suggested. He waited until she did that, then he reached for his pen and pulled a small tablet from another pocket. His tone was business-like. "Address and phone number?"

Still dazed, Hope gave them.

"I have some patients to see right now," said the doctor briskly. "I'll pick you up at seven-thirty."

"But, Dr. Hartman, are you positive that you really—"

He held up a hand to silence her. "The name is Charles, remember?"

At last Hope's irrepressible sense of humor rescued her. "I remember nothing of the kind," she declared pertly. She flashed him a wicked grin. "I'll see you tonight, Charlie."

Chapter Three

Feeling like a naughty child, Hope raided her mother's jewelry box, liberating Grace Evans's wedding pearls from their midnight-blue velvet pouch. Although she had permission to wear the necklace, Hope had never done so.

She fastened the diamond-studded clasp behind her neck and leaned over, twisting awkwardly until she saw herself in the tiny mirror inside the lid of the satin-lined box. Not satisfied with the view, she went to the bathroom mirror for a better look. There she flipped her dark, loose hair away from her shoulders and admired the way the pearls lay against the jewel neckline of her simple charcoal-gray dress.

Blessed with clear skin and blue eyes, Hope rarely wore makeup. But she slicked on a bit of lip color before returning to her own bedroom to check her reflection in a full-length mirror.

She heard movement behind her. "Bob, you won't believe this," she said into the mirror, "but I actually have a date." She flicked a piece of lint off one of her short sleeves. "Well, not a *real* date, but a man is taking me to dinner. And it doesn't mean anything at all, so don't you dare give me that worldly-wise look of yours."

When the doorbell rang Hope was ready to go. Or would be, just as soon as she located her other black pump. On a single three-inch heel she limped to the living room and opened the front door. "I'm glad to see you," she said artlessly, standing aside and allowing Charles to enter. "I was a little afraid you wouldn't come."

"I said I would, didn't I?" he asked irritably.

The prickly physician didn't scare her at all. Having grown up with four older brothers, Hope was used to men and their moods. Early-morning surliness, high-decibel temper tantrums and boneheaded stubbornness were all things she knew how to deal with.

"I just thought you might have changed your mind," she said honestly. "I wouldn't have blamed you. Because—well, I goaded you into this, didn't I?"

He gave her a puzzled frown. "I've had rather a difficult afternoon," he said by way of explanation, if not apology, for his rudeness.

Wearing a beautifully cut and obviously expensive suit in almost the same charcoal shade as Hope's dress, he looked downright elegant. Except for the pearls, Hope hadn't dressed with any special care, which was just as well, because she could have spent a week getting ready and still not have attained *that* level of gorgeousness.

No, not gorgeousness. Charles Hartman wasn't actually handsome. He was…classy. Yes, that was it. Well, if *she* had tons of money, she'd look classy, too. Who wouldn't?

Forgetting her semishoeless state, Hope took a lopsided step away from Charles and promptly lost her balance. As her arms flailed uselessly, he lunged for her, his alert reflexes preventing her from hitting the floor.

An instant later it occurred to Hope that leaning sideways in this virtual stranger's arms was probably as close as she would ever come to dancing the tango. She giggled, stammering an apology as Charles righted and released her.

He stared at her feet for a moment, then raised startled eyes to her face. Hope calmly met his gaze, chewing her tongue while she waited for him to ask.

He cleared his throat. "Is that a new fashion or are you just eccentric?" he queried.

Hope tilted her head to one side. "I'm going to need some more choices."

He nodded, his eyes drifting away from hers as he thought. "Your other shoe's being repaired? You have an ingrown toenail? The store had only one shoe in your size but you couldn't pass up the bargain?"

Hope grinned and waited. He was good.

"Perhaps we should skip multiple-choice and try fill-in-the-blank," he suggested.

For a man who was so reluctant to smile, he had a great sense of humor. Hope rewarded him with the correct answer. "Bob plays with my shoes. I was looking for the mate to this one when you arrived. I'll continue the search now, if you don't mind. I'm guessing you want to go to one of those swanky places where they pretty much insist on their patrons being fully shod."

"It's what I had in mind. Definitely one of those fashionable *two-shoe* establishments. You have a son?"

"N-no, I've never been married," she replied in confusion.

"Well, that wouldn't preclude your having children. I knew that one even before medical school."

She didn't care for his casual attitude. "Yes, it

would," she stated firmly. "I believe the biblical teaching that sex outside of marriage is a sin."

He gave her a noncommittal shrug. "Then who's Bob?"

"Oh!" she said, finally understanding. Looking Charles in the eye, she put two fingers to her mouth and whistled, watching with satisfaction as he cringed. Hope was proud of her whistle. It was exquisitely loud and nerve-shatteringly shrill.

"Hope! You might have warned me," he chided, twisting his fingers in his ears.

She bent to caress the cocker spaniel that had just bounded in from the kitchen. "That was nothing. I can do it much louder," she declared. "I have four older brothers, and I can whistle and spit and belch with the best of 'em. My curveball isn't bad, either."

"I can imagine," he said admiringly. "But are you about ready to go? I haven't had a thing to eat all day, unless black coffee counts."

She removed her solitary shoe and handed it to him. "Check under the sofa and see if you can find something that looks like this. I'll go look under my bed."

A minute later Charles called to her. She returned to the living room, where he handed her both shoes. She inspected them for damage and slipped them on. "Nice work," she said. "And black coffee *doesn't* count, so let's get moving."

Delighted by the massive bouquet of pink roses in the lobby of the small French restaurant, Hope couldn't resist touching one perfect bloom as a hostess escorted Charles and her past the display. When they stepped into the dining room, she was even more impressed to find that each white-draped table was graced by three red roses and a bit of ivy in a small silver vase.

Much was made over Charles and his guest. "You must be a regular here," Hope commented after they were seated.

"It's my favorite restaurant," he acknowledged. "I come here just about every week."

"Do you eat out a lot?" she wondered.

"Every day. I don't cook."

"Not at all?"

He shrugged. "I make coffee."

"What's in your refrigerator?"

"Fruit juice, vegetable juice, bottled water," he recited.

"What else?"

"Nothing else."

"No ketchup? Men always have ketchup."

His mouth twitched. "Is that so? I must be an exception, then."

Hope lowered her gaze and concentrated on not blushing. What she had just said implied an extensive knowledge of men and their refrigerators that she didn't actually possess. Uncomfortably aware of her companion's amused regard, she opened her menu and pretended to study it carefully.

Charles broke the excruciating silence. "Do you need any help deciphering the French?" he asked politely.

Without looking up, she thanked him in that language, assuring him that she was having no trouble reading the menu. She didn't mention the grammatical error she'd spotted.

"Your accent is beautiful. Are you French?"

Hope raised her eyes to his. "I'm a natural mimic. Languages are easy for me."

His eyebrows lifted appreciatively. "How many do you speak?"

"French, German, Spanish, Italian and Japanese."

That obviously surprised him. "Really? Do you speak them all as perfectly as you do French?"

"I'm not that good in Japanese. My accent is pitiful and I have the vocabulary of a ten-year-old."

She looked at her menu again, and this time she noticed the prices. It was all she could do to keep her eyebrows from jumping straight up to the soaring, wood-beamed ceiling.

When she heard a chuckle, she realized she had not managed to conceal her shock from Charles. "Go ahead and have some fun," he said. "It's on me tonight. And the portions are small here, so be sure to try a lot of different things."

Well, why not? Dr. Moneybags could afford it. And if a girl was going to have just one actual date in her entire lifetime, she might as well make it memorable, right?

After their orders were taken, Charles encouraged Hope to talk about her schoolwork and her translating. Then he asked about her family. "Your parents are in Africa, you said?"

"Yes. They're both teachers, and when I finished high school, God called them to the mission field. The boys were already scattered—one in Dallas, two in Los Angeles and one in Pittsburgh. So Mom and Dad sold the farm and bought the house where I'm living now. Am I talking too much?"

His mouth twitched with humor. "I'm getting used to it. What will you do after you get your degree?"

"I hope to travel to conferences all over the world as a simultaneous interpreter. I'm studying medical terms, especially. One day you might go to a meeting in Paris and hear my voice through your earphone."

"It sounds like you'll have some real adventures. Is that why you don't want to marry?"

This was the part she hated. People always asked why

she didn't date, why she didn't want a husband and children. It wasn't something she cared to discuss, yet everyone seemed to think she owed an explanation. She never gave one. God alone knew how her young heart had been shattered. Everyone else could speculate all they wanted.

"I prefer not to talk about it," she said slowly, "but I *am* resolved. And to be honest, I have mixed feelings about being here with you. Since I'm not interested in romance I've made it a rule never to go out with men. This is the first exception I've made in almost seven years."

He raised an eyebrow. "You're against a little harmless fun?"

She regarded him thoughtfully. "What if I went out with a man and he began to love me? My 'harmless fun' could end up hurting someone. Don't you see?"

One corner of Charles's mouth turned up. "Well, don't worry. As charming as you are, there's absolutely no danger of my falling in love with you. So we can be friends, can't we?"

Hope lightly caressed one of the red roses. "I'd like that. But you said… How did you put it?" She looked up, meeting his eyes. "That a friendship with me would take more energy than you're willing to expend?"

He pursed his lips, appearing to consider his earlier statement. "Hmm. Well, perhaps I could exert myself a *little*."

She grinned at him, delighted by the quirk of his mouth that told her he was trying not to smile. "It might be worth your while," she said eagerly. "I'm really good at friendship."

His almost-smile died instantly. "I can't say the same, Hope. Maybe you shouldn't waste your time."

"Waste my time?" she echoed faintly.

"I don't really care about people," he said matter-of-factly. He rapped his chest with a fist. "Heart of stone."

Hope's eyes widened. Did he honestly believe that? He was a doctor, wasn't he? Of course he cared about people. She shook her head. "Nonsense. You gave me parking money."

His eyes held hers easily. "It was an impulse, that's all. I'm not a kind man."

She stood her ground. "Nonsense," she said again, more firmly this time.

"I mean it. There's no 'niceness' in me. I am incapable of love."

His uncompromising words and his earnest, unwavering gaze shocked her. Nervously, she fingered her mother's pearls. "What about your family?"

"I don't care much for my parents. My grandfather is okay, but we're not particularly close. I feel affection for my brother, but sometimes he gets on my nerves. Honestly, I've never loved anyone."

A plateful of steamed mussels was set before her but suddenly Hope had no appetite. "What about God?" she persisted when the waiter had gone.

Charles's lips parted and for several seconds he stared at her without speaking. "I would very much like to believe in something or someone. I wish I knew how. But nothing touches me."

Hope shivered. Never in her life had she heard anyone utter such a bleak sentiment. Speechless with pity, she could only stare at him as tears gathered in her eyes.

"Don't take it to heart, kid," he said with a gentleness she never would have expected from him. "It's nothing I can't live with."

As she continued to study his face, something in it changed. It was as though he had suddenly become aware that he'd inadvertently left a door ajar, and now that door was carefully closed.

"Try your mussels," he suggested. "They're good here—lots of garlic."

Hope looked at her plate, blinking furiously to hold her tears at bay. This poor man was wandering alone in a wilderness. Could she help him find his way to God?

With all her heart, she wanted to. She looked up, straight into the hazel eyes that were now carefully guarded. "Okay, let's get to work," she said briskly. With her fingertips she wiped moisture from the corners of her eyes.

Charles leaned back in his chair as if to distance himself from her. "Get to work on what?" he asked cautiously.

She gave him her sweetest smile. "Our friendship. It's clear that you need me, Charlie, and I've decided to take the job." She offered her right hand so he could shake it.

He turned his head and looked at her sideways. "Not a good idea," he cautioned, ignoring her hand.

She leaned forwards, taunting him, her eyes boring into his. "Scared?"

His head jerked slightly and he gave her a thin-lipped smile. "Of a Girl Scout? Hardly."

She again extended her hand and this time it was clasped briefly. As he started to withdraw, Hope impulsively tightened her grip, holding his large hand captive in her slender one. "You won't regret it, Charlie."

He looked pained. "Must you keep calling me that?"

She released his hand. "Don't worry. You'll get used to it."

That didn't seem to comfort him any. He looked at his hand, flexing it as if she had injured him. "Hope, I'm not a nice guy," he warned.

"I'm a better judge of that than you are, Charlie."

Their gazes locked in a silent showdown, and when he sighed Hope knew he'd given in. For now, at least.

"Eat your mussels," he said, "or I will."

Two nights later he called just before nine o'clock and asked Hope to join him for a late dinner. She'd already eaten, but she told him she could really go for some cheesecake.

He was phoning from his car, and he was not far from her house. "Can you be ready in ten minutes?" he asked.

She could. She hung up the phone and turned to her dog. "Oh, Bobby, I hope I know what I'm doing." She peeled off her T-shirt and shorts and tossed them onto her bed. "It's not actually dating, is it—just having dinner and talking? It's no different from going out with Claire or Barb, is it?"

She stood in front of her closet and wondered which of her six dresses to put on. She didn't know where they were going, but she guessed he'd be wearing another of those snazzy suits. "Must be nice to have money," she mumbled as she pulled a sleeveless, beet-red sheath off a hanger and wriggled into it. The nails of her long, straight toes were already painted deep red, so she eased her feet into strappy black sandals.

Hope couldn't remember the last time she'd enjoyed herself as much as she had when she'd gone to dinner with Charles. She could barely scrape together money for a monthly pizza, let alone a to-die-for meal at one of Chicago's finest restaurants, so it had been a wonderful evening. But the best part had been getting to know Charles. He was amazingly intelligent, remarkably articulate and he had a delicious sense of humor.

Even apart from her facility with languages, Hope had always been considered by her teachers to be extremely bright. But this man's brain could dance circles around hers. She had never known such a stimulating conversation partner.

"I like him, Bob," she said. "I've never come across anyone as interesting as he is. He needs a friend and I'm just a girl, not a woman, to him. So it's really pretty safe, don't you think?"

Bob didn't disagree.

She gave her long hair five licks with a brush, then twisted it into a loose chignon, securing it with hairpins. She uncapped a tube of deep red lipstick and stroked color on her curvy top lip. Hearing Charles's car in the driveway, she gave her bottom lip a quick swipe. Then she blew a smacky kiss to Bob and slipped the strap of a small black purse over her shoulder.

She opened the front door just as Charles touched the bell. "I'm ready," she announced.

He looked down.

"Two shoes," Hope confirmed. "Let's go."

She kept him company while he ate, then he ordered coffee for the two of them and cheesecake for Hope.

"Thanks for joining me," he said after their coffee was brought. "It's boring to eat alone."

How could he possibly know that? Hope seriously doubted that a catch like Dr. Hartman would have any difficulty finding a dinner companion. "Why did you call me?" she asked, suddenly curious. "Were all the girlfriends busy?"

"I wasn't in the mood for a date. I just wanted to talk, like we did the other night."

Suddenly embarrassed, Hope lowered her gaze. She guessed that to Charles, a date involved quite a bit more than dinner and conversation. Although that shocked her, it was reassuring to know she didn't interest him in *that* way. But her cheeks burned and she was uncomfortably aware of his eyes on her.

She sensed a shift in his mood as the silence lengthened between them. She lifted her head and glimpsed a dark, angry stirring in his narrowed eyes. She had a disquieting impression of swirling winds and gathering thunderclouds and she felt a warning flutter in her stomach.

He spoke just a shade too casually. "What makes you think there are so many girlfriends?"

At a loss to comprehend the undercurrent of hostility in his manner, she answered hesitantly. "Well...you're good-looking and brilliant. You probably have to beat them off with a stick."

His eyes flickered dangerously and the storm broke. "I do," he said harshly, "but not for those reasons. Money is what women really go for, and I am disgustingly wealthy."

Upset by his stinging words and his flinty gaze, Hope stared into the rich darkness of her coffee and said nothing.

"Does that impress you?"

Her heart twisted. Did he truly believe money was his only attraction? Did he think she was here tonight because of *that?* She shook her head, aching for him. "Not everyone is like that, Charlie."

"Yes," he said savagely. "Every woman I've ever met."

"I don't believe it," she insisted. He would probably take her head off for this, but she couldn't stop herself. "I don't know where you've been meeting women, Charlie, but I think you've been going out with the wrong ones."

"No, they are perfectly suited for what I want." The

dangerous glint in his eyes made it impossible to mistake his meaning. "And now I've shocked you, haven't I?"

He had, but more than that, he had *meant* to do it. Why was he being so nasty? Hope sipped her coffee, then picked up her napkin and dabbed at her mouth. It wasn't much, as stalling tactics went, but it gave her a few seconds to think. "I guessed that was true, but I never thought you'd say it," she reproached him. "Not to *me,* Charlie."

She saw the regret in his eyes before he lowered them, but he wasn't a man who apologized. Her heart flooded with pity. "You've got a lot more going for you than money, Charlie, and anyone with an ounce of character is sure to see that."

He made a small sound of disgust and shook his head in amazement. "You honestly believe that, don't you? I suppose you're about to tell me what a charmer I am?"

"No." She opted for brutal honesty because he would sneer at anything less. "You're not charming at all. You're about as warm and fuzzy as a porcupine. But I admire you for so many—"

"Oh, don't sugarcoat it, kid," he interrupted. He smiled, oddly entertained. "I'm an ogre and you know it!"

A minute ago he had hurt her, but now he was just plain ticking her off. She was determined to set him straight. "That's just it, Charlie—you're *not*. But you try so hard to make yourself and everyone else believe that you are. It must be a tremendous strain. I wonder how much longer you'll be able to keep up the act."

He wasn't smiling now. "Stop it, Hope," he said in a low, threatening tone.

Refusing to be intimidated, she folded her arms on the table and leaned towards him. "Why?" she challenged. "Are you afraid your mask will slip?"

"There's no mask. This is who I am. You appear to be convinced there's something in me worth redemption. There isn't, and your pretty illusions are in danger of being trampled. I might regret that, but I wouldn't bend over to pick up the pieces."

She was very sure. "Yes, Charlie—you would."

He might snap at her, he might try to shock her a little, but he wouldn't hurt her for the world. Hope knew that even if he didn't. She had decided to be a friend to him and she always stood by her friends. If he expected her to run away just because he was a little testy, he was going to be surprised. She lifted her chin and silently defied him.

"Stop it, Hope," he said again. It wasn't a warning this time, but a plea, and sudden insight told Hope she'd pushed him too far. She had meant only to shake him up a little, but somehow she had disarmed him completely. She looked into his wide, frightened eyes and realized he understood nothing at all about friendship and trust.

Impulsively she reached out to touch his hair. She was surprised that he didn't shy away, but sat perfectly still, watching her face in apparent amazement. She ruffled his civilized, honey-colored waves, coaxing them to stand up rakishly.

Satisfied with her work, she swallowed a giggle and withdrew her hand.

He gazed at her soberly, making no effort to smooth his hair. "What was that for?"

"It needed to be done," she said with an almost-straight.face.

"Are you laughing at me?"

She was. "Don't you think it's about time somebody did, Charlie Hartman?"

His mouth opened slightly and she saw his tongue

move against his cheek. He didn't smile, but he came close.

"You're wondering whether I'm fearless or merely stupid," she guessed, lifting a forkful of cheesecake.

His breath came out in a huff. "You are a most uncommon girl."

"No," she protested, reaching for her coffee. "I'm as ordinary as they come."

He shook his head in slow motion, his eyes on her all the while. "Hope, there is nothing remotely ordinary about you."

She lowered her cup and dropped her gaze. Aware that he was still watching her, she picked up her fork again, toying with her dessert as she prayed silently. *Lord, let me show him what a real friend is. And help me teach him that You are the best friend of all.*

Chapter Four

It appeared that she had passed some kind of test. Hope sat on her porch swing, her purse and her Bible beside her. Rocking gently, she mulled over the events of the past two weeks.

Consciously or not, Charles had done his utmost to push her away. Confronted with his unrelenting cynicism, she'd dug in her heels and fought for him. When the smoke cleared, she'd remained standing, battered but not beaten, still determinedly waving her banner of friendship.

And Charles had surrendered, handing her his trust as if it had been hers by right, a spoil of war.

Hope glanced at her watch—5:50. Provided he had been able to get away from the hospital, Charles would be here in ten minutes. But people didn't stop bleeding merely to suit Dr. Hartman's convenience, and Hope was learning to be flexible.

She still couldn't believe he had actually agreed to accompany her to Tuesday night Bible study. When she'd asked he had merely pressed his lips together for a moment before answering, "Sure. Whatever you want."

It was almost scary. He seemed unable to deny her anything. Did the man think he had to pay for her friendship? Or was this the Lord at work, softening Charles's heart?

She leaned her head back to catch a few slanting rays of the late-afternoon sunlight on her face. Eyes closed, glorying in the sun's warm caress, she listened to the sounds of summer: the hypnotic drone of a neighbor's lawnmower, the delighted squeals of children as they splashed in a wading pool across the street. Her last drowsy thought was to wonder how many times she had danced around the lawn sprinkler with her brothers on hot summer afternoons just like this one....

"Hope."

She opened her eyes and saw Charles ensconced in the wicker chair next to her, one ankle resting on his other knee. His suit coat had been tossed over the porch railing and his tie was loosened. He was refolding her newspaper.

"Hi," she murmured groggily. She struggled to sit up. "How long have you been here?"

He placed the folded paper on a small table and looked at his watch. "Twenty minutes. You must have an awfully clear conscience to be able to sleep that soundly."

Hope rubbed her eyes, thinking it probably had more to do with growing up with four rowdy boys and their noisy friends. She'd learned to sleep through just about anything.

Charles stood. "We'd better go."

They stopped for a quick dinner at Hope's favorite deli, which was nearby. She loved the place not only for its excellent soups and sandwiches, but for the charming outdoor eating area that was crowded with large pots of fragrant herbs and dramatic cascades of colorful petunias.

They got their food and carried it out to the small patio. "It smells good here," Charles commented.

"It's the herbs." Hope ran her hand lightly over the needles of a rosemary plant, then held her fingers under Charles's nose.

He sniffed. "I know that smell."

"It's rosemary. You've probably had it with lamb or potatoes."

He pointed. "What's that one? I can smell it from here. Something minty?"

"Spearmint. You must have brushed against it when you walked by. That releases the scent, especially on a hot day like this."

Hope pointed out several other herbs, telling Charles which dishes they were commonly used in. He touched and sniffed them all, cautiously delighted by each little discovery.

As they ate messy but delicious Reuben sandwiches and crunched enormous spears of dill pickles, Hope wondered again whether anyone had ever seen past her friend's tough outer shell to the gentle heart beneath. Charles denied its existence, but Hope knew better.

It occurred to her that he knew all about her life while she knew next to nothing about his. She tried to draw him out, but it wasn't easy. He deflected several questions about his family before he gave in.

"It's not a sweet story," he warned. "I saw little of my parents while I was growing up. I was always away at school or summer camp, and they were too busy, anyway. I was fed, clothed and educated by a long line of individuals who were handsomely paid to perform those services. And at an early age I was given to understand that the sole reason for my existence was to heap additional glory on the exalted name of Hartman.'' He looked at his plate, his shapely mouth twisting in contempt.

Shocked into speechlessness, Hope waited for him to go on.

He was silent for a moment before he continued. ''Winning important piano competitions, earning perfect scores on my SATs, starting college at sixteen—those were the things that mattered to my parents. There was never any…affection.'' He shrugged as if to say that didn't matter, but Hope knew his indifference was feigned. She watched with an aching heart as he picked up a plastic spoon and carefully stirred his coffee, to which he had added neither cream nor sugar.

''I was five years old when baby Tom came along,'' he said as he laid the spoon on a paper napkin. ''I was absolutely fascinated by that little creature.'' Looking up, he grinned suddenly. ''Maybe because I wasn't allowed to have a dog.''

A smile tugged at Hope's mouth and she gave in to it.

''I used to sneak into his nursery and watch him sleep,'' Charles remembered, his own smile slowly fading. ''He was tiny and defenseless and I vowed to protect him always.''

His expression hardened. ''But our parents can be incredibly vindictive, and when Tom married against their wishes they hurt him terribly. I tried to stop them, but…'' His eyes sparked with barely controlled anger. ''I don't like them, Hope,'' he said fiercely. ''They've done some unforgivable things to my brother and I don't like them at all.''

''Oh, Charlie, how awful!'' she breathed. Looking down, she tried desperately to blink back her compassionate tears.

It was too late. He had already seen them, and his head

jerked impatiently. "What's awful, Hope? That they're monsters or that I don't like them?"

"All of it," she gasped, truly horrified. She lifted shimmering eyes to answer his granite gaze. "It's so sad!"

As she watched his face, his anger slowly dissipated. He shook his head in a silent apology. "It's difficult to talk about," he admitted.

"Do you want to tell me about your brother?"

He nodded. "Tom's an attorney. He was happily married until three years ago, when he lost his wife to a rare form of cancer. It hurt him a lot, but it didn't make him bitter. He's still as good-hearted as ever."

His brother appeared to be a safe subject, so Hope pursued it. "Do you see him much?"

"Yes, he lives here in Chicago. We try to play squash twice a week and we often have dinner together. Right now he's in Italy with friends, but you'll be able to meet him in a week or so. You'll like him, Hope. Everyone does."

On the strength of the warm light in his brother's eyes, Hope *did* like Tom Hartman, sight unseen.

It was time to leave for the Bible study, and as they stood and began clearing off their table, Hope impulsively touched Charles's arm. "I shouldn't have pressed you about your parents," she apologized.

His big hand cupped her shoulder, giving her a brief squeeze. "No, it's okay. Actually, I'm glad you know. I've never told anyone those things." He lowered his voice and made an amazing confession. "And…maybe I needed to."

From the deli they drove to the home of Hope's pastor, where they joined two dozen other people in a cramped living room. Tuesday was the night for choir practice and various meetings at the overcrowded church, so Pastor

Bill Barnes and his wife hosted this informal Bible study in their own home.

The group was a good mix of ages, and in their no-holds-barred discussions Pastor Bill tackled any subject that interested the participants. Tonight's conversation ran along the lines of "How can we know there is a God?" Hope was thrilled that Charles appeared to be listening attentively.

When the meeting ended, they enjoyed coffee and cookies. Hope introduced Charles to several people, including Pastor Bill, a longtime friend of her parents. Charles was scrupulously polite, but after ten minutes Hope took pity on him and linked her arm through his. "Let's go," she whispered.

Enjoying the soft night, they walked to his car without speaking. Charles looked thoughtful as he fastened his seat belt and started the engine. "That wasn't what I thought it would be. In fact, it was rather interesting."

"Really?" She tried not to sound too eager. "What interested you?"

"Your pastor said frankly that he couldn't prove the existence of God. If he had insisted otherwise he would have lost my attention immediately. But now, I almost wonder..." He shook his head. "Pretty shrewd of him, don't you think?"

Hope sent up a silent prayer for wisdom. "Well," she began carefully, "it's not his job—or my job—to reveal God to you. The Holy Spirit does that. But we can help by nudging you a little, pointing you in the right direction. Pastor Bill was trying to pique your curiosity. The rest is between you and God. We can answer some of your questions, Charlie, but we can't make you believe. We can't prove God to you, but if you ask Him, He will prove Himself."

Charles absorbed that in silence.

It was a quiet ride back to Hope's house, and as she sat in the darkness beside Charles, she prayed. Her eyes stared straight ahead, but her lips moved a little as she spoke to her Heavenly Father. *Please, Lord, draw him to You and reveal Yourself to him. Bring him to his knees before You and heal his wounded heart. And show me what I can do and say to help him find You.*

"I know what you're doing," Charles said humorously, glancing over at her. "Do you think it's fair?"

She kept her voice as light as his. "What are you afraid of, Charlie?"

His rich chuckle filled the car and Hope's heart. "You and God," he said, "ganging up on me."

Hope closed her Bible and placed it on the table beside her. It was almost two in the morning, but she hadn't been able to sleep. Curling more comfortably into the overstuffed chair, she tucked her bare toes under the ruffled hem of her long cotton nightgown and patted her lap. Bob answered her invitation and Hope held him close, absently stroking his glossy coat as she thought about Charles.

They were as far apart as summer and winter, as different as potato chips and caviar. She'd grown up on a farm and he'd grown up in a mansion. She was twelve years his junior and her sunny disposition was diametrically opposed to his irascible nature. She was warm and giving while he was aloof.

So why did he constantly seek her company? He phoned her every day, sometimes more than once, and unless he was working or sleeping, he wanted to be with her.

Hope guessed he had no idea why he was so drawn to her. She hadn't understood, either, until tonight. But now she knew why he was unable to stay away. For all his gruff protests, he was searching for love and acceptance, compassion and forgiveness. He was desperately seeking meaning and purpose in his life.

Charles Hartman was looking for God.

He was intrigued by the personal relationship Hope had with Jesus Christ, but he couldn't admit that. Not to himself and certainly not to Hope. But he watched her, listened to her, questioned her, all without any conscious understanding of what he was seeking. Hope saw it now, and she rejoiced.

"He's close, Bobby," she said, fingering one of the dog's floppy, velvety ears. "I have a feeling we're about to see the Lord make a brand-new man of Charlie Hartman!"

Two days later, Hope carried her canvas bag into the visitor's lounge, where she sat at a table to do some needlework. One of her close friends was expecting a baby, so Hope was embroidering a tiny shirt.

Humming softly, she worked for more than an hour before someone spoke her name from the doorway. As she raised her eyes her heart lifted, too. "Charlie. How did you know I was here?"

"I didn't," he said calmly, coming to sit beside her. "But I can't seem to pass Mr. Seltzer's room or this one without sticking my head in to look for you."

She eyed his dark, stylish suit and wondered whether he was starting or ending his workday. When on duty he wore blue scrubs and a lab coat that was emblazoned above the pen-stuffed pocket with Dr. C. Hartman in red script. "Are you coming or going?" she asked.

"I'm off until seven tomorrow night," he said with a satisfied air. "How about you?"

She wound thread around her needle to make a French knot. "I've been with Gramps all morning. He had a rough night, and I didn't want to leave until I was sure he was resting comfortably. I was just about to check on him one last time and then head home.''

''Are you hungry?''

''I'm famished,'' she admitted. ''But it's my turn to buy.''

He looked put out. ''Hope, I understand your wanting to reciprocate when your other friends treat you. But it's different with me. You can't pretend I'll ever miss the pocket change I spend on you. And what am I supposed to do—sit around twiddling my thumbs until you can afford to take your turn? Why should I have to suffer just because you're poor?''

He had her there. ''Charlie,'' she muttered, ''you're downright nasty.'' Shaking her head in pretended disgust, she repositioned her embroidery hoop and tightened it. ''Why don't you go return calls or something?'' she suggested. ''I want to finish this. I'll come down to your office in ten minutes.''

''No, I'm really free. Take your time.'' He reached for his wallet and checked his cash supply. Apparently satisfied, he folded the wallet and replaced it.

''Sure you have enough? I'm really hungry.''

''I have enough for anywhere *you* want to go,'' he answered. With his foot he hooked the leg of an empty chair, pulling it towards him and propping his long legs on it.

Hope cut a length of embroidery floss and separated the strands. ''You think I'm unsophisticated,'' she accused.

''Delightfully so,'' he agreed, shifting to a more comfortable position in his chair. He picked up her tiny scissors and examined them. ''I'm sick of worldly women.''

''Yeah, *right,*'' she mocked as she threaded her needle.

"This from a man who wears Armani suits and drives a Mercedes!"

He ignored that. "How do you feel about Indian food?"

"Mmm—I'm wild about lamb curry. But today we're limited to casual restaurants, unless you want me to go home and change." She held out her arms so he could inspect her coffee-brown T-shirt and baggy black jeans.

She supposed she ought to start dressing more carefully if she was determined to hang out with Dr. Moneybags. He always looked classy and she felt like a waif beside him.

"You're fine," he said with apparent unconcern.

Easy for him to say. He looked as if he'd just stepped out of a fashion spread in one of those magazines she couldn't afford to subscribe to. Just once she'd like to see him in blue jeans and a ratty T-shirt. Maybe with a shoelace untied.

He interrupted her reverie. "It's just lunch, Hope. Nobody's going to call the fashion police on you."

She was unconvinced. "I won't embarrass you?"

"You?" He looked honestly surprised. "Never."

Well, if he really didn't mind, she wasn't going to worry about it. She remembered something. "Charlie, how about letting me take you to a ball game tonight? A friend has offered me his tickets for the Cubs. First row in the club box, right behind home plate. I've already asked three girlfriends, but they wouldn't dream of wasting a Saturday night with me and the Cubbies when they can go out with dashing young men, instead."

"So I'm fourth choice. How very flattering."

"I thought you'd be busy saving people tonight," she pointed out.

"No. Tonight they'll just have to take their chances with Dr. Olmstead."

"I'll drive," Hope offered. "You need to relax. Besides, you probably don't know the best way to get to Comiskey Park."

"Hope, the Cubs are at Wrigley Field. The White Sox are at Comiskey." His eyes darkened with suspicion. "Did you honestly think I wouldn't know that?"

"Just making sure." She sniggered. "I wouldn't want to waste these good tickets on someone who doesn't like baseball."

He folded his arms over his chest and gave her a disgusted look. "Hope, I was playing baseball two years before you were born."

She scooped up her sewing things and bent to stuff them into the canvas bag that sat on the floor. "Play catch with the chauffeur, did you, rich boy?" she asked wickedly.

Lightning-quick, he leaned forwards and gave her ponytail a teasing tug. "Little League," he corrected. "Third base. Of course Mother hated my playing with the 'dirty urchins,' as she called them, but Granddad told her it was a rite of passage for American boys. They let me play for two years, then I had to quit. But later, Tom got to play. I enjoyed watching him, but I was always a little envious. I had some natural ability and I wanted desperately to play."

"Did your parents go to your games?"

"No. Never. But Granddad came a few times, and we appreciated that." His eyes held a faraway look that was a little sad and very unlike the tight, angry expression he usually wore when he spoke of his family. "Hope, that's about as far as I want to stroll down memory lane, if you don't mind."

She nodded, understanding, then she gave him a bright smile and changed the subject. "Let's go say goodbye to Gramps."

* * *

Even though the Cubs were down by three runs going into the bottom of the sixth inning, Hope was having a wonderful time. Charles, appearing completely relaxed as he roundly criticized umpires and shouted helpful instructions to the players, was learning how to eat sunflower seeds like a major leaguer.

Hope directed him to put a handful of shells in his mouth, separate one from the rest, use his tongue and teeth to extract the tiny seed, then spit out the empty shell.

"Hold them in your cheek, like a squirrel," she encouraged. "Then do them one at a time. It's an art form."

He gave her a doubtful look.

She grabbed his wrist as his hand moved to extract a shell from his mouth. "No," she said firmly. "That's not the way I showed you."

"Do you honestly expect me to spit?"

"Look around you, Charlie. You're at a ballpark, not the Ritz hotel. Loosen up!"

He did, literally. He had left his suit coat in Hope's car, but now he unknotted his tie and pulled it off, wordlessly handing it to her. He unbuttoned his collar and rolled up the sleeves of his sapphire-blue dress shirt.

The crowd roared as the Cubs loaded the bases. When the visiting team's manager headed out to the mound, Hope giggled and blew a goodbye kiss to the pitcher.

She draped Charles's tie around her neck and tied a neat four-in-hand knot as he looked on. Then she undid it and tied a half-Windsor, followed by a Shelby.

When Charles's attention wandered she elbowed him. "Don't you want to see my Ronald Reagan Special? When he was president he always did the full Windsor."

He leaned close so she could hear him over the wild crowd. "You're too young to remember President Reagan. And, Hope, I would rethink the navy tie with the brown T-shirt.''

She ignored him, groaning in dismay at a called strike that clearly would have been "ball four" to any umpire with twenty-twenty vision.

"Which of your brothers played ball?" Charles inquired, grimacing as the batter struck out on the next pitch.

"All of them played varsity in high school, but Mark played in college, too. He taught me how to throw a curve."

Charles leaned forwards and spit elegantly.

Hope picked up the shell that landed in her lap and soberly handed it back to him. "Don't spit into the wind," she deadpanned. "It's the mark of an amateur."

He looked sheepish. "Sorry. When I'm finished with this mouthful of seeds, do you think you might buy me a hotdog?"

"Yes," she promised. "And ice cream, if you're good."

"I don't like ice cream, but I'll be good anyway," he offered, spitting another shell as she watched approvingly. "Please don't tell anyone I actually did this."

She hooted at that. "Are you kidding? I've got people taking pictures! You'll have to outbid the tabloids to get 'em. Just how rich *are* you, anyway?"

He patted her knee. "Kid, you can't count that high. Hey, guess who's up next!" he said, drawing her attention back to the game. Another batter had gone down swinging, but the bases were still loaded and the team's home-run champion was approaching the plate.

"We need this!" Charles shouted. "Come on! Give us a grand slam!"

It actually happened, and with the rest of the crowd, Charles and Hope leaped to their feet.

"Do it, Hope!" Charles yelled.

She watched in wonder as he laughed and pounded his hands together.

"Come on, Hope!" he urged again, poking at her ribs.

She'd never been more motivated to whistle in all her life. This would be the granddaddy of them all—a whistle of praise and unrestrained joy. She took a deep breath to steady herself. Then she filled her lungs again and whistled long and loud, shrilly enough to rattle car windows in the parking lot.

Women recoiled and men stared, unbelieving. Little boys watched and worshiped. Three ballplayers turned to look at Hope and one lifted his cap in awed appreciation.

Charles covered his ears and laughed like a tickled ten-year-old.

Gazing up into his face, Hope thrilled to the sight and sound of him. She'd known him for almost a month, but she'd never seen him laugh like this. She hugged herself, thinking that if she accomplished nothing else in life she would still count her time on earth well spent because on this night she had done a marvelous thing: she had made sober, cynical Dr. Hartman laugh until his eyes were wet with tears.

The ball game was over, but Charles didn't want this night to be. He hadn't had this much fun in years. Strike that: he had *never* had this much fun. Not in his entire life.

It was all Hope. In three short weeks the girl had shaken his world.

They strolled back to her car without speaking. It was a balmy, beautiful evening and Hope was happy, humming under her breath, almost skipping beside Charles. Her hands were shoved deep into the pockets of her jeans and he could hear the jingle of her keys and loose change.

"Charlie, where's my car?" she asked suddenly.

"Over there." He pointed.

"Oh!" She giggled. "Now you know why I brought you." As she lifted her arms and executed a giddy pirouette someone behind them shouted.

"Hope Evans! Hey there, Twinkle Toes! How are you, sweetheart?" She was scooped into the arms of a large young man who squeezed her until she actually squeaked.

"Ryan!" Her voice was muffled in his bear hug. "It's great to see you!"

As the man let her go, another grabbed her and soundly kissed her forehead. "How ya doin', Shortstop?"

"Scott! I thought you were in Florida these days?"

Charles watched in amazement as the second man stepped back, allowing another to take his place.

"T.J., how's my boy?" Hope squealed, thumping him on the back as she hugged him. "Oh, it's so good to see you guys!"

She stood back, beaming at each of them in turn, and Charles looked around to see whether there were any more men in line to hug her. He thought briefly about taking a turn himself, but she was already making introductions.

All three of the men had played high school baseball with Hope's two middle brothers, Mark and Luke. They treated Hope like an adored little sister, and Charles guessed she had been something of a mascot to the team.

They chatted for a few minutes, then Hope hugged each of the men and said goodbye.

"They're so grown up!" she marveled to Charles as she unlocked her car. "I haven't seen them since my eighteenth birthday party, when they were just out of college. That was only five years ago, but it makes a huge difference, doesn't it?"

"Not to me. Five years is merely another drop in the bucket."

"Oh, stop talking like an old man," she scolded as she slid into the driver's seat.

Charles wondered, not for the first time, why a charmer like Hope was uninterested in romance. He supposed that someone had broken her heart. He wondered who. And when. And how.

But most of all, he wondered why. It was impossible for him to understand how any man could bring himself to hurt Hope Evans.

Chapter Five

Hope was in the habit of exchanging e-mails with her father at least once a week. In the past three weeks she'd written quite a bit about Charles and had asked her parents to pray for him.

Now she stared at her computer screen, rereading a disturbing message from her father.

> Sweetheart, I'm glad to know so many of our prayers have been answered regarding Dr. Hartman. It is indeed good news that he's attending Bible study and talking to you about spiritual matters. But your mother and I are a little worried about your spending so much time alone with the man. We're quite willing to believe he's as tenderhearted as you say, but it's our daughter's heart that concerns us.
>
> Hope, there's no future for you with a man who doesn't belong to God. We pray you'll see that before you get hurt.

Hope clicked the "message delete" button so she wouldn't have to see the note again. She'd write to her father later, when she wasn't feeling so sad and lonely.

She switched off her computer and wandered into the kitchen, where she heated a cup of water in the microwave oven. She unwrapped a bag of chamomile tea, holding it to her nose for a comforting sniff before dropping it into the hot water. The scent reminded her of her mother, who enjoyed a cup of herb tea and a few verses of Scripture each night before bed.

"Why am I so blue tonight?" The sound of Hope's voice startled Bob. His ears perked up and his golden-brown eyes studied her face, alert for any sign that she wanted him.

Hope understood what her father was saying, but she wasn't dating Charles. She *didn't* date, not ever. Not since Trevor Daniels.

Even now, nearly seven years after the night her heart had been ripped in two, the painful memories invaded her waking hours as well as her dreams.

"No," she moaned. She leaned against the kitchen counter for support. "I can't think about him tonight." But she did....

He had a beautiful smile. He turned it on her now, and she caught her breath. He had perfect teeth, movie-star white, and he was smiling just for her. Hope felt a thrill in her chest.

"You look incredible, Hope. Absolutely gorgeous. And yellow is a beautiful color on you."

She was pleased that Trevor liked her new dress. He moved closer and she lifted her arms as his went around her waist. She leaned against him, glorying in the warm, solid feel of him.

She was not quite seventeen and he was nearly twenty. Her parents were strict about dating, so she and Trevor had never actually been alone. They'd shared only quick, stolen kisses, and Hope had known nothing but the light-

*est brush of his mouth against hers. Tonight, though, he
was finally going to kiss her properly. She'd been dreaming about this moment for weeks.*

Overflowing with love, she lifted her face to his....

Hope's throat tightened and she brushed tears from her
eyes. As she slumped against the counter she heard the
soft jingle of Bob's collar. He came and sat at her feet,
willing to help in any way he could.

"Oh, God," she whispered brokenly. "It's been so
many years. Will it never stop hurting?"

Trevor Daniels was dead, and with him had been buried every girlish dream Hope had cherished about love
and marriage.

She removed the soggy tea bag from her cup and
stirred in a spoonful of sugar. If only her parents could
understand just how immune she was to romance. She
wasn't going to fall in love, not with Charles or anyone
else. Men didn't interest her in that way, not since Trevor.

She wrapped her hands around the warm cup. Closing
her eyes, she sipped slowly as she listened to the loud,
familiar rhythm of Granny Evans's old mantel clock.

On a current of loneliness Hope drifted into the living
room, where she found comfort in touching the well-
loved objects that made this house feel like home. Her
father's favorite chair, her mother's treasured Stafford-
shire china dogs, framed photographs of the boys and
their families—all were balm to Hope's wounded heart.

A lamp spilled soft light over one end of the sofa,
calling attention to the rumpled floral slipcover. Two
small pillows had been squashed against the armrest and
on the table, ice cubes melted in a half-finished glass of
mint tea.

Just over an hour ago, Charles had occupied that corner, listening to a ball game on television as he worked
the crossword puzzle from last Sunday's paper.

Hope smoothed the slipcover and plumped the pillows. Then she switched off the light and picked up the glass. As she headed back to the kitchen, something made her turn and look again at the corner, now dark and empty, and her blues were banished by a single thought: He would come again tomorrow.

On Sunday afternoon as he approached room 6120, Charles heard a commotion. John Seltzer had visitors—was Hope among them? Stopping to look in the doorway, he was overcome with dread. Low voices and quiet sobs told him the family had gathered for a deathwatch.

He hadn't spoken to Hope since late yesterday afternoon when he had watched a ball game at her house. But she had told him then that the old man appeared to be slipping. She had planned to consult with Gramps's doctor before asking Pastor Bill Barnes to notify the Seltzer family.

Now two men and three women surrounded the old man's bed, but Hope was not with them. Biting his lip, Charles looked up and down the hall. Where was she? He addressed one of the men. "I'm sorry to trouble you, but have you seen Hope?"

"Hope?" The man looked blank, but one of the women turned to face Charles. She pushed her eyeglasses up to her forehead and dabbed at her red-rimmed eyes with a ragged wad of tissues. "You must mean Hope Evans. She was here earlier, but she left as soon as we arrived. That must have been a couple of hours ago."

He found her in the lounge, in her usual corner. She had kicked off her sneakers and was sitting cross-legged in an armchair, hugging an open Bible. Her head rested against the high back of the chair and her eyes were closed. Her lips moved slightly, so Charles took the chair next to her and waited.

Her eyes opened. "I'm glad you're here," she said wearily, her voice barely audible. "I wanted you."

"You could have paged me," he chided gently.

She closed her Bible and placed it on the table next to her. "I didn't want to disturb you."

"I was just rounding, Hope. I could have—"

"Oh, Charlie!" Her eyes clouded and her chin quivered. "Gramps is going to—"

"I know," he said softly. In mute sympathy he surveyed her tear-streaked face. His fingers itched to brush back the strands of loose hair that clung to her damp cheeks, but he was afraid to touch her and he didn't know exactly why. He felt relieved when she tipped her head back, caught the errant strands with her fingertips and hooked them behind her small ears.

"Wouldn't you rather be in there?"

"His family is with him," she responded quietly.

He bristled. "You belong in that room if anyone does. I'm sure you've done more for him than—"

She cut him off. "Charlie, please don't." She lowered her wet, spiky lashes, hiding her eyes from him. "They all live out of town, and they don't know me very well. They don't realize how close Gramps and I have become in the past few years, so I can't intrude on them now."

His fists clenched in impotent anger. What had the Seltzers said to make Hope feel her presence was an intrusion? Were they jealous of the sweet young woman who had befriended their father?

Hope looked up, alarm darkening her eyes. "No, Charlie—it's okay," she soothed. "I sat with him all night. He gave me his blessing. And he asked me to thank you for visiting him."

Charles frowned. "I don't visit him. I've said hello a few times, that's all."

"Oh, really?" Hope let him see she wasn't buying it. "Last week he told me you sat with him one night while he ate his dinner. You even cut his chicken for him. He felt bad about being able to eat only two bites after you went to that trouble."

Her tears flowed again and Charles watched in silence as she wiped her eyes with a tissue. "Thank you for being nice to him," she choked. "I'm so grateful that you took the time. I'll never forget it, Charlie. Never."

His throat had closed and he couldn't reply, so he covered her soft, trembling hand with his. Was this how her God took care of her? Was she to suffer this heartbreaking loss all alone?

"He's ready to go home. He's not afraid. It's hard for me to let him go, but somehow, it really is okay, because he's going to God and I'll see him again. In a way, it's really quite wonderful. I wish you could understand."

Charles let go of her hand and stood. He walked to the window and looked out, but he might just as well have stared at the blank, pale green wall, because he saw nothing. "All I understand is that it's making you cry. How wonderful can that be?" He turned abruptly, as if he expected an answer from her.

Her wet blue eyes were enormous in her pale face as she pressed a shaking hand against her mouth. Looking away, Charles silently berated himself for adding to her distress. After a moment he forced himself to face her again. "Do you want me to go check on him?"

"I wish you would, Charlie."

He slid his hands into the pockets of his lab coat and nodded mutely, waiting as she struggled to say something more.

"Would you tell him—" The voice was tiny, tentative. "Would you please just tell him that I—"

"Of course I will," he said, having already read her request in the limpid depths of her eyes.

The memory of her tremulous smile haunted him as he walked back to John Seltzer's room. He paused at the doorway, not wanting to go in, but he carried a message and he was bound to deliver it.

When he entered, he found the men had gone and only two of the women remained. "I'm Dr. Hartman," he told them. "A friend. May I say goodbye to him?"

"Dr. Hartman?" echoed one of the women. "He's been asking for you. We couldn't think who he meant."

Charles approached the bed and slumped into the chair beside it. When he put his hand on John's, the old man's eyes opened.

"Can I do anything for you, Gramps?" Charles had surprised himself by using Hope's name for the man, but it had been exactly the right thing to do. The dull blue eyes opened wider and a weak smile of recognition lit the haggard face.

"Hope sends her love," Charles said, low enough so that only Gramps could hear.

"And mine to her," the old man replied in a feeble whisper. "Take care of her, Charles."

Charles looked at him in bewilderment. Who was he to be charged with such a responsibility? What could he possibly do for Hope? All he had to give her was money, but she wouldn't take that, however much she might need it.

"We'll just step outside for a minute," one of the women said to Charles. He half turned, but didn't look at her as he nodded.

The old man was whispering again, so Charles bent closer. "She's for you." Gramps sighed.

Charles panicked. "No, you don't understand. It's not like that with Hope and me."

"I understand…everything now" was the man's answer. "She's…for you, Charles." The weary eyes closed again and a few minutes later John Seltzer's last breath went out in a fluttery sigh. Charles was still holding his hand.

Was it just an old man's fond wish? How could anyone who cared for Hope wish Charles Hartman on her? The dying man couldn't possibly have known what he was saying.

I understand…everything now.

No. It simply wasn't true. Hope wasn't for him. She was far too young. Too sweet. And too good for him, in every way.

Charles had made it clear that he had nothing to give a woman, but Hope wasn't looking for romance. He knew very well what she saw in him: he was a friend who needed saving. Hope's compassion knew no bounds and she was going after Charles like a lifeguard after a drowning man.

What she stubbornly failed to accept was that he couldn't *be* saved. And he wasn't worth saving, anyway.

He had pretty much come to terms with their odd relationship. From the beginning he'd been helplessly drawn to her. She was an amazing kid, someone interesting to talk to. A breath of fresh air in his stale life. Her faith and her personality appeared to be fully integrated somehow, and that intrigued him.

He gave her everything he could, though that wasn't much. She could command him to do anything, and she knew that, but he was perfectly safe with her. And she was safe with *him,* just as long as he continued to think of her as a kid. If he ever began to look on her as a woman, it would be all too easy to hurt her.

Charles looked at the fragile hand he still held in his own. With everything in him he wished Gramps could hear and understand. And forgive him for not being the kind of man Hope needed.

When a nurse entered the room, Charles sighed and got to his feet. "Just now," he said quietly, answering her unspoken question. He left without another word.

Hope looked up as he entered the lounge. She read his face in an instant. "He's gone home?" she asked in a surprisingly steady voice.

Nodding miserably, Charles took the chair beside her. He watched her face, bracing himself for a torrent of tears, but her eyes were calm and, incredibly, the corners of her mouth were slightly turned up. Her peaceful expression intensified the confusion he felt. "Hope?" he ventured. "Can it really be wonderful?"

Her smile widened and her bright blue eyes sparkled like clear mountain lakes under the summer sun. That was all the answer she gave him.

"But it hurts, too?" His mind labored over the paradox.

Her smile faded. "It hurts a lot."

Charles watched her face, knowing that in another moment her chin would quiver and she would reach for the box of tissues at her elbow. Hope was a curious mixture of strength and vulnerability, and Charles understood Gramps's concern for her.

He rubbed his face with both hands. "I'm so very sorry," he murmured. He wasn't speaking to Hope, but to Gramps, who with his last breath had asked for something that Charles just couldn't give.

Charles escorted Hope to the funeral. He watched from across the room as she approached the Seltzers, politely offering her hand and her condolences. Then she greeted several friends, hugging each of them.

He was bitterly angry that Gramps had been taken from Hope. And he was furious that she'd been shut out by Gramps's children, just as if she had been nobody to the man.

Charles knew firsthand of Hope's devotion, and he firmly believed Gramps's family owed her a debt of gratitude. But the neglectful Seltzer daughters, each dressed head to toe in sober black, made a great show of their suffering and were given every attention while Hope, who deserved a medal for her selflessness, was left alone with her grief. The injustice of it burned like acid in Charles's throat.

The service was short and Charles didn't hear much of it. His attention was centered on the young woman at his side. Hope was a hugger, a hand-holder, and he longed to put his arm around her to show his support. But he didn't know if she wanted that from him, especially in front of her church friends.

During a prayer, she surprised him by leaning close and winding her arm through his. He softened instantly, turning towards her, showing her that he didn't mind.

It was a long way home from the cemetery, over an hour's drive, but Hope didn't speak until Charles pulled into her driveway. Then she thanked him but didn't ask him to come in.

He couldn't bear the thought of her spending the long afternoon alone, especially as the family was now gathering at Gramps's house, just across the street. Hope, who had mowed the man's lawn and stocked his refrigerator for nearly five years, had not been invited.

"Let me come in and sit with you a while," Charles urged.

"I won't be very good company," she warned.

"Then the doctor will finally have a taste of his own medicine, won't he?"

She managed a wan smile. "Oh, I don't suppose you're all that bad," she teased gently. "After all, you *are* a Charlie. I'm going to keep telling you until you believe it."

She persisted in believing something about him that was completely untrue. It was no reflection on him—he knew very well that he wasn't a nice man. That she so steadfastly clung to her convictions about his "goodness" said nothing about him and everything about her: Hope's loyalty was unfathomable. Charles had no idea what he could have done to inspire it.

It had been two days since Gramps's funeral and Hope was doing her best to get back into her routine. Groaning in exasperation, she flicked the power switch on her computer. She didn't know what to do next: it was a toss-up between laughing hysterically and sobbing uncontrollably. She was still trying to decide when the phone rang.

She picked it up immediately, hoping it would be Charles. It was, and as usual he didn't waste time on "hello."

"Hope, my brother wants to have dinner with you."

"Really? I thought Tom was a big-shot attorney," she said, trying for a lightness she didn't feel. "Can't he get his own dates?"

Charles made an amused sound. "I'm invited, too. He wants to meet you, that's all. Because he thinks you're a good influence on me."

"Oh, that's nothing," she quipped. "Attila the Hun would be a good influence on *you*, Dr. Hartman."

"Probably," Charles agreed. "Tom likes Japanese food. Is tomorrow night good for you?"

"Yeah." She patted her knee and Bob jumped into her lap. "Just promise me I won't have to eat fish bait."

"I promise. We'll get you a steak."

She forced a chuckle. "*Cooked,* I hope?"

"As 'cooked' as you want it. Now stop playing games and tell me what's wrong."

It was both comforting and unnerving that he could read her so effortlessly. Hope sighed. "I'm having a really bad day."

"I'm not busy," he said gently. "Talk to me."

She fingered one of Bob's silky ears as she vented her frustration. Her brain just wasn't working. She'd been making stupid mistakes all afternoon and her computer was acting up. Nothing was right and she was tired and she had a headache.

Charles zeroed in on the real problem. "You're missing Gramps," he stated. "Hope, I'm so sorry. I wish I could make it easier for you."

Hope wished that, too. How was she supposed to go on without Gramps? The pain of five years ago came back in a rush and she felt abandoned all over again.

She had always been remarkably mature for her age. Although she'd been barely eighteen when her parents left the country, they had no qualms about leaving her alone in Chicago. She was a responsible young woman with a safe place to live, money in the bank and a church home.

But Hope was lonely. She stopped eating dinner because it was just too hard to sit at the table all by herself. Bedtime was difficult, too, because there was no one to say good-night to. She put on a brave front, but Gramps had seen through her. He encouraged her to talk about her doubts and fears. Then they began to focus on her goals and dreams.

Hope told Charles all of it: how God had used Gramps to comfort her. He'd been her counselor and her encourager, but now all that had been taken away and she was alone again.

"But you *had* him," Charles pointed out. "You had him for five years and he helped you through a difficult transition. According to your theology, God put you and Gramps together—partly, at least—because you needed him at that particular time in your life. But if God has separated you now, doesn't that suggest the purpose for bringing you together has been accomplished?"

Hope was astounded. Where was he getting this? Of course he was right, but she was too shocked to say so.

Charles correctly interpreted her silence and gave a self-deprecating chuckle. "If I dropped a pearl of wisdom just now, let me assure you it was entirely accidental."

A sweet warmth stole over Hope. "What kind of doctor are you, again?"

"They say I'm a very good one."

He truly was. And he was a better friend than he would ever know. "Thank you, Charlie."

"Anytime, kid."

She squeezed Bob, but he wasn't in the mood to be loved on. He jumped down from her lap and trotted out of the room. "You're not busy tonight?"

"No. We're tossing a football and playing darts. And a first-year surgery resident is entertaining us by making balloon animals out of examination gloves. He's really quite talented, I had no idea. I'm sure he hasn't demonstrated that level of manual dexterity in the OR."

Hope smiled. Lifting a shoulder to trap the phone against her ear, she drew her legs up into her chair and hugged her knees. She heard an "Oof!" from Charles, then a banging and clattering that told her he'd dropped the phone.

She heard his voice as he picked it up. "One more time, Hastings, and I'll cut your heart out!" he growled. Then he spoke into the phone. "Sorry, Hope. He thought I was open for a pass. The football game is getting out of hand."

"Well, good. Maybe somebody will get hurt and you'll get to stitch up a gored gizzard or something."

He made an amused sound in his throat and Hope could imagine him shaking his head in that slow, mocking way of his. "At this point, if one of them complained of a hangnail I'd be perfectly willing to scrub. What I wouldn't give for a nice, juicy trauma right now."

Hope was shocked. "Charlie, what are you saying?"

"Oh, I'm not wishing disaster on anyone. But it's a fact that all over Chicago, people are getting hurt. I simply want them to bring the hurt ones to *me* tonight. Okay?"

She chuckled. "Okay. And thanks again for listening."

Her head still ached, her computer was probably on its last legs and, at the rate she was going, she would not be able to finish this translation by tomorrow as she had hoped. But she wasn't feeling sorry for herself anymore.

She marveled that God had used Charles to send a message to her. While her tired mind still struggled to make sense of her suffering, she firmly believed that her Heavenly Father knew exactly what He was doing.

Chapter Six

Thomas Hartman had the same build and coloring as his brother. His hair was lighter, nearly blond, and he wore it shorter than Charles did, but they had the same hazel eyes. Even their voices were almost identical, Hope noted, except Charles's was deeper. But their dispositions were poles apart.

Tom was friendly and outgoing and he had a ready smile. Although Charles was smiling more and was noticeably less abrupt since Hope had known him, the difference between the brothers was starkly apparent. But while it was impossible to resist Tom's easy charm, Hope was more convinced than ever that there was something rare and valuable in Charles. If only he would open his heart and allow God to reveal it.

Dinner at the Japanese restaurant was proving to be a marvelous adventure. After removing their shoes, Hope and the Hartman brothers had been led to a small, private room with a low table. There they sat on colorful cushions on a floor covered with tatami mats.

Their server, a willowy young woman dressed in a

luxurious kimono of emerald-green silk, seemed delighted when Hope greeted her in Japanese. Hope shot a pleading look at Charles, knowing he would understand her desire to converse in Japanese with this native speaker.

He gave her a good-natured shrug. "Go right ahead." With a wink and a grin that Hope didn't quite understand, he explained to his brother, "She wants to practice her Japanese."

Hope glimpsed a flicker of interest in Tom Hartman's bright eyes, but she didn't catch his response. She was already chattering to the young woman. *"I am learning your language,"* she said eagerly, *"but I know too little about your customs."*

Smiling broadly, the woman offered *oshibori* towels from a bamboo tray. In Japanese she explained that Hope should refresh her hands—and even her face, if she liked—with the hot, moist towel, just as the men were already doing.

Tom replaced his towel on the tray, then turned to Charles. "I'll bet they're talking about how handsome we are," he confided in a stage whisper.

When the Japanese woman darted a glance at Tom and giggled, Hope thought delightedly that it sounded like a hundred little silver bells tinkling all at once. *"They are handsome,"* said the woman in her own language. *"Are they brothers?"*

It was Hope's turn to giggle. *"Yes, and they're both single. Shall I introduce you to the doctor or the attorney?"*

Hope had asked that outrageous question solely for the pleasure of hearing the Japanese woman laugh again. She was treated to another ringing chorus of the silvery bells, then the woman bowed gracefully and backed out of the room, still holding her tray.

Turning back to the men, Hope caught Tom whispering to his brother. They both laughed and turned expectant faces to her.

Suspicion dawned. Blushing furiously, she forced herself to meet Tom Hartman's dancing eyes. "You speak Japanese," she accused faintly.

"Maybe just a little," he suggested. "So, which of us do you think she's interested in? Of course Trey has all the money and brains, but I've got him on looks and personality, don't you think?"

As the men laughed again, Hope eyed the low table, wishing it were a few inches higher off the floor so she could crawl under it. But Tom quickly put her at ease and within minutes they were chatting like old friends.

Hope wasn't sure how it happened, but somehow Tom had persuaded her to order sashimi. When a beautifully arranged plate of raw fish and unusual vegetables was set before her, she thought it looked more like a work of art than a meal. "This is exquisite," she admitted to Tom. "Do you look at it or eat it?"

"Both," he said amiably. "That's the fun, don't you see?"

Charles was having sukiyaki. "Beef," he said, answering Hope's unspoken question. "Definitely cooked." She gave him a here-goes-nothing look and picked up her chopsticks, determined to taste everything on her plate.

She tried three kinds of fish, some octopus, a couple of odd-looking vegetables and a nibble of pickled ginger that was actually quite refreshing.

"Well?" Tom waited for her reaction.

"I don't hate this," she said, surprising herself. "It's not awful. I'm not sure that it's delicious, but it's…fun."

"That's a start," he said approvingly.

Near the end of their meal Charles flinched and Hope

understood that his pager had signaled him by vibrating. He read the message, then excused himself from the table.

When Charles had gone, Tom turned his infectious smile on Hope. "I can't believe he actually allows you to call him Charlie. I used to try it when we were kids. He knocked me down a few times to help me remember not to do it anymore."

Hope grinned. "He doesn't like it much."

"But he likes *you*. A lot."

Hope was beginning to get the distinct impression that Tom thought he was interviewing a potential sister-in-law. She didn't know exactly how to disabuse him of that idea.

"You've done him a world of good," Tom asserted. He leaned forwards, speaking confidentially. "I understand you taught him to spit."

She felt her cheeks grow warm again. "Uh…"

"Yeah, I can't believe the moron didn't know how to eat sunflower seeds. I could have taught him years ago if only I'd been aware of his deficiency. Thank you for seeing to his education, Hope."

Thomas Hartman was too good to be true. Hope shook her head. "Are you and Dr. Hartman actually *blood* relations?"

He laughed. It was a wonderful sound, rich and throaty. "Boggles the mind, doesn't it?" After a moment he turned serious. "Yes, we're different. Trey's five years older than me, you know. When we were kids he took it upon himself to carry the burden."

"The burden?" Hope's hands twisted in her lap.

Tom nodded soberly. "Our family can be a bit much, I'm afraid. Our lives were mapped out for us and naturally we both resented it. But Trey did their bidding because of me."

Hope glanced at her agitated hands, willing them to be still. "Because of *you*, Tom?"

His eyes, so like his brother's, held hers easily. "Trey shielded me from our parents. He made concessions to them for my sake. They could have anything they wanted from Trey as long as they left me alone." Tom lowered his gaze, but not before Hope had glimpsed his deep sorrow. And something more: a profound admiration for his brother that warmed her heart.

After a short silence Tom again met her eyes. "Hope, I've never admitted this to anyone," he confessed in a low tone, "but I've always wondered what dreams Trey gave up so that I could have mine."

It wasn't easy to speak past the knot that had formed in her throat. "Didn't he want to be a doctor?"

Tom seemed to consider carefully before he spoke. "I've never been sure of that. All I know is that he'd have gone to medical school whether he wanted to or not. They expected both of us to go, but I decided at fifteen that I wanted to study law. Trey promised if I made the grades in high school and college, he'd see to the rest. So I buckled down. And he started medical school that fall."

The fluttering in Hope's stomach had nothing to do with the raw fish she'd just eaten. "But he's a good surgeon, isn't he?"

Tom nodded. "They say he's the best. I know he gets a lot of satisfaction out of his work."

Hope looked at her plate and blinked rapidly, willing her unspilled tears to dry. "Thank you for telling me," she murmured, not looking up. "It explains a lot."

But there was more, and Tom told it. The Hartmans had disapproved of the girl he'd fallen in love with. She was bright and beautiful and funny, but she'd lacked the pedigree a Hartman bride was expected to possess. Tom's parents had vowed to disinherit him, but he'd married Susan anyway.

"And did they do it?" Hope asked breathlessly.

"Absolutely. They don't make idle threats, and I knew that. They've barely spoken to me since the day I told them I was married. Still, it was the right thing to do. We were both just twenty at the time, but we were very much in love."

He unfolded his legs and shifted to a more comfortable position on the floor. "Susan and I finished college and we both went to a good law school. Trey paid for all of it."

"How did he manage that?"

Tom looked at her in surprise. "His inheritance. Don't you know about that?"

Hope shook her head.

"Well, it's no secret. Our father's sister died a month before I was born, but she doted on little Trey. The big family scandal was that she snubbed both her father and her brother, leaving her husband's entire fortune to Trey, to be held in trust until he was twenty-five. So you see, Trey came into his money just as I was cut off. But even without the inheritance, he'd have found some way to help Susan and me."

"Yes, I think he would have," Hope murmured. She swallowed painfully. "He's told me so little about your parents. I gather he doesn't see them much?"

"Just a few times a year. It tears him up, but he won't admit that. Hope, I couldn't begin to make you understand how cold our parents are."

"But *why?*"

Tom lifted his hands in a helpless gesture. "I don't know, really, but I think they've been unhappy in their marriage since the beginning. Maybe that explains why they never cared much for Trey and me, apart from the status they might gain through our accomplishments. And our marriages, I suppose. But except for Trey's stellar career, they haven't had much to brag about.''

Hope reached across the table, touching his wrist with gentle fingers as she looked into his sad eyes. "Charlie said your wife died. I'm sorry.''

He smiled wistfully. "Susan hoped I would marry again. I'd like to, and I'd love to have children. But I can't make myself look at another woman. It's not fear of being disloyal, it's just that I have no enthusiasm for it.''

Hope patted his wrist. "Three years isn't really very long, you know. I have a feeling somebody will get to you one day. But I'm glad you loved your wife so much.''

"Susan was everything wonderful. She anchored me, and she made me want to be a better man. She was to me what you are to Trey.''

Deeply shocked, Hope withdrew her hand. "Oh! No, you've misunderstood, Tom. We're not a couple.''

He shrugged and let that go. "Whatever. But I've seen the changes in him since he's known you. There's an amazing difference, Hope." He started to say something more, but his brother entered the room.

"You two look serious," Charles commented.

Tom shook his head and grinned. "We've just cemented our friendship, that's all. We're allied against you, united in the struggle to turn you into a living, breathing human being. Right, Hope?''

She followed his lead. "If it can be done, we'll do it!''

Tom propped his elbow on the table and leaned his chin on his hand. He looked steadily at Hope and she knew they *were* friends, solid ones. "We might as well dream big," he said cheerfully.

* * *

On Friday morning Hope finished a huge translating job. She delivered the documents, picked up a sizable check and decided to give herself a minivacation.

"I'm not even going to cut the grass this weekend unless I just happen to be in the mood," she told Charles when he called shortly before noon.

"Good for you, kid. Sorry I can't help you celebrate." He sounded exhausted, so Hope asked what he'd been up to.

"I just humiliated Tom on the squash court and now I'm going to bed. I'm on for twenty-four hours starting at six tonight. I'll call you late tomorrow afternoon, and then I'll take you to dinner and a movie if you want."

She had a better idea. "Why don't you just get a good night's rest and then take me to breakfast on Sunday?"

He grunted. "I suppose you'll want to go to that new restaurant that is so very conveniently located just across the street from your church?"

She tried to swallow a giggle, but it stuck in her throat, making her voice waver. "Charlie, they make the best French toast."

"Kid, I may be laboring under a profound sleep deficit, but I still know when I'm being conned. Isn't it enough that I go to your Bible study just about every Tuesday night?"

Hope shrugged, even though he couldn't see. "I'm greedy," she admitted.

"Have pity on me, Hope," he said in a weary tone she knew was only half-teasing. "I'm too tired to fend you off right now. We'll discuss it tomorrow."

She'd talk him into it, Hope thought smugly. She could talk him into anything.

At seven o'clock, her good friend Claire Baker arrived with an overnight case, a couple of rented videos and a bag of chocolate-covered pretzels. The plan was to watch movies, order a late-night pizza and talk until the wee hours. They would sleep late on Saturday, then they'd go out to lunch and indulge in some recreational shopping.

"Just don't let me spend too much money," Hope said to her friend. "This is a big paycheck, but it's all I have to live on for a while."

Claire filled two large mugs with coffee while Hope dumped the chocolate pretzels into a glass bowl. The young women made themselves comfortable at the kitchen table, on which they'd placed a tray of manicure supplies and a dozen colorful bottles of nail polish.

For several minutes they munched pretzels and savored their coffee, chatting quietly. Then Hope opened a bottle of nail color. "It's been too long since we did this," she complained.

"Yeah," Claire agreed. She uncapped another bottle and stroked burgundy-red polish on a thumbnail. "I guess I should consider myself fortunate that Dr. Hartman was busy tonight," she teased. Tossing her shoulder-length, pale blond curls, she turned clear green eyes on Hope. "Do you like this color?"

"Too dark for you. Try this one."

Claire accepted a small rose-hued bottle and twisted off its cap. "You haven't had a lot of time for me lately."

"I'm sorry," Hope said honestly. "I've been working like a maniac, and it's true that I've been spending every spare minute—not that there have been a lot of them—with Charlie."

They were silent for a few moments, each intent on her work, then Claire sought her friend's eyes. "Hope, what's going on between you and Dr. Hartman?"

"I'm not sure what you mean," Hope said innocently. She held up her left hand and twiddled her fingers, displaying five differently colored nails.

"He's not a Christian and you're dating him," returned Claire. Her lovely face was troubled. "I think we both know what your father would have to say about that."

Hope sighed. "I'm not dating him. Not like *you* mean. I've told you a hundred times that love and marriage aren't for me. Honestly, Claire, I'm not romantically involved with him."

Claire's loose curls swayed softly as she shook her head. "It's great that you're bringing him to church and Bible Study, but the two of you are getting awfully close. And if you can hang out with a man like *that* and not be tempted to become involved, there's something wrong with you!"

Hope was baffled. "What do you mean?"

Claire rolled her eyes. "Wake up, Evans!" she said impatiently. "He's gorgeous. He's rich. He's brilliant." She counted on her long, tapered fingers as she made each point. Then she lowered her hands and her voice, looking her friend straight in the eye. "And he's in love with you," she accused.

"Well," Hope said thoughtfully, determined to address each of Claire's points, "he's definitely rich and brilliant, but I can never quite decide whether he's handsome or not. But he's not in lo—"

"Then you're stupid," Claire interrupted. "He *is* handsome. Not in the pretty-boy Hollywood way, I'll grant you—but in a real-man kind of way."

Hope let that pass because she had something more important to settle. "But he's not in love with me, Claire. He doesn't want that any more than I do. We don't kiss or flirt. We just talk, and he won't talk to anybody else the way he talks to me. He comes to Bible study with me, but he wouldn't with anyone else."

Claire opened her mouth to speak, but Hope hurried on. "You know Dr. Bates from the Bible study?" she queried. "He's an oncologist or something like that. He and Russ Mackenzie asked Charlie to go for coffee with them, but Charlie brushed them off. Don't you see, Claire? I have influence with him that nobody else has. I have to try, don't I?"

Claire sighed. "I don't know. I just can't help thinking that you're playing with fire."

"I'm not 'playing' at all. I pray for him and talk to him about spiritual matters. If I turned my back on Charlie, he'd have nobody at all. I won't do it, Claire. I *can't.*" Surprised by her own vehemence, Hope gave her friend a weak but apologetic smile.

"Well, I'll pray for him," said Claire, backing off. "And you, of course." She held up another finger. "Too pink?"

The next evening Charles and Hope were being shown to their table in a crowded restaurant when someone called Charles's name. He paused to greet two men, offering each a hearty handshake.

"Are you alone, Charles? Join us!" one man boomed before he noticed Hope, who had been hanging back.

Charles made the introductions. Physicians from St. Louis, the men had just wrapped up a two-day conference in Chicago.

"This year has flown by," one of the doctors remarked. "I guess it's time for us to think about heading south, isn't it?"

"I'll be there," Charles confirmed. "Is Marge Silverman going to make it this year?"

"Yeah. And a new guy from Dallas."

Charles gave a satisfied nod. He told his colleagues he'd see them next month, then he led Hope to their own table.

She placed her napkin on her lap. "What's next month?"

He hesitated. "A business trip."

"Going anywhere interesting?"

"Not particularly," he said, looking a little uncomfortable. "Just to Mexico."

Hope was puzzled by his reticence. "A conference, you mean?"

"Something like that," he said dismissively. "I'll be gone for three weeks." He glanced at his menu. "Want to try the seared scallops? Tom says they're good here."

He obviously didn't want to tell her about the trip, so Hope tried to contain her curiosity. "Okay, put me down for the scallops," she said. "Did you have a good day? Work lots of wonders in the OR?"

"Yes, it was a good day. But I don't think you really want to hear about it," he said with a smile that was gently teasing. "Every time I try to tell you about an interesting case, you turn pale and shudder."

It was true. She really *didn't* want to hear about his work. Not the grisly details, anyway. When she was eleven she'd seen her grandfather lose three fingers to a piece of farm machinery. Even now, the memory of his bloody, mangled hand made her stomach churn and her knees go weak....

Something was coming together in her mind. Something about Charles and his doctor friends. And Mexico.

At last she had it. "I know why you're going to Mexico!"

"Do you?" He eyed her warily.

"You're meeting a bunch of doctors in Mexico," she said eagerly. "If it's not a conference, there's only one other thing it could be."

He tilted his head back. "And that would be...?"

Like an excited child, Hope bounced on the edge of

her chair. "It's a medical mission! You're going to provide care to poor people who wouldn't get it otherwise.
Oh, that's wonderful of you!"

"It's challenging work," he said defensively. "The
cases are interesting." Carefully avoiding her eyes, he
drank deeply from his water glass.

She leaned forwards, shaking her head. "That's not
why you go. You go because you're *nice*. You go because you, Dr. Hartman, are a Charlie among Charlies."

He opened his mouth to protest, but he gave up and
smiled at her instead. He'd been doing a lot of that lately.

But his face still looked drawn and tired. She gave him
a pitying look. "You're exhausted, aren't you? Let's skip
the movie and make it an early night."

His smile vanished. "You want me to take you to
breakfast in the morning. And then to church."

Charles was taking the Tuesday Bible study in stride,
but the Sunday service appeared to unnerve him. He'd
attended twice, and both times Hope had seen him visibly
rattled. Although he didn't participate in the hymn-
singing, the powerful music seemed to tug at his heart.
Having glimpsed the hunger in his eyes, Hope understood
why he wasn't eager to go again.

"Will you, Charlie? Please?" She nodded, encouraging him.

"Hope, I really—"

"Please?"

His finely sculpted mouth tightened as something bor-
dering on frustration flickered in his eyes.

"What's bothering you, Charlie?"

"My absolute inability to say no to you" was his gruff
reply. "It annoys me no end."

Hope smiled. He was so close. She couldn't let up
now.

Chapter Seven

He couldn't save her. No one could have saved her. But that didn't stop the anger that rose like hot bile in Charles's throat.

It had been a car wreck. They'd kept her alive, got her into surgery to address the massive internal bleeding, but two minutes after they opened her up, her blood pressure plummeted.

"No, don't do this!" Charles had thundered. "No!" But they couldn't hold on to her.

Her name was Kelli and she was twenty-seven, although she looked much younger. She had black hair and delicate features and fine dark eyebrows. Just like Hope.

In the emergency room she had clutched Charles's hand and begged him not to let her die.

Just yesterday at church, one of Hope's friends had asked Charles how he handled losing a patient. "Not very well" had been his terse reply. People assumed the hardest part of this job was losing a patient, but that wasn't so. More difficult was hearing the pleading voices, seeing the frightened eyes of people who realized they weren't

going to make it. Charles was continually amazed that
they seemed to know. More often than not, when a
trauma victim spoke of death, he or she was already circling the drain.

He turned his back on Kelli, swearing harshly as he
tore off his surgical gown and gloves. Another doctor put
a consoling hand on Charles's shoulder but it was immediately shrugged off.

In a far corner of the operating room he collapsed onto
a chair and picked up a telephone. He dialed Medical
Records and dictated his surgical notes in a flat voice.
Then he steeled himself and went out to face Kelli's father.

When that difficult task was accomplished Charles
went to the doctors' lounge and poured himself a cup of
coffee. Twice he picked up the telephone and put it down
again. Finally he gave in and dialed Hope's number.
"I'm sorry, but could we rethink our plans for the concert
tonight?" His voice sounded tight and unnatural. She
wouldn't miss that.

"Whatever you want, Charlie," she responded instantly. Her voice throbbed with compassion. "You lost
someone, didn't you?"

"Yes." His clipped tone conveyed his unwillingness
to discuss it.

"I'm sorry. Please come over, Charlie, just as soon as
you can. I'll cook something and we can talk or not
talk—whatever you want. Please come?"

His mouth opened but the word *no* stubbornly refused
to pass his lips. He leaned his head against the wall and
stared at the worn blue carpet, hating his weakness.
"Yes, all right," he said softly.

It frightened him that he was beginning to need her.

When Charles arrived, Hope took his arm and steered
him to the sofa. He didn't protest as she arranged pillows

around him. He looked surprised but offered no objection when she loosened his tie and slipped the button on his shirt collar. She even removed his shoes and propped his feet on the coffee table.

She brought him a glass of iced tea with a sprig of fresh mint in it. As he drank greedily, she called softly to Bob. "Sit here, Bobby," she ordered, patting the sofa, and the dog snuggled against Charles's thigh. Charles automatically lifted a hand to caress Bob's silky head.

"Dinner is almost ready," Hope said quietly.

Meeting her eyes, Charles nodded. He hadn't spoken at all.

Hope had prepared beef-vegetable soup, and she had a loaf of good, crusty bread and some soft cheese to accompany it. She'd even thrown together an apple tart, and the cinnamony fragrance wafting through the house suggested it was almost ready to come out of the oven. She filled the coffeemaker and set the table.

When she finished in the kitchen, Hope peeked around the corner and was deeply satisfied to find that Charles had fallen asleep. Bob's liquid gold-brown eyes gazed calmly at her, but he made no attempt to move out from under the heavy arm that rested on his back.

Dinner could wait. Charles needed the rest. Hope watched him for a moment, her heart aching with pity, then she reached for her Bible and the comfort of the Psalms. She settled onto a kitchen chair to read.

Half an hour later Charles padded into the kitchen, shoeless and sleepy-eyed. The smile he gave Hope was oddly boyish and appealing. "Aren't you going to feed me?"

He made light conversation over dinner. They were halfway through the meal before he got to the subject that was uppermost in their minds. "People die, Hope.

We see it all the time and we each have our own ways of dealing with it. Dr. Olmstead goes skydiving, and Dr. Murray rebuilds classic cars and races them. My coping strategy is to play squash until I drop from exhaustion.'' He gave her an apologetic smile. ''And I growl a lot, don't I?''

Hope set the soup tureen in front of him and silently refilled his bowl.

''We learn very quickly to close off parts of ourselves. Otherwise we'd never be able to do the job. You can see that, can't you? When we lose someone, I'm always angry and disappointed, but sometimes—'' He shook his head and began again. ''Today, something got to me in a way that rarely—'' Again he stopped. ''It's just that this one…hurt me.''

It was a lot for him to admit. Hope's heart swelled with compassion. ''I'll pray for you, of course,'' she said honestly. ''But is there anything else I can do?''

He reached for her hand and squeezed it in wordless gratitude. Hope was surprised but greatly pleased by the uncharacteristic gesture. She squeezed back, then she went to pour his coffee and cut him a generous slice of warm apple tart.

Hope saved a file to her computer's hard drive and got up to answer the summons of her doorbell. Charles stood on the porch looking as if he hadn't slept since she'd last seen him three days ago.

When she stepped aside, he went straight to the sofa and collapsed on it. ''May I sleep here?'' he asked without preamble.

''Sleep here?'' Hope parroted. ''What do you mean?''

He rubbed his face with his hands. ''I have to be back at the hospital in six hours. I'm supposed to be off but I rashly promised to cover for Olmstead tonight. Will you let me crash on your sofa?''

She still didn't understand the question. His apartment was closer to the hospital than her house was. And if all he wanted was a sofa, there was a very comfortable, extralong leather one in his office at the hospital. Why was he here? She sat beside him and waited.

''I've been having nightmares,'' he explained. ''The same thing over and over, every time I close my eyes. Now I have five hours to sleep and I desperately need—''

''But how will it help you to be *here?*'' she interrupted.

He tipped his head forwards and squeezed the back of his neck with both hands. ''The dreams are about you,'' he said simply. ''You remember the other day, when I was so upset? Her name was Kelli. She was twenty-seven, and she reminded me of you. She begged me not to let her die, but then she—''

''Charlie, no!'' Hope put her hand on his knee and shook him. ''You didn't fail Kelli. You can't blame yourself for her death.''

He leaned forwards, resting his elbows on his knees and dropping his head into his hands. ''I know that, Hope. But in my dreams it's all jumbled up and Kelli is you. I have no idea what it means, but I'm exhausted, and I thought if I could just sleep at your house today I wouldn't—''

''Charlie.'' She waited for him to raise his head and look at her. ''It's okay. I'm working on the computer in the guest room, and I have books and papers all over the bed. But you can have my room. This sofa is comfortable enough, but it's too short for you.''

''It doesn't matter. I can sleep anywhere.''

''Good,'' she said briskly, rising from the sofa. ''Then

you won't mind a nice, comfortable bed, will you?'' She took his hand and pulled him to his feet.

Hope drew back the bedcovers and fluffed pillows as Charles waited in the doorway of her room. When she moved past him, he thanked her and asked her to wake him in five hours.

She returned to the other bedroom, where she closed the door and said a prayer for him. Then she sat down in front of her computer, but was unable to concentrate on her work. She felt vaguely uneasy about the fact that there was a man in her bed. What would her parents think of this arrangement?

She decided to turn her attention to housework.

An hour later she was headed to the bathroom linen cupboard with an armload of freshly laundered towels when she noticed Charles had neglected to close her bedroom door. She put the towels away and went back to pull it shut.

As she leaned into the room and reached for the doorknob a rustle of sheets and a deep sigh riveted her attention to the sleeping man. He lay on his stomach with the bedcovers bunched around his waist, revealing a muscular back. His face was buried in the pillow and one long arm dangled over the edge of the bed, its fingertips just brushing the carpeted floor. His hand twitched slightly, and Hope wondered whether he was dreaming.

It had been a few years since she had seen any of her brothers in a similar posture, but the memories rushed back. She leaned against the doorframe and gave herself over to remembering Sunday mornings in her family's farmhouse.

Matthew, the eldest, could never seem to get his tie straight. Mark was always out of clean socks. Luke invariably ran late, missing breakfast because he stayed too long in the hot shower. And it was nearly impossible to get lazy John, the youngest, out of bed. They'd think he was up, and the minute they turned away, down he'd flop, pulling the covers over his head as if that would prevent anyone from disturbing him again.

It had been a forty-minute drive from their farm to the church, so they'd had to get an early start on Sundays. It had been no small feat to get the boys ready on time. Hope had been her mother's helper, cheerfully serving the big brothers whom she idolized.

Now all four of the boys were making memories with families of their own. Hope hugged herself, thinking gratefully that her family had been—still was—exactly what God intended a family to be.

She remained in the doorway, watching Charles sleep, and a painful lump formed in her throat. He had everything, but he had nothing at all. He was good-looking and rich, talented and successful, but there was no joy in his life. He didn't know God and he didn't like himself. He tried not to care, but he *did* care, deeply. Hope knew it, and so did Tom. Were they the only ones who understood?

Indignation surged in Hope. How could the world have rejected a jewel like Charles Hartman?

She strode purposefully to the chair beside her bed. She scooped up his clothes, bent to pick up his shoes and left the room. She didn't close the door.

At the appointed time she went in to wake him. His face was still in the pillow, so she lightly touched the back of his head. Of their own volition Hope's sensitive fingers dug deep into his thick, silky hair, exploring the lush waves for several seconds before reluctantly following her brain's command to withdraw.

His eyes opened, fully alert. He rolled to his side, pulling the covers up to his chest. When he smiled, Hope's heart lurched strangely.

He made a deep, growly sound of contentment. "I slept like a rock," he murmured, blinking at her.

She remembered this. The sleep-softened eyes, the wild hair, the froggy morning voice. Now a hand would come out to yank her ponytail and she'd hear a playful command. *What are you waiting for, brat? Bring me some coffee.*

Hope gave herself a mental shake. This man wasn't one of her brothers.

Charles spotted the neat stack of clean, freshly pressed clothes on the chair. "Hope, I never expected you to—"

"It's okay," she assured him. "I wanted to help. You can shower while I make you something to eat."

He propped himself up on an elbow and stared at her. "You're sweet," he said, then his mouth stretched wide in a silent yawn.

Sweet? Since when did Dr. Hartman use words like *sweet?* With an effort Hope hid her surprise. "The bathroom's through there," she said, pointing. "I've put out a new toothbrush and a disposable razor and a couple of other things you might need, but I don't have any shaving cream." She eyed his face critically. "And you look like you could use some."

"I'll make do, thanks. But I was planning to shower at the hospital, Hope. I never expected you to go to this trouble."

"It's no trouble," she said over her shoulder as she left the room. This time she closed the door.

Twenty minutes later he strolled into the kitchen, whistling under his breath as he knotted his tie. When he sat down, she put a plate of ham and eggs in front of him and poured his coffee.

"Hope, did you…?" He looked at her curiously. "Did you actually polish my shoes?"

"Yes. Do you mind?"

"No, they're perfect," he said in a strange voice. "It's just that nobody has ever done that for me before. Not just as a favor, I mean."

"I used to do it for my brothers. I know it's nutty, but I always liked polishing shoes. Something about the leathery smell, I guess."

The look on his face nearly broke her heart. "Thanks," he said wonderingly. "It makes me feel—" He searched for the word. "It makes me feel good."

Abruptly she turned away, glad to have the excuse of returning the coffee carafe to its warming plate. With her back to Charles, she took a deep breath and attempted to swallow the outrage that rose in her.

The man was honestly amazed that someone had polished his shoes. It angered Hope that such a small gesture could move him like that.

Two days later, they made the most of a rainy Saturday afternoon by browsing in a cozy little secondhand bookshop. Carrying three books and a paper cup of cappuccino, Hope was walking immediately behind Charles when he stopped suddenly to examine a display. She ran into him, pouring her full cup of coffee on his lower back.

"Yow! Ah! Kid, you're downright dangerous!"

"Charlie, I'm sorry!" Hope cried, deeply shocked by what she had done. "Are you badly burned?"

He closed his eyes briefly. "I'll live," he said in a tight voice.

He had left his suit coat in his car, and Hope cringed as she realized a dress shirt offered little protection against a hot-coffee assault on a man's back. She dearly hoped his wool slacks had cushioned the insult to the area below his belt.

A salesclerk approached, concern and suspicion mingled in his eyes.

"We'll pay for the damage," Charles growled. "Would you please find something to mop this up with?" As the clerk retreated, Charles turned to face Hope. "I can't believe you threw coffee on me."

"Well, you should signal before you make a sudden stop like that."

"I always brake for Hemingway. You should have remembered."

She took a soggy book from his hand. "Well, it seems you dumped *your* coffee on poor Mr. Wordsworth." She thought about what she had just said. "You were looking at Wordsworth, Charlie?" She gave him a teasing grin. "Isn't he a little sweet for a hard-boiled egg like you?"

"I was going to buy it for *you.*"

"You were?" Enormously pleased, she examined the hundred-year-old, cloth-bound book. "It's beautiful. And the pages aren't wet at all, just the cover. I don't mind that." She grinned again. "Besides, the stain will give me something to chuckle about when I'm ninety."

"Yes. And I will treasure the memory of my second-degree burn."

Hope grew serious again. "I really am sorry." She parked her books and her now-empty coffee cup on a nearby table. "Come on," she urged, putting one gentle hand on his waist and resting the other on his arm. "Nobody can see us back here in the corner. Pull out your shirt and let me have a look."

"No, it's okay," he said shortly, backing away from her. His tone was strange, a husky one she'd never heard him use, but she ignored it in her concern for him.

She stepped towards him and started to tug the shirt free, but she was afraid of hurting him. "Come on, Charlie, just let me—"

"Stop it, I'm fine!" He twisted away from her as if she had burned him a second time.

"I'm sorry," she murmured, unable to hide her shock.

"Hope, I didn't mean it," he said quickly, his expression unreadable. "It's not bad, really."

She stared, shaking her head in a silent apology.

He placed his hands on her shoulders, his eyes wide and dark now, seeming to beg for understanding. "Hope, you know I didn't mean it."

But she *didn't* know that. A minute ago there had been something strange, something deeply disturbing in his eyes and in his voice. She looked away from him, biting her lip in consternation.

The clerk returned with several towels, offering one to Charles before he began wiping coffee off several books. Hope had to get away before she burst into tears. "Charlie, I'd like to wait in the car," she said in a small, unsteady voice.

His hand went to his pocket and he silently offered his keys. Hope took them and whirled away from him.

Her tears were already falling as she wrenched open the passenger-side door of the Mercedes and slid into the soft leather seat. She pulled the door shut, then closed her eyes and forced herself to take several deep breaths.

Whatever had just happened had nothing to do with her clumsiness, she was certain. But what *was* it? She racked her brain and still came up clueless.

Lost in her troubled thoughts, she was startled when Charles opened his door. He slung a shopping bag onto the back seat before easing his lean frame behind the steering wheel. Although Hope had put his key in the ignition, he didn't move to start the car. He stared through the windshield as a drizzling rain made the transition to a downpour.

"Hope, I'm sorry." His voice was barely audible over

the loud, angry splattering of the rain on the car's roof and windshield.

She laced her fingers together and stared at them.

Charles moved suddenly, reaching over the seat for the bag he'd just thrown back there. He fished out a small book and placed it on her lap.

It was the Wordsworth. Its cover was damp, but the damage was surprisingly minimal. At his urging she opened it and saw what he had penned on the faded, marbled paper of the flyleaf: "For Hope, a better friend than I could ever deserve."

The inscription was signed and dated, but the signature was not his usual one. For the first time he had signed a name that no one but Hope had ever dared to call him: "Charlie Hartman."

He watched the rain. "Hope, you've always taken my surliness in stride. Not that you should. It's just that you always have."

He had a point. She knew his sharp words came from habit, not from his heart, and she had learned to ignore them. Why did they bother her now?

It was something about the way he had looked at her, but she didn't understand it, so how could she tell him? She sighed. "Please take me home, Charlie."

He moved to start the car, then suddenly dropped his hand and sat back in his seat. He stared straight ahead for a moment before turning to her. "Why do you spend so much time with me?"

"I...want to," she faltered.

A spark of frustration leaped in his eyes. "My salvation is not your responsibility."

Hope sucked in a breath, but said nothing.

"Do you think I don't know that you see me as a project?" he ranted, pushing his words like pins, straight into her heart.

Why was he doing this? She fought to keep her voice steady. "You're not a 'project' to me. You're my friend."

"Hope, you have a lot of friends. Maybe it's time to—"

"No, there's nobody like you." Didn't he know? Hadn't he guessed that? "I mean it, Charlie. You're my best friend." She closed the book and hugged it to her chest. "Please, let's not argue. I'm sorry for burning you and for—well, for whatever else I did."

He let out a long breath. "No, don't apologize," he said quietly. "You've done nothing at all. It's just something in me. A kind of wildness." Avoiding her eyes, he shook his head sadly. His wide shoulders slumped and he turned away from her, looking out his window at the slackening rain.

Hope was silent, praying desperately for insight and direction.

A minute later Charles's head came up and he seemed to shake off his dark mood. Hope waited, holding her breath, and finally their eyes met, held, communicated. Forgiveness was asked and granted without a word being spoken aloud.

Charles pressed the tip of her nose with his thumb. "You're not going to believe this," he said, "but I'm really in the mood for a good cup of coffee."

"Me, too," Hope admitted with a giggle. "But let's *drink* it this time, okay?"

Until tonight the Tuesday Bible study had never been boring. Pastor Bill and the others seemed to be enjoying a lively discussion, but instead of following it, Hope was doodling elaborate ice-cream sundaes in her little notebook. She couldn't stop yawning, although she tried hard to hide it, and she had peeked at her watch at least three times during the past twenty minutes.

Charles appeared to be giving even less attention to the meeting than Hope was. It was obvious that he had something on his mind, but every time she tried to catch his eye, he looked away. He was probably just tired, she thought. She was tired, too, after spending several long days and late nights in front of her computer. Maybe they shouldn't have come tonight.

When the meeting finally ended, Pastor Bill asked to speak privately with Hope. She couldn't help giggling when Charles nudged her and whispered, ''Now you've done it, kid. You got a detention for doodling in class.''

He had come straight from the hospital, so Hope had her own car tonight. She told him not to wait, but Charles lingered, speaking politely to several people as he downed two small cups of orange juice and three chocolate-chip cookies. ''This is dinner,'' he explained with a grin that didn't quite reach his eyes. He left a few minutes later, at Hope's insistence, but it was another fifteen minutes before the five or six people who remained finally trickled out into the night.

As Pastor Bill's wife rinsed coffee cups and put the kitchen to rights, Hope and the pastor straightened the living room. After they put away the small folding chairs and returned several errant sofa pillows to their rightful places, Pastor Bill picked up a heavy oak chair under each arm and headed down the short, wide hall to the dining room. ''Hope,'' he said over his shoulder, ''I've known you since you were a baby. Will you accept some fatherly advice?''

''I know what's coming,'' she said warily. She picked up two chairs and followed him. ''Dad has already reminded me that dating an unbeliever is a bad idea.''

Pastor Bill set down his chairs and pushed them up to

the dining room table. "I haven't talked much with Dr. Hartman, but if you like him, he must be something very special." He placed his palms on the table, leaning forwards and giving her a long, direct look. "But, Hope, he's not a Christian. Where do you expect this relationship to go?"

She put her chairs down and let out a weary breath. "Oh, Pastor, we enjoy being together, that's all. I pray for him and I talk to him about spiritual matters. But we're not in love."

"And how much longer will you be able to say that?"

She shook her head impatiently. "Pastor, you must have noticed that I have never dated."

"Yes, I've wondered about that." He removed his glasses and placed them on the table. Rubbing his eyes with stubby, wrinkled fingers, he went on. "I've seen several very fine young men gaze wistfully at you." He picked up the glasses, settled them once again on his face and looked expectantly at Hope.

She took a deep breath. "I can't honestly say that I have felt a 'call' from God, but for reasons I prefer to keep to myself, I'm certain that I'll never marry. So where's the harm? This is a friendship. I'm trying to lead him to God."

Her pastor gave her a stern look. "Hope, you know very well that people often find themselves in love without meaning it to happen. And you may have convinced yourself that your heart is in no danger, but have you thought about his?"

How could she make him understand? "I'm not the type of woman Charlie could ever be interested in," she said honestly. She turned away, starting back to the living room.

Behind her, Pastor Bill cleared his throat. "Maybe I

should tell you what I saw in his eyes tonight. They were on you every moment.''

"No," she protested. "There's nothing romantic going on, not on either side. You're mistaken, Pastor."

"I hope I am." He started to pick up another chair, but leaned against its tall back, instead. He looked old and tired.

"Pastor Bill, I'm sorry." Hope reached for his hand and gave it a brief squeeze. "You're just looking out for me, I know. Thank you for caring enough to speak up."

A few minutes later Hope went out to her car and found the Mercedes still parked behind it. Charles was leaning against his car, apparently lost in thought as he gazed up at the stars. He startled at her approach. "I just wanted to make sure you were okay," he offered in explanation. "You look awfully tired."

"I *am* tired," she said, meaning it.

His hand went to his pocket for his keys. "Welcome to the club, kid. Drive carefully, will you?"

"You too, Charlie. Good night."

"Hope?"

She turned, puzzled by his urgent tone.

"I mean it," he said. "Be careful, okay?"

She walked back to him. He'd been quiet all evening, but she'd been too tired to think much about it. Now she put a hand on his shoulder and spoke softly. "What happened today?"

He turned his head, avoiding her questioning gaze. She lowered her eyes, absently watching the steady rise and fall of his broad chest as she waited for him to find words.

"A woman ran a red light and got broadsided by an eighteen-wheeler," he said at last. "There were three small children in the back seat of the car. We saved the woman," he said with difficulty, "but she won't thank us for that when she wakes up in her hospital bed. She has only one leg now. And her kids…'' Shaking his head, he finished in a shocked whisper. "Oh, Hope, they're *gone.* All three of them are gone.''

How much longer was this man going to be able to delude himself that he didn't care about people? Hope leaned her forehead against his shoulder, where her hand still rested.

"All it takes is a second," he said. "You're tired or you're distracted and you—''

"Charlie, don't,'' she commanded. "You need to sleep.''

His head moved up and down. "Yeah. Both of us.''

"I'm careful,'' she assured him. "You be careful, too.'' She gave his shoulder a friendly pat and stepped away from him.

Their eyes met and held briefly, and Hope was nearly overcome by a sudden urge to slip her arms around his waist and hold on tight until all confusion, all weariness, all sorrow melted away. For both of them.

But he was already opening his car door.

Chapter Eight

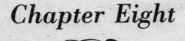

"**S**top pestering me, Charlie." Hope cradled the phone between her ear and shoulder as her fingers danced over the computer keyboard. "I'm working under a tight deadline, as you very well know."

"You can talk to me for five minutes," he insisted. "You need a break anyway. You've been working too hard this week."

Her fingers never slowed. "Oh, that's rich," she said, mildly irritated, "coming from the guy who considers four hours a sufficient night's rest."

"You're awfully cranky this morning," he returned pleasantly. "How much sleep did *you* get last night?"

She gave him no reply but the clacking of keys as she typed.

"Yes, I thought so," he said. "Kept the coffeepot going all night long, didn't you? Whereas I, on the other hand, got a solid eight hours of blissful slumber."

"Really? That's wonderful," she said, forgetting to be annoyed with him. "When was the last time you did that?"

"When I was still sleeping in a cradle, probably."

Well, she wasn't like Charles. He was a confirmed workaholic for whom there was no excuse. Hope was simply an unfortunate student who occasionally had to pull an all-nighter. She'd been out of school for more than a week now, but she was still scrambling to catch up on a couple of translating jobs.

The document she was working on had to be in Montreal by nine tomorrow morning. At this point she had no idea how she was going to accomplish that. She'd probably have to charter a jet, she thought grimly. She glanced at the tiny clock at the bottom of her computer screen and noted with a pang of dismay that it was already past noon.

"I'm free tomorrow," Charles said. "Want to go to the art museums?"

"Umm," she replied absently, her fingers flying.

She was translating a purchase agreement between a small Canadian shoe company and a Mexican manufacturer. Reading in French, she was typing rapidly in Spanish while speaking with Charles in English. Man, I'm good, she thought.

"Hope, get your fingers off that keyboard and talk to me," Charles insisted. "It's annoying to listen to that clatter."

She sighed and picked up her oversize coffee mug, taking a long drink of the too-strong brew. "Did you call for some *reason*, Charlie?"

"Yes. Will you attend an awards dinner with me?"

She pressed her weary forehead against the hot mug. "You know I will," she said. "Just tell me when."

"Seriously, Hope, I'm asking you to do me a huge favor."

She put the mug down, then arched her back, rotating

her shoulders one at a time. "How huge can a dinner be?"

"It's important, Hope. Do you have an evening gown?"

"No, but I know where I can borrow one. Claire has a closet full of them, all conveniently in my size." Just as long as she wore four-inch heels and a padded bra, but Charles didn't need to know those details.

"I'll buy you a dress," he said smoothly. "You should have one of your own."

Hope resumed her key-tapping. "I don't much like the idea of a man buying clothes for me," she said honestly.

"Pretend I'm your brother. You have so many you'd never notice another one."

"Never mind that right now. Why is this dinner so important?"

He hesitated. "My parents will be there."

Hope's fingers came to a complete stop and her mind whirled. "Your parents?" she croaked.

"You heard correctly."

No. Meeting Charles's parents was definitely *not* on her list of fun things to do. "Why on earth do you want me to have dinner with your parents? From what you and Tom have hinted, they'd eat me alive!"

Charles wasn't listening. Hope heard someone speak to him in an agitated tone and he replied, "No, let me take a look. I'm right behind you." When he spoke into the phone again, there was an urgent edge to his voice. "Hope, I have to go. May I come over around seven?"

"I'll be here," she promised. "Bring a veggie pizza if you want to be sure of a warm welcome."

Pizza. It didn't take much to please Hope Evans. Charles placed the large cardboard box on the passenger seat and turned the key in his car's ignition.

He was used to women who pouted for expensive jewelry and insisted on the finest champagne, but this one would be thrilled that he'd thought to pick up a few cans of ginger ale.

He liked that about her. Once when she'd teased him about being rich he had asked her, as a joke, what she would do with a million dollars. She was in a silly mood that night, so he had expected a hilarious reply. But although she laughed, he knew she wasn't really kidding.

"Well, I'd give it to foreign missions," she said. "Just as soon as I bought new tires for my car. And a celebratory pizza, of course."

That was when he'd started worrying about the tires she was driving on. At the earliest opportunity he'd slipped out, unobserved, to check them. He'd been relieved to find that while they definitely needed to be replaced, they were not yet a safety hazard. That was good, because she would never allow him to buy her a set of tires, he was certain.

It was frustrating because she was so insistent that she needed to make her own way in the world. "God will provide for me," she'd told him once. "I'm young and strong and able to work. Maybe I can't have everything I want, but I've never had to do without anything I truly needed."

She was a puzzle to Charles. He admired her, but he just couldn't figure her out. Where did a girl like that come from? Was she born that way, or had her parents taught her?

He thought bitterly of his own parents. He had pleaded with them not to disinherit Tom, but they stubbornly insisted that at twenty, Tom was too young to be married, especially to a girl who was not "Hartman material." When Susan died seven years later, Charles begged his parents to reconcile with Tom. His father's resolve had wavered, but his mother's fierce pride would not allow her to back down. That night Charles had sworn he would never again ask them for anything.

And he would never marry. Because even if by some miracle he found a woman he could tolerate for more than a few hours at a time, he never wanted to be a father. He would not risk doing to a child the things that had been done to Tom. There was a very real danger of that, Charles thought, because he had become every bit as hard and cold as his parents.

He wondered if he'd ever had a chance. Was he set on this path at birth, or had he just taken a wrong turn somewhere?

His edgy mood evaporated as he pulled into Hope's driveway and cut his engine. He closed his eyes to welcome the gentle waves of relief that washed over him. It was always like that when he came here.

He looked up and studied the little house. Behind two enormous blue-blossomed hydrangea bushes was a welcoming front porch with a comfortable swing on it. Inside the house was a friend who was always glad to see him and a chocolate-colored dog who thought Charles was the next best thing to pork chops. Was this what "home" felt like? He could only wonder.

He heard Hope singing as he came up the walk, something in German, and through the open window he smelled chocolate. Her famous brownies? Maybe this time they'd be for him and not a friend or neighbor who'd just had a baby. For some inexplicable reason Hope believed new babies called for chocolate.

Charles rang the bell. The singing stopped abruptly and he smiled. A few minutes ago his mind had been a tangle of fear and doubt, but now he was here, and somehow she would make everything all right.

* * *

When Hope opened her door, a great-smelling card-board box was thrust under her nose.

"Dinner is served," Charles announced.

The tantalizing aroma made her knees weak, but Hope perked up instantly when a six-pack of canned soda was handed to her. "Hey, ginger ale!" she squealed. She closed the front door and followed Charles—and her pizza—to the kitchen. "You don't like ginger ale, Charlie."

"You like it."

She bristled. "You don't have to ply me with ginger ale, Charlie. I already agreed to go to your stuffy dinner, parents and all. I am not a weasel."

He smiled. "It's not a bribe, kid—it's a reward."

As he put the box on the table, Hope eagerly threw back the lid. Not bothering to set out plates and napkins, she simply dove in, grabbing a slice and taking her first huge bite even before the seat of her jeans connected with her chair.

Charles watched in apparent amazement. "Hope, when was the last time you saw food?"

She wiped her mouth with the back of her hand. "Just a minute ago, when I took your brownies out of the oven," she said with her mouth full.

"*My* brownies?" He looked inordinately pleased.

"Yes." She unhitched a can from the six-pack and snapped it open. "But if you hadn't arrived with the pizza just when you did, I'd be halfway through that pan by now."

He gave her a look of stern disapproval. "So you haven't been sleeping *or* eating?"

"Stuff a sock in it, Doctor. I've had a rough couple of days, but it's over now. It was an aberration, I assure you."

That did not appease him. "How much trouble is it to pour a glass of milk and peel a banana?"

She took a long pull from her soda. "I haven't had time to run to the store, and I'm completely out of food. I thought long and hard about scrambling the last three eggs, but I knew you were bringing dinner. So I sacrificed them to make brownies."

He made an impatient noise and looked away from her. "The girl's a brainless wonder, Bob," he said to his furry friend. "How do you put up with her?"

Hope was too busy scarfing pizza and gulping ginger ale to defend herself, but she watched in fascination as Charles lifted a slice of pizza from the box. He had the most beautiful table manners she'd ever seen, but here he was, calmly eating pizza out of a box without so much as a paper napkin. He managed it with an air of unstudied elegance.

"What are you looking at?" he inquired.

"I'm waiting to see if you'll lick your fingers," she answered truthfully.

"Why?"

"Because you have exquisite manners and I haven't offered you a napkin. I was just wondering how you'd handle it."

His eyes twinkled as he produced a handkerchief from his pocket. "Prepared for every contingency," he said suavely. "Are you disappointed?"

"No, I'm delighted. I dearly wish my mother could see you. She'd cry tears of joy. She did her best, but my brothers are still animals." Hope downed half a can of soda in a single breath, then she again wiped her mouth on the back of her hand.

"Hmm. It would appear that she didn't wholly succeed with *you,* either. I suppose you're going to belch for me now?"

Hope loved the way his mouth moved when he was trying desperately not to smile. "Charlie, for a guy who's been up to his elbows in blood and guts all day, you are ridiculously easy to gross out."

"Hope, I have been performing surgery, not butchering beef. Credit me with a *little* finesse, won't you?"

Her mouth was stuffed again, so she put her index finger and thumb together and flashed him an okay sign.

"Thank you. Want to hear about the dinner?"

Hope raised her eyebrows and nodded vigorously.

"Tom's being honored," Charles began. "He has managed single-handedly to raise an incredible amount of money for the new burn unit at Lakeside. I have to give a speech and I want you to be there for Tom."

Hope was deeply interested. "That's wonderful," she said with feeling. "I'm not at all surprised that Tom did something so nice. But I don't understand why you want *me* to go."

Charles opened a can of ginger ale. "He and I will be alone at a table with our parents. They will barely speak to him, and Tom wouldn't dream of taking a date. If you come, I know he'll relax a little."

So Charles was still protecting his brother from their parents. Hope's heart ached for the mixed-up family. But it still didn't make sense. "I'm surprised your parents have consented to go," she said.

"That's the funny part—Mother is honorary chairperson of the organization that's giving the award. She's not going to be in a very good humor, I'm afraid. She was asked to introduce Tom, but she declined. I don't know what excuse she gave them, but I'm sure she made it sound perfectly reasonable. She excels at that sort of thing. Anyway, I'm going to do it."

Hope fought an urge to grab him and hug the stuffing out of him. "Of course you are," she said staunchly, angry that Tom's own mother would slight him. "So they'll sit with him for the sake of appearance?"

"That's it exactly. But they won't give another inch."

Hope's spine stiffened in fierce loyalty. "I'll do whatever I can."

"Thanks. I knew I could count on you." Charles wiped his fingers on his handkerchief and leaned forwards to extract his wallet from his back pocket.

"No," Hope said firmly. "I won't allow you to buy me a dress."

Hazel eyes flicked over her. "Actually, you will," he said with maddening certainty. "I knew you'd dig in your stubborn little heels, so I've developed an ingenious strategy for handling you."

Hope's eyes narrowed and her cherry-red fingernails drummed threateningly on the table. "*Handling* me?"

Charles selected a credit card from his wallet and laid it on the table before her. "You will take this to the finest store in town and buy something hideously extravagant."

She jeered at him. "Ha! I'd like to know what makes you think you'll be able to get me to do that!"

He gave her a smug look. "This is where my superior intellect comes in. However much you spend, I plan to double it and write a check in that amount to your church's missionary society."

He had her undivided attention.

"Brilliant plan, don't you agree?" His tone was annoyingly reasonable. He sat back in his chair and watched her intently.

She opened her mouth, but no sound came out. She took a sip of ginger ale and tried again. "Since when are you so interested in missions?"

"I'm not at all interested in missions. But you scrape to give them every penny you possibly can, so I don't believe you'll be able to resist an offer like this."

She had to admire him. "Charlie, you're an evil genius."

"Yes," he said contentedly, reaching for another slice of pizza. "I take pride in my work."

She continued to watch him. "But I don't understand. Putting an expensive dress on me won't impress your parents."

The teasing light faded from his eyes. "It has nothing to do with my parents," he said. "I just don't want you to feel like an interloper in a borrowed gown."

She stared.

His voice deepened. "Hope, I'm asking you to have dinner with people who would gladly go out of their way to slight you. I have every confidence that you'll be able to handle it, but it won't be pleasant. Wouldn't a pretty dress of your own help you feel more relaxed?"

His thoughtfulness amazed her. She'd been planning to borrow a dress from Claire, but Charles was right—she would feel like a gauche little girl playing dress-up. How was it possible that he understood?

He watched her, waiting for her decision. It wasn't a difficult one to make. She picked up the credit card. "So what's your limit?" she asked mischievously, running a fingernail over the raised numbers on the card.

"Limit?" He looked blank.

"Your credit limit."

He was still confused. "Why would I have a credit limit?"

She laughed. "Oh, I forgot! You probably own the bank."

He reached for her hand and rotated her wrist so he could read the name on the card she held. "No, not that one," he said seriously. "Not that I know of, anyway. But I don't always know what Tom is up to."

"Tom?"

"He manages my financial affairs so I can play surgeon. Occasionally he shoves a pile of papers under my nose and I sign them. Tom's a fiscal genius, so I don't usually bother him with questions."

He sipped his ginger ale and grimaced. "Yuck. This is definitely not an acquired taste." He got up and opened the cupboard next to the sink, removing a drinking glass. "Hope, I'm serious about this," he said over his shoulder as he turned on the faucet. "Have some fun, okay? Get your nails done or whatever it is that women do for these things. Take a friend with you and buy shoes and everything else you need. You can treat your friend to lunch and buy her a present for helping. Make a day of it."

He returned to the table with his drink. "Just be sure to keep all your receipts so you can add them up and let me know what to make the check out for."

Hope recruited Claire for the shopping excursion. A dental hygienist, Claire was off on Wednesdays, so that day had been set aside for their "girlish fun," as Claire called it. Over a breakfast of coffee and chocolate-filled croissants, they mapped out their shopping strategy.

By noon Hope had tried on five dresses. She and Claire had just made their decision when their salesclerk returned to the dressing room with a sky-blue silk they had overlooked. "Would you like to try this one? You seem to like clean, simple lines, so I have an idea this will please you. And the color will show off your lovely blue eyes."

Hope obligingly ducked her head and raised her hands, allowing the woman to ease the dress over her. Claire watched in the mirror as the gown was zipped and fastened. "Oh, Hope!" she breathed. "You're gorgeous!"

The saleswoman concurred. "I like the other one a lot, but this dress was made just for you."

It was by far the priciest one she had tried on, so Hope asked them to give her a moment to think about it. Left alone in the spacious dressing room, she stood on the platform and gazed wonderingly at her reflection in three large mirrors.

She had often been called pretty, but Hope had never felt that way. Now for the first time, she saw it. A solitary tear rolled down her cheek and she wished with all her heart that her mother could see her in this beautiful dress.

She took another look at the price tag and shuddered. But the gown was perfect in every way, and Charles *had* stressed that she should buy something "hideously extravagant."

"Claire," Hope called. "Tell her to hurry and ring this up before I change my mind."

Half an hour later they purchased a silvery pair of evening sandals and a tiny crystal-beaded bag. After that, Claire led the way to the cosmetic counters.

"Hope, try this lipstick." Claire had definitely entered into the spirit of the expedition. "And you need perfume, don't you?"

Of course she did. And a pair of dangly earrings.

"No." Claire was adamant. "I'll put your hair up for you, and with your long, slender neck you'll be plenty elegant without any jewelry at all. I imagine you'll make a lovely contrast to all the society matrons dripping with diamonds."

Hope consulted her watch. "Our manicure appointments are for three-fifteen, so we'll have time for a leisurely lunch."

Claire's bow-shaped lips curved up. "Sounds good. Is lunch on Dr. Hartman, too?"

"Naturally." Hope nudged her friend with an elbow. "I trust you're hungry for something expensive?"

* * *

The next evening, Charles sat at Hope's kitchen table and opened his checkbook. When he raised his eyebrows, waiting, she took a steadying breath and named an astonishing figure.

"Really?" His deep voice registered surprise. "Well, good for you. To be honest, I wasn't sure you'd have the guts."

She and Claire had enjoyed themselves tremendously. But late last night, Hope had added up the receipts and got the shock of her life. He couldn't have meant for her to spend *that* much.

She gave him a weak smile. "It's an awful lot, isn't it?"

"Not to me," he said comfortably.

He uncapped his fountain pen and Hope watched as he dated the check and made it out to the missionary society. "Are you really going to double it?" she asked.

"Oh, I might just round it up a little," he said casually. "Because I'm so pleased with you." His pen scratched lightly across the paper, then he signed the check and tore it free, folding it in half before placing it atop the stack of bills beside Hope's telephone.

"Thank you," she murmured. "It's very generous."

"No, not particularly." His eyes swept slowly over her as he slid the checkbook and pen into a pocket of his tuxedo jacket. "I have to say it again, Hope. You look beautiful. The gown is just perfect, and I really like your hair that way."

Hope smiled to herself. Of course she was beautiful. Dr. Hartman's magic credit card could make *anyone* beautiful.

"You look pretty gorgeous, yourself," she replied. What was it about the starchy black-and-whiteness of a tuxedo that made a man look so dashing? Charles was always nice-looking, tall and straight in his usual Italian suits, but tonight he was positively handsome. Hope had never thought that about him before. Could a wing collar and a bow tie do all that?

She couldn't stare at him forever, much as that idea appealed to her, so she dropped her gaze and examined her fingernails. Cut fashionably short and squared a little, they were painted the subtlest shell-pink.

Charles stood. "Are you going to admire your pretty hands all night, or may we go now?"

Suddenly Hope wanted to run. "Charlie," she squeaked. Her hand closed around his wrist in a desperate attempt to convey her nervousness.

He took her other hand and pulled her to her feet. "Don't fold on me, kid. Tom needs you. Just be yourself and everything will be fine."

Hope read the uncertainty in his hazel eyes and was stung by shame. This man had never denied her anything. He would move a mountain if she wished it. How could she deny this small request, the only thing he had ever asked of her?

She took a steadying breath and squeezed his hand. "I'm okay," she said, flashing him a confident smile. "Let's go."

Chapter Nine

$\backsim$

As she and Charles entered the glitzy banquet room of a venerable old downtown hotel, Hope sternly reminded herself not to gawk. Magnificent crystal chandeliers glowed overhead and tall candles flickered among the stunning floral arrangements that decorated each table. In the soft pink light of the room every man was handsome and every woman beautiful. And Hope noticed more than a few older women who appeared to be, as Claire had suggested, "dripping" with diamonds.

She felt a light touch on her elbow and heard Tom's voice. "Trey, why don't I take charge of the ravishing Miss Evans while you go find Donovan? Apparently there's some change or other about the timing of your speech."

Nodding at Tom, Charles touched Hope's shoulder, wordlessly excusing himself. Then Tom took Hope by the hand and introduced her to several of his friends before leading her to their own table, where he presented her to Dr. and Mrs. Winston Hartman.

Tall and slim like his sons, Dr. Hartman had neat gray

hair and the leathery brown face of a golfer. He gripped Hope's hand firmly. "A pleasure, Miss Evans," he said, but his bored expression strongly suggested otherwise.

"How do you do?" asked Mrs. Hartman, a trim, attractive blonde. Her handshake was as cool and impersonal as her face, which was a real shame. Hope thought she would be a beautiful woman if only her smile would reach her eyes instead of remaining confined to her flawlessly painted mouth.

Hope murmured the appropriate greetings and expressed polite regret at not being able to meet Dr. Hartman, Sr., who was home with a cold.

They had just seated themselves when Charles arrived. "Good evening, Mother," he said, bending to drop a perfunctory kiss on the smooth cheek that was offered. "Father," he said politely, shaking Dr. Hartman's hand, "is Granddad all right?"

"It's nothing that concerns us," said his mother crisply. "He didn't feel up to a late evening."

"Of course," said Charles in a tone every bit as starchy as hers. He took the empty chair between his father and Hope. "Shall I look in on him tomorrow?"

"Thank you, but he's fine. Dr. Jennings saw him today."

Shocked by the cold formality of their exchange, Hope darted a look at Charles. She was appalled by the hostile glint in his eyes.

"Mother, I wasn't offering to make a house call." His voice was low, but every word had a razor-sharp edge to it. "I was merely suggesting that I might visit my grandfather."

Tom looked at him in undisguised alarm. "Trey…" he began in a warning tone.

Hope's hand quickly moved under the table, finding Charles's knee and silently communicating an urgent message: *Not here, not tonight. Remember Tom.* Charles turned towards her, his harsh expression softening as he met her eyes. Hope removed her hand, silently thanked God and resumed breathing.

"I apologize for my tone, Mother," Charles said in a perfectly ordinary voice. "If it's not inconvenient, I would like to visit Granddad tomorrow morning."

"As you wish," said his mother dismissively. She looked at Hope. "You're from the hospital, I suppose, Miss…Everett?"

Hope smiled sweetly and let the error, which seemed to be intentional, pass. "No, I'm a grad student."

"Hope is a remarkably talented linguist," Charles said with a hint of pride that warmed her heart.

"Oh, how very interesting," said Mrs. Hartman, sounding not at all interested.

Both Charles and Tom had warned Hope about the impenetrable reserve of their parents. She had thought herself prepared to meet them, but the reality was much worse than she had braced herself for. Determined to meet the challenge, she squared her shoulders and turned on the charm full force. "Dr. and Mrs. Hartman, this must be a very proud night for you," she gushed.

"*Must* it?" Charles's father asked with palpable sarcasm.

Charles draped his arm across the back of Hope's chair, a warning. She ignored it, fixing a bright smile on her face. "Yes, Tom has accomplished quite a lot, hasn't he? And his brother, too, of course. I'm sure you're delighted with both of them. It must be terribly thrilling for you to know your children have turned out so well."

Tom gurgled and abruptly set down his water goblet. Charles gazed at Hope with unabashed admiration. Dr. Hartman ignored them all, turning in his chair to speak to a waiter.

"Thrilling," echoed Mrs. Hartman woodenly. "Of course." She delicately sipped her water.

Hope went on, perfectly aware of Dr. Hartman's indifference, Mrs. Hartman's scorn and the rapt attention of Charles and Tom. "Mrs. Hartman, there are many things I admire about each of your sons, but I am profoundly moved by the generosity of spirit I see in them. At the risk of embarrassing them—and you, of course—I just have to tell you that they inspire me!"

"How very kind of you to say so," murmured Mrs. Hartman, looking very unkindly at Hope.

Hope was unstoppable now. "Tom has achieved something truly remarkable by getting the burn unit financed, don't you think?" She tossed her head. "Oh, what am I saying? Here I am, rattling on like a fool, telling the man's very own mother that he's an incredibly generous individual! You must be beside yourself with delight."

"Indeed," said Mrs. Hartman icily. "*Beside* myself."

"Aw, cut it out, Hope," said Tom, obviously pleased.

Charles said nothing, but his eyes gleamed with satisfaction. When he removed his arm from the back of her chair, Hope experienced the same nervous thrill she'd felt years ago when her father had let go of her bicycle and sent her off, balancing on her own for the very first time.

As dinner was served, Charles inquired about the lectures his father had given at a recent medical conference. Then Tom mentioned Charles's upcoming trip to Mexico.

"Trey, you seem to be out of the country rather a lot," Mrs. Hartman reproved. "Shouldn't you be focusing more on your career?" Her steel-blue eyes issued an unmistakable challenge.

"Oh!" said Hope brightly. "But think what his services mean to those unfortunate people. I believe the doctors who do that work are bona fide heroes, Mrs. Hartman. Don't you agree?"

Mrs. Hartman's mouth made a firm, thin line. After a frigid silence, she spoke again. "Miss...Everstone, I'm interested in hearing where you met Trey."

"Well, we weren't formally introduced," Hope said airily, breaking a piece off her roll and buttering it. "I'm afraid I hit him."

She pretended to be unaware of the sensation her words had created. Three pairs of eyes were on her as she took a bite of her roll and chewed carefully. She sneaked a look at Charles and found him smiling at his plate as if his smoked salmon had just performed some clever trick.

Tom broke the stunned silence. "I knew it!" he said to his brother. "I never bought that wild tale about your disagreement with an escalator."

"It was an elevator," Charles corrected without looking up.

"Yeah, whatever. So, what did you do to Hope?"

"Oh, he didn't do anything," Hope replied casually. She lifted a forkful of salmon to her mouth and chewed thoughtfully. "This is very good."

"Yeah, sure—it's great," said Tom, who had yet to taste the salmon. "Why'd you hit Trey?"

Hope didn't know where the parents were in all of this; she was afraid to look at them. She kept her eyes on Tom and drank deeply from her water goblet before continuing. "I ran into his car in the hospital parking lot and I broke his taillight, that's all. Naturally, it was an accident, but I must confess that I ran away from the scene!"

Hope finally glanced at Mrs. Hartman. A minute ago she'd been convinced that the woman's eyebrows couldn't possibly be ratcheted up another notch, but she had been mistaken.

"Well, to be fair, you did toss me your wallet as you dashed by," Charles reminded Hope.

"Why did you do that?" Tom wanted to know.

"Because I was terribly upset and in a hurry," she replied. "I just meant for him to copy the information on my driver's license and then leave the wallet in my car. But he came looking for me, instead. He'd noticed that I didn't have enough money to pay for parking. So he sneaked a fifty-dollar bill into my wallet and then brought the wallet to me. Of course he tried to get away before I found the money."

"Sounds like something he'd do," said Tom, his head bobbing up and down.

Charles rolled his eyes. Hope looked at Mrs. Hartman for a response, but there was none, so she turned back to Charles. "Oh, stop making those faces," she ordered. "You just hate it, don't you, when somebody catches you being nice? Honestly, Charlie, sometimes you really—"

"Charlie?" Mrs. Hartman had spoken at last, and she looked like someone who had just inadvertently swallowed an insect.

Hope beamed at the woman. "I know everyone calls him 'Charles,' but I think that sounds just a little bit stuffy."

"Stuffy?" the woman echoed in undisguised disapproval.

Hope nodded emphatically. "Haven't you ever noticed that rich men always seem to be called 'Charles' and never 'Charlie'? Or is that just in the movies?"

"I'm sure I have no idea" was Mrs. Hartman's chilly response.

Charles suddenly lifted his napkin and Hope suspected him of wiping off a smile. She shrugged and went on. "Of course I could never call him 'Trey,' as you do, because of my grandfather. He lived in Tennessee and he raised hunting dogs. He had a favorite hound called Trey. He was third in the litter, of course. The dog, I mean—

not my grandfather. I believe Grandpa was actually a deuce...."

Tom made a strangling noise and dropped his butter knife on the tablecloth. Charles's eyes closed tightly and he shook with soundless mirth. Their father forgot himself entirely and chuckled.

Mrs. Hartman's elegantly painted mouth fell open most unattractively, but she made a quick recovery. "Miss...Everest, my son's name is an honorable one," she said frostily.

"Certainly it is," Hope affirmed. "But even if the name wasn't already in use by two fine men, Charlie would have made it honorable all by himself, don't you agree?"

"Absolutely!" Tom boomed. He leaned back in his chair, his wide grin testifying that he was having a marvelous time.

Chewing an inside corner of his bottom lip, Charles studied Hope in silent amazement. She was breathtakingly lovely tonight—not sexy or stylish, but undeniably elegant in a simple gown of pale blue.

Her poise was as remarkable as her beauty; but Charles, seated close beside her, had seen the telltale pulsing at the base of her throat. He could almost *hear* the wild hammering of her heart, and he marveled at her courage. Smiling brightly and chattering madly, she ignored the barbs that were so skillfully aimed at her. Every blow glanced off her armor of good humor.

In the dim light her vibrant blue eyes had darkened to indigo. And there was fire in them—not just reflected candlelight, but something that came from within her. To Charles's immense satisfaction, her indignation had been aroused on Tom's behalf. Hope had all the protective instincts his mother lacked. Tonight she had figuratively put her slender arms around Tom and she was telling his parents in no uncertain terms to back off.

They were getting the message, certainly; but the way Hope was delivering it was nothing short of brilliant. Charles could barely contain his admiration—it threatened to spill out of every pore of his body.

Profoundly grateful that no one was aware of her clammy hands and her nervously curling toes, Hope chattered nonstop, daring the Hartmans *not* to be entertained. Every time her courage began to falter she glanced at Charles and was strengthened by the warm approval in his eyes.

Picking up the thread of their earlier conversation, she turned to Tom. "There's just one thing that bothers me," she said. "I think Charles Winston Hartman is a beautiful name and Charles Winston Hartman, Jr. also has a lovely ring to it. But Charles Winston Hartman, III is problematic."

"Problematic? In what way?" challenged Mrs. Hartman.

"Well," Hope drawled, "you don't fully appreciate the difficulty until you look at his signature."

"I've never been able to read his signature," Tom confided. "He's a doctor, you know."

"Yes, of course. But think what his signature looks like. The first name is a squiggle, the middle name is a scribble, the last name is almost a straight line and then at the end you see the problem."

Charles took the bait. "What problem?"

"Well, it's all those pesky Roman numerals," Hope said reasonably, spelling it out for him. "I-I-I." She looked at Tom again. "How can a man be expected to maintain any semblance of modesty when his own name whips up his ego like that?"

Tom chuckled. "It explains a lot, doesn't it?"

Dr. Winston Hartman had been watching Hope steadily, a half smile on his tanned face. But the smile was no longer cynical. He was genuinely amused.

For a fleeting moment Mrs. Hartman's eyes shone on Hope with grudging admiration and she looked as if she, too, wanted to laugh. But the impassive mask slid over her features once more.

"Hope." Charles looked at the ceiling, trying desperately but failing utterly to keep a straight face.

"Is something wrong, Charlie?" she asked innocently.

His shoulders shook. "You're killing me!"

"Oh, I wouldn't worry," she said tranquilly, looking around her. "You know, I'll bet you couldn't toss an olive in this room without hitting a doctor. Want me to get one for you? A doctor, I mean. I know you don't care for olives."

That brought a peal of helpless laughter from Tom, and Charles lost what little control he had left.

They managed to calm themselves as the room lights dimmed and the master of ceremonies spoke into the microphone. Hope turned in her chair, ostensibly to see the speaker, but actually to escape Mrs. Hartman's unnerving gaze. She closed her eyes and took a steadying breath. Her heart was pounding, but Tom and Charles were perfectly at ease.

How nice for *them;* Hope was a mess.

Charles leaned towards her and put his mouth next to her ear. "And you called *me* an evil genius!" he whispered. "That was quite a performance, kid."

Several speeches and awards followed, then Charles got up. He seemed to enjoy himself immensely as he shared a string of humorous anecdotes about his brother. "I've been saving up these stories for years," he confided to the audience, "just waiting for my chance to embarrass Tom publicly.'' He looked at his brother. ''How am I doing so far?''

Tom gave him a wry grin and a thumbs-up, then covered his face with both hands, shaking his head. The audience loved it and Hope was pleased that even Dr. and Mrs. Hartman laughed.

Finally Tom went forwards to accept the award and express his thanks, and the evening's program was at an end.

When they rose from the table, Dr. Winston Hartman held out a hand to Hope and actually said he had enjoyed meeting her. Mrs. Hartman smiled enigmatically and, casting a speculative glance at Charles, told ''Miss Everheart'' that she was ''a most unusual young woman.''

As his parents left the room, Tom positioned himself directly in front of Hope. He dropped dramatically to one knee and pounded his right fist against his heart. ''Hope Evans,'' he declared ardently, ''from this day forwards I am your devoted slave!''

''The line forms behind me,'' Charles announced quietly.

Hope reached for Tom's hand and pulled him to his feet. ''Well, my first command is that there be no more awards dinners. I don't think my nerves could stand another evening like this!''

Tom squeezed her hand before letting go. ''The folks are pretty terrible, aren't they? I thought Mother would eat you alive, but Trey assured me you could handle yourself. What he neglected to mention was that you could handle Mother, as well!''

''I've never seen anyone tie a knot in Mother's tail like Hope just did,'' Charles commented.

''Wasn't she great?'' Tom enthused. ''I wish dinner could have lasted longer!''

Hope groaned. "My heart still hasn't returned to a normal rhythm," she confessed.

Charles consulted his brother. "Is that place across the street still open? You know, the place Susan liked so much?"

"Yeah, till midnight." Tom turned to Hope. "We know the best ice-cream parlor in the universe. Are you interested?"

"It sounds wonderful," she said with enthusiasm. She'd been too nervous to eat much dinner. "Is it the kind of place where they do incredible things with hot fudge and pecans?"

"They'll do anything you want," Tom Hartman promised. "And so will we."

"Now and forever," Charles confirmed. "We owe you, Hope. We won't forget."

She gulped. "Right. Let's just hope your mother forgets what *she* owes me!"

Hope slipped off her silvery sandals and tucked her feet up beside her. This was luxury. She had a whole side of the comfortable red-velvet booth to herself and across the table from her, two handsome, elegantly dressed gentlemen were going out of their way to charm and entertain her.

She dipped a long-handled spoon into a deep parfait glass and brought up a glob of hot fudge and melting vanilla ice cream. She savored the warm-cold sweetness and then plunged her spoon in again, digging for a fat pecan. Acquiring the treasure, she glanced up, straight into Tom's dancing eyes.

Tom was a peanuts man, and it had disappointed Hope a little to learn that about him. She felt strongly that all right-thinking individuals acknowledged the superiority of pecans. Still, Tom harbored a commendable appreciation of hot fudge, so he was as worthy a pig-out partner as she was ever likely to find.

Charles didn't care for ice cream, so he sipped coffee and scowled in mock disapproval as his brother and Hope dug into their enormous sundaes with unbridled enthusiasm.

Holding a maraschino cherry by the stem, Hope admired its plump redness before dropping it into her mouth and pulling the stem through her teeth. Deeply satisfied by the sensation of slowly squeezing the luscious cherry between her molars, she handed the stem to Tom. "More," she commanded.

"Absolutely!" he agreed, waving the cherry stem to signal their attentive waiter. "Isn't this a great place, Hope?"

"Too good to be true. There must be a catch."

Charles lowered his coffee cup and offered his professional opinion. "I think the catch is that you're consuming about half a million calories' worth of something that has no redeeming nutritional value whatsoever. Then of course there's the cholesterol issue…"

"Killjoy," muttered Tom, licking his spoon in a greedy way that would have shocked his fastidious mother.

Hope frowned at Tom. "Nice going, Hartman!" she scolded. "Why'd you have to bring Dr. Doom to our ice-cream party?"

"I thought he was with you," Tom returned.

They both glared at Charles until he laughed. "Okay," said the doctor. "I take it back. I don't suppose ice-cream sundaes, in moderation, will do you any real harm."

"You moron," said Tom with feigned contempt. "Ice-cream sundaes 'in moderation' are no fun at all." He winked at Hope. "Give me ice-cream sundaes in reckless abundance! Pile them high with cherries and nuts and then drizzle unspeakably gooey things on top of them!''

"Hear, hear!" Hope contributed eagerly, rapping her spoon against the side of her half-empty water glass and loving the tinkling sound it made. "Oat bran may help us live longer, Dr. Hartman, but I would not *want* to live without ice cream!"

"I'm with the lady," said Tom, pointing his spoon at her.

Charles smiled. "The lady has chocolate on her face." He reached across the table and dabbed at Hope's chin with his own napkin. She sat perfectly still, delighted by the happy light in his eyes. It occurred to her—and she gave silent thanks to God—that smiling was becoming a habit for Charles Hartman.

He was still smiling as, with a flourish, their waiter placed a small silver bowl on the table.

It was full of cherries.

Hope's body melted gratefully into the butter-soft leather seat of the Mercedes. Her eyelids drooped to half-mast and she was only dimly aware of the colorful city lights that flickered past them as Charles drove her home in an easy silence.

She was startled awake when he opened her door. "Let's go, Cinderella. You can't sleep in my car."

She yawned. "Well, I believe I was doing a pretty good job of it." She accepted his hand and was pulled to her feet. They strolled up the walk and climbed the porch steps, by an unspoken agreement heading to the swing instead of the front door.

"It turned out to be quite a lovely evening," Charles said, pushing with his feet to rock the swing.

"Yes," Hope agreed, yawning again. "Thank you, Charlie."

"I knew it was right to take you," he said. "I'm sure Tom hasn't enjoyed himself like that since before Susan died. Hope, I'm more grateful than I can say."

She leaned her head against his shoulder, acknowledging his thanks, and for ten minutes they listened together to the night sounds and the rhythmic squeak of the moving swing. Then Hope slipped off her sandals and put them on the seat between herself and Charles. "These are pretty, aren't they? I balked at spending so much, but Claire said, 'It's not a two-hundred-dollar pair of shoes. It's a four-hundred-dollar donation to the missionary society.'

"Claire's an intelligent young woman."

"Not to mention drop-dead gorgeous."

"I suppose so."

Hope giggled. "Want her phone number?"

"Isn't she a little young for me?"

"Young? Claire's twenty-six."

"Practically middle-aged," he teased. His eyes flicked over Hope and his voice deepened. "Would you really throw your friend to a wolf like me?"

She slapped a mosquito off her bare arm. "Claire would be sorely tempted, but she wouldn't go out with you."

Charles gave her the tight-lipped smile that she hated because it always seemed to precede a nasty remark. "Why is that? Because I'm not a Christian?"

"Yes," she said uncomfortably.

"You go out with me," he accused.

"That's different."

"How is it different?"

She didn't know quite what to say. "Well, it's not like we're dating," she said finally.

"Isn't it?" His eyes glittered in the dim light and he stopped the swing. "What *are* we doing, Hope?"

"I...well...we're friends, aren't we?" She watched him closely, trying to understand why he was pressing her this way. "I enjoy your company and you enjoy mine, so we spend a lot of time together. But we're not—" she yawned "—dating."

"Go to bed," he said gently. "I want to sit here and look at the stars for a while. Turn off the porch light, will you?"

"Okay. Good night, Charlie. Be careful driving home."

The porch light went off and Charles tilted his head, listening to make sure she turned the dead bolt.

What *was* he doing with Hope? He'd been asking himself that question for weeks. She'd been only partly correct when she said he enjoyed her company. The truth was, he needed her company like he needed air to breathe.

He didn't understand it. All he knew was that her gentleness, her remarkable good sense, her unquenchable optimism, everything about her soothed him. Just saying her name, Hope, somehow tamed the angry beast in him.

Tom said he was on dangerous ground, walking around the edges of love. But good-hearted Tom was incapable of understanding how much a man could despise himself. How a human heart could be as cold and hard and unyielding as a stone. The problem was that Charles *couldn't* fall in love, not even with Hope, and that knowledge filled him with despair.

But what about Hope? Sometimes he saw a tenderness in her eyes that frightened him. He longed to pull her into his arms, but he would allow himself to do nothing that might encourage a deeper feeling than the warm friendship she gave so freely.

He'd come dangerously close to kissing her that day

in the bookstore when she spilled coffee on him. She'd wanted simply to check his burned back, but when she put her hands on him he'd nearly lost control. Shocked by his sudden desire, he'd barked at her in a desperate attempt to keep her at a distance. That mistake had almost cost him her friendship.

He felt like a man walking a tightrope, and it was becoming increasingly difficult to maintain his balance. He had to be with her, but he couldn't afford to get too close. He couldn't let her go, but if tenderhearted Hope ever began to imagine that she was in love with him he would *have* to. Somehow.

For a long time Charles watched the stars dance to unheard music in the black-velvet sky. The night was deceptively calm, he thought; surely this quiet universe was only a heartbeat away from spinning out of control.

He was filled with fear.

"Don't let her love me," he whispered to the distant points of light. "Please don't, because I'll never be able to give her anything in return. Do anything to me—I will bear it. Just don't let Hope love a man who has no heart."

Chapter Ten

"Two, please," Charles told the woman behind the lemonade stand. "Big ones. Lots of ice."

On a sunny Friday morning they'd driven to the country for an antique auction and flea market. Hope was scouting for a sturdy sewing basket she could refurbish for her mother's upcoming birthday. Charles was getting an education.

"Auctions, I know about," he had said to Hope over breakfast. "I've bought paintings at Sotheby's. But what exactly is a flea market?"

"You'll see when we get there" had been her reply. "Brace yourself for a culture shock."

He seemed to be enjoying himself immensely as they pondered over mysterious gadgets and shook their heads at some of the junk people were so eager to buy. He'd even purchased an antique pocket watch for his grandfather, who collected and repaired them.

Hope hadn't found what she'd been looking for, but it was worth the ninety-minute drive just to see Charles's stunned expression when he witnessed two middle-aged women emitting squeals of girlish delight and eagerly plunking down their money for the privilege of taking home a black-velvet painting of Elvis.

It was hot. There wasn't a cloud in the sky and the merciless sun was taking no prisoners. Even in khaki shorts and a sleeveless white cotton shirt, Hope was sticky with sweat. Only occasionally was there a soft puff of wind, but it was a perfect day, Hope thought, for sipping freshly squeezed lemonade and munching peanut-butter cookies in the deep shade of an enormous oak tree.

They escaped the crowd by hopping a fence and climbing the steep hill that was crowned by the ancient tree. Hope sank into the tall, almost-cool grass and watched as Charles dropped gracefully beside her. "You look so different," she told him, accepting the large cup of lemonade he offered and handing him a cookie. "Are you boycotting Armani?"

He looked down at his plain gray T-shirt and faded blue jeans. "You don't approve of my outfit?" He removed his Chicago Cubs ball cap to finger-comb his damp hair. "You told me to dress 'scruffy' today. I thought I did pretty well."

"You did great. I like it. It's just such a novelty, you understand. When you're not wearing your doctor outfit, you're wearing a suit. I've never seen you in anything else, have I?"

"Not true. Last week you saw me in black tie."

She gave him an exasperated look.

He leaned back on his elbows, stretching out his long legs and crossing them at the ankles. He studied the green canopy above them. "You're trying to tell me I work too much."

"Would it kill you to make room in your life for a few more T-shirt days?" she asked wistfully.

"Not if they could all be as nice as this one," he said, still looking up. "Got another cookie?"

"I only bought two," she apologized, handing him the last bite of her own. "I didn't know they'd be this good. Besides, we haven't had lunch yet."

He took the tidbit she offered, then sat up and reached for his lemonade. He watched with lazy interest as a honeybee inspected his bare forearm before discovering the cup of sticky-sweet liquid in his hand. "I'm going for more cookies," he decided. "Let's forget about lunch. Unless you want a sandwich or something?"

She didn't. She enthusiastically embraced the cookies-for-lunch proposal. It had to be a nutritionally sound idea, she reasoned, since a doctor was suggesting it.

She gulped her icy lemonade and wiped the corners of her mouth with her thumb, watching as Charles descended the hill. He waded through the rushing river of people, making his way back to the baked-goods table.

It was true, what Tom had said. Charles *was* different. He was calmer, not as easily irritated. He was smiling more, and now he laughed easily and often. In the two months since they'd met, he'd changed in so many small ways that only now, when she studied him from a distance, did Hope see it.

With hands in his pockets, he sauntered through the crowd. Fascinated, Hope watched his long, easy strides. A tiny child darted in front of him and Charles stopped suddenly, bending to lay his large hand on the little blond head. Hope smiled as he gently steered the toddler out of harm's way and back to its mother.

"Yes," she said under her breath. She looked up at the hot blue sky. *You're working on him, aren't You, Lord? Please keep it up. And show me what I can do to help.*

* * *

With a full bag of groceries in one arm, Hope answered her kitchen telephone on the sixth ring. The deep, familiar voice made her smile.

"Hello, Hope. This is—"

"Tom Hartman," she finished for him.

He sounded pleased. "How did you know? People say our voices are identical on the phone."

She eased the heavy bag onto the counter. "It was the 'hello' that tipped me off. He never says that. He just starts talking."

"That's true. Listen, Hope—how about doing me a favor?"

"I already did you one," she teased. "How quickly you men forget!"

"Now, there you're wrong, honey. I will *never* forget. But did Trey tell you they took our grandfather to the hospital for surgery yesterday morning?"

She tucked the phone against her shoulder and began pulling groceries out of the paper bag. "Yes. I understand he broke his hip." With her foot she gently nudged Bob out of the way so she could open the refrigerator. "How is he today?"

"He'll be fine. But he needs cheering up and I have an idea," Tom said carefully. "Why don't you visit him tomorrow?"

What? Hope dropped a bag of frozen peas on the floor. It split on impact and tiny green balls bounced and rolled in all directions, much to Bob's delight.

Was Tom out of his mind? She hadn't yet recovered from her harrowing encounter with Dr. and Mrs. Hartman. Was he really asking her to go back into the lion's den?

That's what it sounded like. But she couldn't say no to Tom. If he thought she could do some good, she ought to go.

"Aw, come on, Hope," he encouraged. "You may as well know the entire family, right? And I really think you could do wonders for the old man. He's not exactly a teddy bear, but he's not as bad as my parents, either."

She caved. "Okay. But you'll owe me ice cream for this."

Tom pressed his hand into the small of Hope's back, urging her to approach the hospital bed. "Good afternoon, Granddad. May I present Hope Evans?"

"I believe you just did," the old man snapped.

Hope stifled a giggle. He was a Hartman, all right. But he looked like a fairly harmless one, old and thin and bespectacled. What hair he had was not gray but snowy white, and it was short and neatly combed, leaving a perfect pink circle in the middle of his head. He was dressed in a pair of luxurious royal-blue silk pajamas.

"What do you want?" the man growled at Hope.

"Tom says you need cheering up. I happen to be good at that."

Dr. Hartman grunted. "I don't need cheering up."

He didn't look all that dangerous. Hope inched closer. "Isn't that a little like saying, 'I am not insane'? Nobody believes you."

He almost smiled. "Young woman," he said, enunciating every word, "I am *not* insane."

"Okay. But what if you were? Would you admit it?" Without being invited to do so, Hope took the chair beside Dr. Hartman's bed. She was aware of Tom slinking around the corner and out of the room, but she wasn't too concerned.

"Who are you?" the old man demanded.

"You're not a very good listener," she scolded. "My name is Hope."

"And why are you here?"

He'd already rejected the truth, that she'd come to cheer him up, so Hope thought a dose of the ridiculous was indicated. She leaned forwards and gave him a saucy smile. "I heard you were filthy rich and single," she said. "My nefarious scheme is to charm you and get you to marry me. Then I'll push your wheelchair off a cliff and run away with a handsome but penniless young man."

He was smiling. "Isn't that a little like saying 'I am insane'? If you're willing to admit it, it probably isn't true."

This was going to be easier than she had dared to hope. He was just a lonely old man, after all. He was fairly rough around the edges, but he reminded her of Charles and she just couldn't help liking him.

Charles spotted his brother just outside the door of their grandfather's hospital room. "How's the old man?" he asked in a low voice.

"Don't go in. Hope's with him now."

Charles's eyes opened wider. *"Hope?"*

Tom shushed him. "Keep your voice down. I asked her to come. She's doing great."

Charles shook his head. Nothing surprised him about Hope anymore. He leaned forwards with Tom, straining to hear snatches of the conversation inside the room.

"Can you believe we're eavesdropping on Grand-dad?" Tom whispered. "Hey, let's try your stethoscope on the wall."

Tom reached for the instrument that was draped across his brother's shoulders but his hand was slapped away. "I have work to do," Charles said indignantly.

A peal of feminine laughter emanated from the room. It was followed closely by an old man's surprisingly energetic chuckle.

Tom was awestruck. He put his hands in his pockets and rocked back on his heels. "Can you *believe* this?"

"Easily," Charles replied. "She has a knack for—" He was interrupted by the insistent beeping of his pager. He removed it from his pocket and read the message. "It's a trauma," he announced. He spun around and started down the hall. "Clever of you to bring her," he called over his shoulder.

They visited for almost forty-five minutes, then Hope told Dr. Hartman she was leaving so he could rest.

"But I am enjoying this," he protested. "Don't go."

"Dr. Hartman, you're not the only unmarried rich old man in town, you know. I want to look around a little before I settle for you. I might find one I like better. One with more hair, maybe."

He laughed again. "Come back tomorrow, Hope. You're good medicine."

She blew him a flirty kiss, then she went out to find Tom. She didn't have to look very far—he was just outside the door, where he had been listening shamelessly, and she almost tripped over him.

"Hope, there's some kind of magic in you," he said admiringly. "I've never heard Granddad laugh like that."

She jabbed him in the chest with her index finger. "You owe me ice cream, mister."

He draped an arm around her shoulders and gave her a friendly squeeze. "Honey, I'm yours to command. Would you like to have lunch first, or do you want to head straight for dessert?"

She considered. It didn't take long. "Dessert."

Tom looked pleased. "Exactly what I was thinking," he said.

Old Dr. Hartman was in the hospital for more than a week. Hope visited him every day and they became friends.

"Will you come see me after I go home?" he asked one day.

She hesitated. "I'd like to, but I'm not sure it's a good idea. I don't think Mrs. Hartman likes me very much."

"I can't believe you're afraid of them," he said witheringly. "You were tough enough to face *me,* weren't you?"

She smiled. "Well, you were pretty much immobilized in that bed, and Tom was just outside. The risk was negligible."

"So what about that God of yours? Can't He take care of you?"

He was so like Charles, turning her inside out, challenging her to prove that she believed. Hope sat up straighter in her chair. "You're absolutely right. I'll give you a couple of days to get settled and then I'll come. That is, if the butler hasn't been given orders to bar my entrance!"

"Well, you needn't worry about that. The house belongs to me, you know."

"Yeah, but who pays the butler?"

"Uh-oh," he teased. "That could be a problem. Do you think you could shimmy up a drainpipe?"

A few days later, Hope parked her car in front of the biggest house she'd ever seen. No, it wasn't a house. Calling that imposing structure a house was like calling the Crown Jewels of England a nice little collection of baubles.

Hope was more curious than impressed. Did people really live like this? Did maids roller-skate in the hallways as they went from room to room changing bed linens? How many days did it take to dust every picture frame in the place? Wasn't the food cold by the time it traveled from the kitchen to the dining room table?

She gave herself a mental shove and climbed the front steps. For some reason, she counted. Seventeen.

The door was opened by a pleasant-looking middle-aged man who greeted her by name and said that Dr. Hartman, Sr. was expecting her. She was ushered through the front door and across an enormous hall, up one side of a wide double-staircase, down the east hallway to the fourth door on the right.

Dr. Hartman was in his wheelchair, parked by a window. "I watched you come in," he said by way of greeting. "It took you a couple of minutes to get up your nerve, didn't it?"

She told him her fancies about maids on roller skates and he laughed. "My father built this house for his bride in 1917, two years before I was born," he said. "Do you like it?"

"I'm not sure," Hope answered honestly. "It's beautiful, but overwhelming. But I like it that the same family has lived here for so long. That's nice."

"No, my family is not particularly nice at all," he said roughly.

Hope thought of Charles and Tom and the way their parents had hurt them. Her eyes grew moist and she pretended to look out the window so Dr. Hartman wouldn't see. "This house was built in 1917?" she asked absently. "There are seventeen steps out front, you know."

He seemed delighted. "That was my father's little joke. I noticed it as a boy, but nobody else ever has."

As usual, the old man alternated between snappishness and kindness, but he seemed to enjoy her visit. An hour passed quickly and Hope thought she'd better go. Dr. Hartman said he'd have her shown out.

"No, I can find my own way," she said lightly. "I dropped bread crumbs as I came in."

He chuckled. ''Rodgers will have had them swept up by this time. Shall I draw you a map?''

She leaned down to kiss the bald spot on top of his head. ''You forgot to beg me to come back soon, but I will anyway.''

He really could be a sweet old man, Hope thought as she descended the broad staircase. He just needed some encouragement, like Charles had. Why did nobody love these people? And why didn't they love each other?

Near the bottom of the stairs an enormous full-length portrait of a dark-haired woman in a long, white dress captured Hope's attention. Was this Charles's great-grandmother, the bride for whom this house had been built? Her dress and hairstyle seemed to belong to that era. She was standing before the staircase Hope had just come down and she held a small, open Bible in her right hand.

Was the book just a prop or had it meant something special to the young woman? Hope drew closer. Lost in her thoughts, she was startled by a voice behind her.

''Are you interested in art, Miss Evans?''

Hope's heart jumped into her throat, but she fixed a smile on her face and turned to greet Charles's mother, who was dressed in an immaculate white linen pantsuit. ''Interested, but absolutely ignorant,'' she replied as she stepped forwards and took the woman's outstretched hand. ''Will you call me Hope?''

Cool blue eyes flicked over her as her hand was grasped briefly and impersonally. ''Certainly,'' answered Mrs. Hartman after a short pause. ''I understand you've just seen my father-in-law. Will you stay and have tea with me?''

''Thank you,'' Hope said, a little too brightly. ''I'd like that.'' She was amazed that the lie tumbled so effortlessly from her lips.

Mrs. Hartman led the way to a lavishly furnished sitting room where four impossibly tall windows on one side were balanced by a massive, ornately carved fireplace on the opposite wall.

Hope was invited to take a chair and Mrs. Hartman settled on the sofa opposite her. Tea was brought in immediately and after it was poured, Mrs. Hartman pushed a plate of exquisite little cookies towards Hope. "Please help yourself."

Clutching the beautiful teacup and saucer as if they were life preservers, Hope tried desperately to think of something intelligent to say. Why was she suddenly so tongue-tied? Why were her palms so clammy?

Mrs. Hartman turned an artificial smile on her guest. "How long have you been seeing Trey?"

Hope lowered her cup into its saucer and smiled nervously. "Oh, we're not dating. We're best friends."

The woman lifted one elegant shoulder. "Is that what they're calling it nowadays?"

Hope didn't understand. "I beg your pardon?"

Mrs. Hartman's chin jerked impatiently. "You're sleeping together, of course."

Hope was positive that her heart had just stopped beating. It was several seconds before she was able to speak. "Mrs. Hartman! We're *not!*" With shaking hands, she placed her cup and saucer on the table in front of her.

Mrs. Hartman was unperturbed. "Of course I don't approve of all the bed-hopping you young people engage in, but I am aware that it goes on."

Hope's heart had started again; only now it was beating much too fast. Her cheeks felt hot and she knew they must be flaming red. Why on earth had she insisted on coming here without Charles? "Mrs. Hartman," she managed finally, "I am a Christian and I believe sex outside of marriage is wrong."

Charles's mother crossed her slim legs and gave Hope a look of utter disgust. "You can't possibly imagine that he will marry you?"

"Of course I don't imagine that."

"Then what do you want?"

Hope told the truth. "I want to be his friend and help him in any way I can. But most of all, I want to see him find peace with God."

"Ah," the woman said knowingly, "so you're a little evangelist." Her words were as cold and brittle as icicles.

Hope lifted her chin. "I am Charlie's friend. And Tom's. And old Dr. Hartman's. And if you wanted, I could be *your* friend, too."

"Thank you," the woman said shortly. "I have plenty of friends."

"Do you?" Hope's temper flared. "Do you really? I'm sure you know a lot of people, Mrs. Hartman, but I don't believe that you have any real friends at all!"

Mrs. Hartman's mouth dropped open and she actually looked wounded.

Hope's hand flew to her own mouth, covering it too late to stop the ugly words. Had they really come out of *her?* Tears stung her eyes as she thought how ashamed her mother would be of her at this moment. "Oh, Mrs. Hartman! Can you ever forgive me? I had no business saying—"

"Hope?" Charles spoke sharply as he strode into the room. "What's going on here?" he demanded of his mother.

If Mrs. Hartman had been hurt, she made a quick recovery. She wore the look of an outraged queen. "I don't believe you were brought up to interrupt private conversations, Trey," she said haughtily. "Neither were you taught to storm into a room and bark at your mother."

"It was my fault, Charlie." Hope hurried to his side and linked her arms through one of his, desperate to soften him. "I said something horrible."

"Don't worry about it, kid," he said roughly. "I can well imagine how you were provoked." His eyes bored into his mother's.

Mrs. Hartman sniffed and tossed her head indignantly.

"Please, Charlie," Hope begged, tugging on his arm. "There's no need to—"

"Go home, Hope," he interrupted, still glaring at his mother. "I'll have a short visit with Granddad and then I'll stop by your house on my way to the hospital."

Frightened by his flashing eyes and the ruthless set of his jaw, Hope tightened her hold on his arm. When he finally looked at her, she shook her head, freeing a tear to make its way down her hot cheek. She gave him a long, pleading look. She had to make him understand how it would shame her if he defended her by verbally abusing his own mother.

He averted his eyes, biting his bottom lip, and when he turned a calmer face back to her she pulled a shaky breath and sighed gratefully. He gently disengaged her arms from his.

Hope faced Mrs. Hartman. "What I said was rude and hurtful. I hope one day you'll be able to forgive me." With all the dignity she could muster, she walked out of the room.

Charles crossed the sitting room to one of the long windows and pushed aside a chintz curtain, leaning one hand on the window frame and thrusting the other into his pants pocket. As his mother sipped her tea in sullen silence, he watched Hope run to her car and throw herself into it. When she folded her arms on the steering wheel and buried her head in them, something inside Charles twisted painfully and he had to look away.

"How could you do it, Mother?" He was more bewildered than angry now, his tone pleading rather than scolding. He half turned to look at her. "How could you make her cry? Are you really so cruel that you could hurt a gentle thing like Hope without any remorse at all?"

An eggshell-thin teacup rattled against its saucer as both were abruptly set down on the table. "Are you in love with that girl or not?" Mrs. Hartman demanded.

"Love," Charles echoed in disgust. Regret tore at his soul. "There's no love in me, just like there's none in you. But Hope matters to me in a way I can't explain." Not even to himself, and he had honestly tried.

His mother made no reply.

Charles turned back to the window and watched Hope drive away. "Mother, there's something extraordinary about her. Even Granddad has seen it." He leaned his forehead against a cool windowpane and his voice softened. "She'd be friends with you if you'd let her. You'd never deserve her friendship any more than I do, but Hope wouldn't trouble herself about that. She'd find things in you to admire, not because you're so wonderful, but because she is."

"You *are* in love," said his mother. The hard edge was gone from her voice. She sounded curious, perhaps even a little envious.

Turning away from the window, Charles shook his head. As he moved to the chair Hope had just vacated he saw that she'd dropped her sunglasses beside it. He bent to pick them up, then he sat down heavily. He toyed with the glasses for a moment before he folded them and dropped them into his coat pocket.

He wasn't in love. But Hope had done something to

him, shaken something loose inside him, made him *feel* things.

He was a brilliant surgeon, a certifiable genius. He was saving lives and advancing the science. That had always been enough. Or at least, it had kept him so busy he never had time to wonder whether it *was* enough.

Now he knew it wasn't.

He was thirty-five years old and in all his life, he'd never confided in his mother. But somehow he was moved to share this with her. Suddenly he ached to tell his mother about his secret pain, the confusion in him. He was so much like her, and he wanted to know if she had ever felt this way.

"I wish I *could* love, Mother. I wish I could believe in God and see the world the way Hope does. I wish you could, too."

Chapter Eleven

Hope was especially pretty tonight. Glowing. And Charles was trying to figure out why. He brought the Mercedes to a smooth stop at a red light and turned to her. "What are you so happy about?"

She looked out her window and sighed as if she'd just gained her heart's desire. "I didn't ask you to come to Bible study tonight, but here we are."

He frowned, still clueless. "I don't have a standing invitation?"

She turned towards him, her blue eyes shining with excitement. "Of course you do. But I was going to skip tonight because I'm behind schedule on a translating job."

"Why are we going, then?"

She turned an incredible smile on him and his pulse quickened. He wondered why. She gave his shoulder a friendly pat. "Because you called and asked whether you should pick me up or meet me there."

"So?" Hope didn't usually talk in riddles. What was she trying to say?

The cabdriver behind them honked impatiently, alerting Charles that the light had changed.

"You're awfully dense tonight, Charlie," Hope teased. "Can't you imagine what that means to me? To know that if you're not working, you just assume we'll be going to Bible study?"

That struck him as hilarious. He tossed her a quick glance as he changed lanes. "You're the only woman I've ever met who appreciates being taken for granted. You're positively abnormal, Hope."

Minutes later he parked in front of Pastor Bill's house. They hurried inside, entering quietly when they realized the meeting had already begun. Pastor Bill was speaking as they took a couple of chairs on the outer edge of the group.

"…and please don't misunderstand. This isn't a shakedown. I'm just telling you so you can pray that we will follow God's will, whatever it is. I think a lot of our people have already given more than they can afford to the building fund, but you all know we agreed not to move forwards with buying this property unless we could pay cash for it. We're still three hundred thousand dollars short and it looks like we just won't be able to go ahead. Apparently the Lord is saying this isn't the right time."

"But we can do more," said Claire. "Some of us can do a lot more."

A middle-aged woman scoffed. "We're not going to collect three hundred thousand dollars at this late date!"

Pastor Bill rubbed the back of his neck. "Far be it from me to limit God. Remember the loaves and the fishes? But the fact is, we've known for some time that the sellers want our answer a week from tomorrow. Let's pray about this right now, and may the Lord do as He sees fit."

Charles bowed his head politely, but he didn't close

his eyes. He watched as Hope wrote something in the small notebook she always carried with her. "For the building fund," she printed, and she quietly tore the page free.

Charles was still peeking as she reached for her purse and opened her wallet. She looked up briefly to make sure she was not being observed, then she counted her money. Four tens and two ones. Her chest rose and fell in a silent sigh. She rummaged in the bottom of her purse, but apparently she found no more money.

She rose from her chair and slipped into the dining room. Leaning back in his own chair, Charles watched her through the wide doorway. She folded the money inside the note and placed it in the center of the large oak table.

Charles felt an odd tightness in his chest. Did she really imagine forty-two dollars could make a difference? Hope couldn't even buy tires for her car—how could she afford to throw away forty-two dollars on this doomed project?

When she returned to her chair she closed her eyes and prayed with the others. Her face was lit by a secret smile.

"You're quiet tonight," Hope commented as Charles drove her home from the Bible study.

"There's something on my mind," he admitted. "Hope, I saw what you did."

"What I did?" she repeated cautiously.

"The forty-two dollars," he said. "You can't afford to give away that kind of money, especially to a hopeless cause."

She grinned. "Well, since I'm participating, it can't be a Hope-less cause, now can it?"

He refused to be sidetracked. "Please, Hope. What will

you have to go without now that you've given away your last forty-two dollars?''

She looked uncomfortable. ''That's personal, Charlie.''

''Is it? I would have thought you'd be eager to explain. Don't you want me to understand that aspect of your relationship with God?''

She seemed to be amazed by the question. ''Is that why you want to know, Charlie? I thought you were just worried about me having gas money.'' The corners of her pretty mouth eased down.

''Yes, I'm worried about that,'' he conceded. ''But I really want to understand what made you do it. And why you looked so happy afterward.'' A wistful note crept into his voice. ''Won't you explain it to me?''

''I don't know if we'll get the money on time,'' she said slowly, looking out the window as she spoke. ''But if we don't make our goal, I want to know that at least I did everything I could.''

Stopping for a red light, he turned to look at her. ''And if you *do* make the goal?''

The busy city intersection was awash with colorful lights. They illuminated Hope's face, and when she turned to Charles her eyes glittered like stars, throwing sparks into his own eyes and making his breath catch in his throat.

''If we get three hundred thousand dollars by next week I'll be thrilled to have been a small part of the effort,'' she said eagerly. ''I'll have a share in the joy— don't you see?''

He nodded thoughtfully. He *did* see. But what was she going to do for gas money?

And why did that sparkle in her eyes make him forget to breathe?

* * *

Hope had promised to cook dinner for Charles the night before he left for Mexico. She made veal parmigiana and waited.

He was forty-five minutes late when someone from the hospital called to relay Dr. Hartman's apologies and inform Hope that he was still in surgery. "There was a bus accident and things are really hopping here," the nurse explained. "Dr. Hartman will probably be here most of the night."

Half an hour later Hope was at the hospital, picnic basket in hand. She located the nurse who had phoned her, explaining that she'd brought dinner for Dr. Hartman and that she'd be waiting in his office.

"We'll tell him you're here," the nurse promised. "But I warn you, it could be some time before he gets a break."

Hope occasionally picked up Charles's dry cleaning or brought sandwiches to share with him, so she had a key to his office. She let herself in and turned on the lights, feeling perfectly at home. She helped herself to a bottle of orange juice from his tiny countertop refrigerator, then she sat at his desk and went over some of her thesis notes. Just before midnight she dimmed the lights, slipped off her shoes and curled up on the comfortable leather sofa.

Charles was passionate about this sofa, which he had purchased expressly for sleeping on, and now Hope understood why. As she snuggled her head onto a goose down pillow, she felt like a baby lying in her mother's arms, warm and safe. She closed her eyes and whispered her thanks to God, then she prayed for her friend the surgeon.

Lord, he doesn't realize that his abilities come from You. Make him see that. Give him strength and wisdom and guide his hands tonight....

She was asleep before she got to "Amen."

* * *

Hope was awakened by the wail of a siren. Opening her eyes briefly, she remembered where she was. Warm and deliciously comfortable, she settled down again, pulling the blanket more closely around her.

What blanket? Her eyes flew open. Where had the blanket come from? She sat up, noticing immediately that her picnic basket was on the desk, not on the chair where she'd left it. She peeled off the blanket and went to investigate.

He'd been there. Okay, so she wasn't the lightest sleeper in the world, but how had he managed to eat dinner without waking her?

Her heart thumped with pleasure as she saw that he'd turned her notebook to a blank page and written a message. She held the notebook under the desk lamp and read.

You look adorable when you're asleep. I didn't have the heart to wake you.

Thanks for dinner—cold veal is not bad. The cheesecake was fabulous. (Were both pieces for me, or did I eat yours?)

I've got a couple of things to wrap up before I can knock off for the night. If you leave before I come back in, I'll call you from the airport. My flight leaves at ten in the morning, and I fully intend to make it. I'm looking forwards to the flight to Mexico and all those blessed hours of sleep.
Charlie,
1:45 a.m.

Hope smiled at the signature. It was the second time he had called himself that.

She returned to the sofa and made herself comfortable again. Lying in the semidarkness, she wondered what he was doing at that moment. She prayed for him again, until she felt a sweet peace that all was well.

She was awakened by orange-red sunlight streaming through the large window behind Charles's desk. She moved slightly, and something wasn't right. She turned her head and realized with a pang of delight that a warm head lay against her shoulder.

Hope didn't understand how he could sleep in that position. He sat on the floor, his body oddly twisted so that his chest was against the edge of the sofa. One arm lay across the pillow, just above her head, and except for the face against her shoulder, he was not touching her at all. But she savored the warmth of his nearness and she held her breath, not wanting to break the wonderful spell.

In that moment Hope realized something that filled her heart with equal parts rapture and dismay. She loved him.

It couldn't make any difference, she told herself sternly. Even if he loved her, she could never marry him. But he *didn't* love her, and it was actually a relief to know that.

The deep, even sound of his breathing filled her with unspeakable joy. Just one time, she promised herself. Just this once and then never again. What could it possibly hurt?

Slowly, carefully, she moved a little so she could kiss his head, just above his temple. She put her mouth against his soft, honey-colored hair and squeezed her eyes tightly shut as her lips applied a gentle pressure.

"Mmmm," Charles murmured sleepily. "Thank you."

Hope stiffened in shock.

"It's okay," he said softly, his words muffled between her shoulder and the pillow. "I like it." He yawned. "Do it again."

Somehow she managed a light tone. "No, it's time for

you to wake up. You can't be very comfortable, anyway."

He hadn't budged. "On the contrary, I am extremely comfortable. So please don't move, unless of course you have another wild urge to kiss me."

Hope had all sorts of wild urges, but she wasn't about to give in to any more of them. She didn't move a muscle.

A minute later he yawned again and sat up. He flashed her an ornery grin. "I hope you're not planning to tell your four big brothers that we slept together."

"That's not funny," she scolded.

"I take it you're not a morning person," he said amiably. He stood and stretched his arms towards the ceiling. When Hope saw a flash of bare skin between the hem of his scrub shirt and the drawstring waist of his pants she quickly averted her eyes. In the next instant she wondered why.

She'd seen him shirtless the day he slept at her house. But she'd been thinking of her brothers then, and things were entirely different now. She couldn't look now because she *wanted* to look. And those feelings had to be denied, for so many reasons.

He crossed his ankles and bent at the waist, easily touching his toes. "Want some coffee?" he asked, crossing his ankles in the other direction and repeating the move.

She sat up and rubbed her eyes. "No, thanks. How can you be so wide-awake?"

"Years of practice."

"Was it a rough night?"

"It was pretty wild," he admitted, rubbing the back of his neck as he looked out the window. "We had four people from a bus accident. Then there was the kid who found Daddy's stash of target pistols and accidentally shot himself not once but *twice*. I still haven't figured that one out. After that they brought in a guy on drugs who got hit by a newspaper truck while he was directing traffic on Lake Shore Drive. He was stark naked. Or *mostly* naked. As I understand it, he was wearing a cowboy hat and black leather gloves.''

He rubbed his face with both hands. ''People were streaming into that ER so fast, you'd have thought we were running some kind of sale. But they're all going to live happily ever after because all the best people were on duty last night, including your good friend, the breathtakingly brilliant Dr. Heartless.''

''I'm glad it went well. I prayed for you.''

''Did you?'' His tone was sharp, but he seemed to realize immediately that he'd startled her. ''Sorry. It's just that something strange happened last night and now I wonder…''

Hope's heart beat faster. ''What happened, Charlie?''

He shook his head. ''I want to think about this for a while, okay? And I have to leave in a minute, so we don't have time to discuss it, anyway.'' He ran his hand over the stubble on his jaw. ''But when I get back, ask me about last night. I want to tell you, Hope.''

She tried to suppress her disappointment. ''Okay.''

Charles glanced at his watch. ''I'd better go toss some clothes into a suitcase.''

She smiled. ''Do you really sleep on airplanes?''

He pushed a hand through his hair. ''Sure. It's great. I always buy two seats so I'll have plenty of room. That's probably why I keep signing up for these trips. That long flight is the best sleep I get all year.''

''Yeah, right,'' she said skeptically. ''I'm sure *that's* the reason. Because you'd never do anything out of the goodness of your heart, would you?''

"I thought we'd established the fact that I don't *have* a heart," he said.

"Somehow you have failed to convince me. Give it up, Charlie."

He actually smiled at that.

Hope made a dive for her purse. "I almost forgot," she said eagerly. "I have something for you." With a thrill of pleasure she handed him a small white box.

He lifted the lid. The box held a long braided chain made of sterling silver. He pulled it out and examined the pendant that hung from it, an exquisitely detailed silver eagle.

Hope had seen it a month ago in a display case at her favorite Christian bookstore, and she had known immediately that she had to have it for Charles. The price had stunned her, but she cheerfully made several small sacrifices and just yesterday she had marched back into the store, money in hand.

Charles turned troubled eyes to her. "Oh, Hope. You can't afford presents like this."

"I had to pinch some pennies," she said truthfully, "but I wanted you to have it. I thought you might wear it while you're in Mexico."

"Sure, I'll wear it all the time," he promised, fingering the outstretched wings of the eagle. "It's nice."

"It's just a reminder that I'll be praying for you constantly. The eagle is a reference to a Bible verse about strength."

"Which verse?"

"Isaiah 40:31. 'But they that wait upon the Lord shall renew their strength; they shall mount up with wings as eagles; they shall run, and not be weary; and they shall walk, and not faint.'"

He smiled. "You'll be praying that I won't grow weary?"

As she nodded he slipped the chain over his head, allowing the eagle to hang outside the vee neck of his dark blue scrub shirt. "Thank you. I like it." He inclined his head, not looking at her. "Now say the verse one more time and I'll remember."

He listened intently as she repeated it. "You think it means nothing to me," he said slowly. "But it does, because it matters so much to you." He lowered his voice to just above a whisper. "Hope, I wish I could be a Christian for your sake. I know it would ease your mind."

Her heart was too full to allow any response but shimmering eyes. He was so close—why couldn't he just give in to God?

He laid a warm hand against her cheek. "It's going to be the longest three weeks of my life. Thank you for coming last night. I liked knowing you were here."

She managed to nod. As she did, the hand on her cheek moved slightly and his thumb brushed one corner of her mouth. His mouth opened suddenly, as if he would speak, but he didn't. He swayed towards her, and for one heart-stopping moment she thought he would kiss her.

As much as she wanted it, that couldn't happen between them. She backed away, smiling bravely. She picked up her picnic basket and her purse, and left him.

Hope dropped her car keys on the kitchen table and reached for Bob's leash. She wanted to sit down and cry, but her pet had been alone all night and he needed to be walked and fed. She went through those motions and then she was finally free to fling herself onto her bed and sob into a pillow.

It had happened. The thing her father and Pastor Bill and even Claire had warned her about. Could she bear it?

She had to. She was the only one he'd talk to, the only one he'd listen to. He'd come so far; she couldn't give up on him now. Common sense told her to back away, protect her heart, but she knew that whatever it cost her, she would stick by him.

She didn't know how long she'd be able to keep her secret. He might have guessed already. But now she had three weeks to pull herself together.

She sat up and reached for the Bible on her bedside table. For more than an hour she read and prayed, then the phone rang.

"Hope, it's Tom."

She smiled. "Your brother's been gone for less than two hours. Isn't it a little soon for you to be checking up on me?"

He chuckled softly, but there was a wistful note in his voice. Hope's own troubles were forgotten as concern for Tom squeezed her heart. "What's wrong?" she asked urgently.

It was a moment before he answered. "Hope, I'd really like to talk to you about something," he began slowly. "You're the only Christian I know, and I have some questions. About God."

Her favorite topic of conversation. "I'm free right now," she replied eagerly. "Come over and have a cup of tea."

When Tom arrived, he seemed agitated and a little embarrassed. Hope noticed that he carried a Bible, but she said nothing about it. She led him to the kitchen and made light conversation as she prepared a bracing pot of Irish Breakfast tea. Then she set a plate of oatmeal cookies on the table and poured the tea, smiling encouragement at Tom.

He shook his head and made a soft sound of amusement. "It's not difficult to understand why Trey spends so much time here. But what *is* it about you, Hope? What's the magic?''

She smiled, pleased that he had asked. ''I hope you see a glimmer of God's love in me. What did you want to talk about, Tom?''

Resting his elbows on the table, his left hand clasped around his right, Tom leaned his chin on his hands. ''Today's my tenth wedding anniversary,'' he said quietly, not looking at Hope. In an unconscious gesture that tore at her heart, he leaned his face forwards until his lips rested against his gold wedding band.

''Oh, Tom. I'm so sorry.''

''I couldn't sleep last night,'' he said with obvious difficulty. ''So I went through some of her things.'' He sighed, reached for the Bible and pushed it across the table to Hope. ''I found this.''

Hope couldn't hide the moisture in her eyes, but Tom's were shimmering, too. Sending up a silent prayer for guidance, she bit her lip and waited.

''Near the end of her life Susan was very interested in this Bible,'' Tom continued. ''She was always reading it and listening to religious programs on the radio. When she tried to talk to me about what she was learning, I cut her off.'' With one finger he absently traced the ear-shaped handle of his teacup. ''I was just too upset about losing her to talk about the afterlife.'' He looked up, meeting Hope's teary eyes. ''Can you understand that?''

''Of course I can.'' Hope put her hand on his.

''But I loved her so much.'' His voice broke. ''I just can't believe I was that selfish. I wish I had let her talk about what was so much on her mind.''

Hope squeezed his hand and gave him a compassionate look that said he need not be ashamed of his tears. ''That was grief, Tom. Susan must have understood that.''

''Maybe you're right. She understood everything.''

"Can I do anything for you, Tom?" Hope placed her free hand on the Bible.

His eyes followed her movement. "This morning I found that she had written things in that Bible. It almost looks as though she was trying to leave messages for me. A road map to follow so I can find her again. Could that be it, do you think?"

Hope's heart pounded as she opened the Bible and leafed through it. She turned several pages, reading margin notes that had been written in a small, neat, rounded hand, and she rejoiced. A woman gone for three years reached out to Hope, spoke to her heart. They were sisters.

It wasn't easy to speak past the huge lump in her throat. "This is very wonderful to me," she said slowly. "The way you and Charlie talk about Susan, I have regretted not being able to know her. What this Bible tells me is that I *will* know her one day, in heaven. Susan was a born-again believer, Tom. Didn't you know?"

"I don't really know what that means," he confessed raggedly. "Can you explain it to me, Hope?"

She fought to keep her voice steady. "Let's start with one of the verses Susan underlined. Will you read it out loud? Right here," she said, pointing. "John 3:16."

Tom leaned forwards and began to read the life-changing words, "For God so loved the world…"

Chapter Twelve

"Charlie? I can barely hear you." Hope pressed the telephone hard against her ear and strained to hear past the wild crackling on the line.

"Hope, we've...bad connection...raining hard here, and...calling from...in the mountains...hear me now?"

Sort of. She closed her eyes and listened harder. "Yes, go ahead. What's wrong?"

He'd been in Mexico for two weeks, and she had no idea why he was calling. Concern pulled her eyebrows together as she concentrated on his voice. There was something in it that she couldn't make out. Shoulders hunched, she gripped the phone with both hands, as if that would pull him closer.

"...so many wonderful...going on here...Hope, something amazing is...I don't understand it, but... Can you hear me?"

Her heart raced. "Say it again, Charlie."

"Hope, keep praying for...I just...and everything...so please keep praying, okay?"

"Yes! Of course I'm praying! Are you all right, Char-lie?"

"Yes, but I…going extremely well here and we…to another village… Hope, it's so strange and wonderful! I wish…be here to see it for yourself."

Wonderful. Something was strange and wonderful. The work was going well and he was excited. He wanted her to pray. Oh, she could do *that!*

"Charlie, I can't understand you very well, but it sounds like exciting things are happening there. I'm so pleased for you! I can't wait to hear all about it."

"Yes, it is exciting…wait to tell you about…you next week, okay? I have to get off now, but I just…hear your voice, Hope."

The line was dead, so she put the phone down. She tried to fill in the blanks, make sense of what she'd heard. Then she bowed her head and poured out her heart to God.

As he had the week before, Tom picked up Hope on Sunday morning and drove her to church. He'd met her Sunday school teacher and several of her friends, but both Pastor Bill and Claire had been absent the previous Sunday. This morning Hope was eager to have them meet Tom.

After the service she introduced him to the pastor, explaining that Tom was Charles's brother and that he had just become a Christian. Pastor Bill shook Tom's hand warmly, thumped him on the back and asked whether he needed any kind of help.

"I need all kinds of help," said Tom genuinely. "Your sermon this morning answered a lot of questions, but I have plenty more."

Pastor Bill pulled a business card out of his pocket and

pressed it into Tom's hand. "You call me tomorrow," he said, "and we'll have coffee sometime this week."

Hope glowed with pleasure as Tom thanked the pastor and promised to call.

"I pray for your brother," said Pastor Bill.

Tom lowered his gaze and nodded. "Thank you," he said in a husky voice. "He's a better man than anyone realizes."

"Oh, I think Hope realizes it," said the pastor, smiling as he peered at her over his eyeglasses. "She's constantly pestering me to keep Dr. Hartman at the top of my prayer list."

Other people were clamoring for the pastor's attention, so he shook Tom's hand again and excused himself.

Claire approached and gave Hope a friendly hug. "Who's your new bud?" she asked, smiling in Tom's direction.

Hope introduced him, and the three chatted for a few minutes before Claire looked at her watch. "Hey, we'd better get going," she said. "What are we doing today?"

Hope was blank. "Doing?"

"It's your workday," Claire reminded her. "We changed it, remember? Because of my vacation. Did you really forget?"

She really *had* forgotten. And she had just agreed to have lunch with Tom. She apologized to him.

"No problem," he said easily. "Let's make it dinner."

"This is an all-day thing," Hope said. "I'm sorry, Tom."

He appealed to Claire. "So, what is this 'workday' that I'm being stood up for?"

Claire turned her thousand-watt smile on him and Hope, whose arm was loosely linked through Tom's, felt him twitch as though he had just received a small electrical shock. "I dare you to come with us and find out," Claire challenged.

As Tom returned Claire's smile it occurred to Hope that he might soon be ready to take off his wedding ring. His face reminded her of the way Bob looked whenever she opened a box of doggy treats: definitely interested, but trying hard to hide it.

"I happen to be free," Tom replied casually.

"Great." Claire looked at Hope. "I'll get Barb. We've got our clothes, so we'll change at your house. And if you guys aren't starving, why don't we work for an hour and then make a hamburger run?"

On their way home, Hope explained to Tom that the monthly "workday" had started as a ministry to her friend Barb Connors. Married at twenty-one, Barb had been widowed when an industrial accident killed her husband just three years later. Wanting to help in some practical way, Hope and Claire had gone to their friend's house one Sunday after church. While Claire did some minor maintenance on Barb's car, Hope mowed the lawn. Then they washed windows and did several smaller chores. At the end of the day they made a huge salad, grilled some steaks and dined by candlelight on Barb's tiny patio.

They'd done it twice more after that, and it did wonders for their grieving friend's spirits. But Barb wanted to return the favor. She insisted that Claire and Hope, both single women living alone, could use workdays of their own.

"We decided to do it the first Sunday afternoon of every month," Hope told Tom. "After each of us has had her turn in the rotation we choose someone else, usually an old widow, and give her a workday. So every four months it's my turn again. We have a lot of fun together and we get a lot accomplished, too," she concluded. "If you want to laugh at us, go ahead. But if you stay, you're going to work."

"I'll work," Tom said cheerfully. "I have my gym bag with me, so I can change. I don't know how to fix leaky faucets, but I can cut grass and things like that."

Hope couldn't resist ribbing him. "Now where would a rich boy like you have learned how to push a lawn-mower?"

He smiled enigmatically, his attention on the road as he pulled over to allow a fire truck to pass him. Momentarily stopped, he turned towards Hope, pulling his dark sunglasses low on his nose and peering over them. Somehow he managed to look comical and devastatingly handsome at the same time. "New Jersey," he answered.

She flashed him an impudent grin. "No."

He winked at her. "Yes."

The sunglasses were pushed back up and he tossed his head in a way that suggested he was proud to be a member of that bourgeois brotherhood, the Men Who Cut Grass. "I get over to see Susan's folks a couple of times a year," he explained as he pulled back onto the road. "Their backyard is nearly half an acre."

Hope liked it that he was still visiting his former in-laws. But that was Tom Hartman. And Susan's people were probably more to him than his own parents had ever been, anyway.

She looked out her window. There was a sweetness in Tom—and in Charles, although it was much less obvious—that Hope just couldn't explain. Where had it come from?

It must have arisen from their devotion to each other, she mused. Charles had always looked after his brother and Tom, for his part, had always believed the sun rose and set on "Trey." It both wounded and warmed Hope's tender heart to know that when no adult had stepped forwards to accept the job, the Hartman boys had nurtured each other.

But she didn't want to think sad thoughts on such a pretty summer day. Today Tom had ditched his sedate BMW for his sports car, a zippy little Italian number in screaming yellow, and Hope was determined to enjoy the ride. First she slipped off her shoes, then she pinched the back of Tom's hand as it rested on the gearshift. "Music," she commanded. "Loud."

"Yes, ma'am," he said instantly, reaching for the controls.

They arrived at Hope's house just ahead of Barb and Claire. As Hope climbed out of Tom's car, Claire leaped out of Barb's, slammed the door and waved energetically. "Hope!" she squealed. "You got to ride in a Lamborghini!"

Hope shrugged at her, then turned to Tom. "Did they really name a car after pasta?"

"Hope, it's 'Lamborghini,' not 'linguini,'" he said, rolling his eyes skyward. "Is your friend a car nut?" Tom seemed unable to take his eyes off Claire as she reached for something in the trunk of Barb's car.

Claire *was* a car nut, and Hope had an idea. "Hey, Tom…"

"Uh…right here, honey," he said absently. It was all Hope could do not to giggle at his obvious preoccupation with her beautiful friend.

"Remember you offered to let me drive your car?"

"Yeah," he said easily. "Anytime you want."

She gave him an appealing look. "Could Claire have my turn? She knows just everything about cars."

Hope had never tried her hand at matchmaking, but this first attempt looked quite promising.

* * *

Hope unplugged the blow-dryer and dropped a kiss on Bob's well-groomed head. "There you go," she said with satisfaction. "Now you look and smell better than I do."

With his long tongue the dog gave her chin a quick, grateful swipe.

"You're welcome," she said as she glanced at her watch. "Now we'd better get *me* cleaned up, or I'll be late for my visit with old Dr. Hartman."

She hoped she would run into Charles's mother again today. She'd seen the woman twice since their argument, and Mrs. Hartman definitely seemed to be unbending. While she was not actually friendly, her demeanor towards Hope had been carefully polite.

Hope couldn't help but wonder what Charles had said to his mother to effect that change. But she had resolved to put the ugly incident behind her and smother Mrs. Hartman with kindness. Maybe one day the woman would forgive and forget.

Charles's grandfather was becoming more receptive to conversing about spiritual matters. When he expressed an interest in meeting Pastor Bill Barnes, Hope eagerly arranged for the pastor to pay him a visit. Tomorrow was the agreed-upon day.

Hope marveled at what the Lord was doing for the Hartmans. Tom had become a Christian, and surely Charles was close. Old Dr. Hartman seemed to be opening his heart, too, and Pastor Bill would know just how to talk to him. Mrs. Hartman was thawing towards Hope, and maybe one day they could be friends. So now Hope set her sights on Charles's father. She'd already begun praying for opportunities to see him and talk to him.

"Because You know, Lord," she said aloud, "You might as well save the whole family while You're at it!"

* * *

If the first two weeks without Charles had crawled by, the last one moved even more slowly. Hope was thrilled when he called from the airport late on Sunday evening.

"Hope, I'm at O'Hare, waiting for my bag. Just wanted you to know I'm back. How about an early breakfast in the morning? I've got so much to tell you!"

"No—come right now," she insisted. "I can't wait."

When she opened her door a short while later, he surprised and delighted her by wrapping his arms around her and squeezing hard. "I missed you, kid," he said fervently, resting his chin on top of her head. "I missed you every single day."

He took a chair in the living room and Hope plopped happily onto the sofa. She grabbed a pillow because Bob was in the backyard and she needed something to hug. "Start with the night before you left," she suggested. "What was it that you wanted to talk to me about?"

His eyes darkened with excitement. "I'll try to tell you what happened. A sixteen-year-old kid had a gunshot wound to the chest. I was tired, but I did my job, just like always—the adrenaline kicked in and I felt like a superhero. Things were going okay, but then we hit a snag and I started to worry. I glanced up to speak to someone and when I looked down again there was something strange about my hands. I felt—I don't know—detached from them. Like they weren't *my* hands at all."

His voice trembled with emotion as he went on. "It was strange, I tell you. I didn't know what was happening. Hope, it had nothing to do with being tired. And I wasn't overdosed on caffeine, either. Afterwards I found an empty room and sat down to think. The next thing I knew, my head was in my hands and I was sobbing like a child. I don't even know why—the boy was fine."

Joyful tears filled Hope's eyes and she did nothing to

hide them. She fingered the silky fringe on her pillow and waited for Charles to go on.

"After that I went to my office. I sat on the floor beside you and I was going to wake you. But you looked so peaceful, I couldn't do it. And I didn't know how to explain what had happened, anyway. So I laid my head on your pillow and fell asleep."

Hope beamed at him. "And in the morning I told you I had prayed for you while you were operating."

His head dipped as he swallowed. "Yes. And I began to think that I had been…touched…by God."

Hope's breath caught in her throat. "You thought that?"

"Yes, I did. But it was so shocking, I couldn't allow myself to dwell on it. So I got on the plane, had a good sleep and then went to work in Mexico. And, Hope, everything we touched was golden. Every surgery was a success beyond what we believed possible. Everyone there commented that we'd never seen so many patients, never had that kind of success. One of the new guys was a Christian and he annoyed us more than once with his remarks about how God was 'moving' among us. I tried to dismiss it, but I just couldn't get out of my mind what had happened that last night."

Squeezing the pillow against her chest, Hope fought to slow her heartbeat and catch her breath. "Did it happen again, in Mexico? Is that what you were trying to tell me on the phone? I could barely make out what you were saying."

He nodded eagerly. "I thought I was going to burst if I couldn't talk to you about it. I was so excited and the connection was awful, but I heard you promise to keep praying and I was wild with joy."

He had been touched by God. He was wild with joy. Hope's heart was about to explode. "Tell me more," she begged, gazing deep into the hazel eyes that seemed almost to be on fire. She wanted to jump in, be consumed by it. "Charlie, please tell me everything!"

He shook his head. "I can't—it would take forever. But I'll tell you about the boy. He was eight years old and he had fallen off a moving truck while he was holding a machete. It nearly sliced him in half, Hope. You wouldn't believe how bad it was. It happened just thirty yards from where we were working, so the people carried him in immediately. We didn't think he was going to make it. And suddenly it mattered to me, like nothing had ever mattered before."

Hope had to be closer, touching him, so she moved from the sofa to sit on the floor next to his chair. She put her hand on his knee and looked up into his face.

"Hope, he wasn't a 'case' at all. He was just a little boy, and for some reason I thought of Tom at that age. I was thirteen when Tom went off the high diving board into our pool. He came off sideways and cracked his head on the board. When I pulled him out of the water he wasn't breathing, so I—"

"You saved Tom?" she interrupted.

"Yes," Charles admitted. "He's probably forgotten about that. But that's why I had to become a doctor. Somehow in the back of my mind I felt that Tom might need me again one day. But it was Susan, instead, and I couldn't—"

"Don't, Charlie." She patted his knee and pulled him back to the present. "Tell me about the little boy."

He took a couple of breaths and calmed himself. "I couldn't bear it that he was going to die. So I prayed to God."

"How wonderful," Hope whispered, not minding the tear that slid down her cheek. "What did you say?"

"I said, 'I don't know You and I have no right to ask,

but please take over my hands like You did before and save this boy.' Right after I said that I looked up and met the eyes of the Christian. Hope, I *know* I didn't speak out loud, but that man looked me right in the eye and said 'Amen!' Everyone turned to stare when he said it. That was when I knew it was happening again. It was incredible.''

Hope sniffled. ''And the boy was all right?''

He nodded. ''The mother and father thanked me like I had done some wonderful thing. But the hands that saved him were not mine! I tried to tell them, but nobody understood.''

''I think the Christian doctor understood.'' Hope smiled, accepting the handkerchief Charles offered her.

''He did. I longed to talk to him about so many things, but there was work to be done. We finally had ten minutes together and he asked whether I had someone to talk to back in Chicago. I told him all about you and I showed him your eagle. I even told him the verse.''

He paused, which was fine with Hope, because she didn't know how much more she could take. Surely he was about to surrender to the Lord. A ripple of eager expectation rushed through her as she met his intense gaze.

And then something went horribly wrong.

As she smiled into his eyes, his excitement faded. He looked bewildered, then dismayed. Abruptly he rose from his chair. ''I need some water,'' he said. He stepped over her and headed for the kitchen.

It was a minute before she followed, and what she found made her heart turn over. He clutched the edge of the sink with both hands, his head down. His eyes were tightly closed and his face was contorted with pain.

Hope understood immediately. She moved behind him and put her arms around his waist, leaning her head against his strong, stiff back. Then she stepped into the silence and spread her heart out before him. "You *know,* don't you?"

When he spoke, his voice caught. "I saw it in your face just now."

She forced herself to ask the question even though she already knew his answer. "Do you mind?"

"Yes, I mind!" he rasped. He spun around to face her, but his clenched fists went to his sides and he made no move to accept or deny her embrace. His stormy eyes met her frightened ones. "I don't *want* you to love me!" he grated. "Because I'm not capable of—"

"Oh, Charlie! Do you still think you're heartless?"

He sighed heavily. "I've tried, Hope. I just can't make it happen. I've gone to your church and I've even tried to pray. But it's too late for me."

"No, it isn't!" She leaned her forehead against his chest. Her arms were still around him, but he was as cold and unyielding as a marble statue.

When he spoke again, his voice was deadly calm, flat as a windless sea. "I'm no good for you, Hope. We could talk all night and that fact would remain." His hands reached behind his back, closing gently over her wrists. When she raised her head, his tortured eyes pleaded with her. "Hope, you have to let me go," he said in a heart-breaking whisper.

Without waiting for instructions from her brain, her arms tightened around him. But the hands holding her wrists tightened, too, hurting her.

"Let me go, Hope. We can't be friends anymore. Not after this." Still gripping her wrists, he forced her arms to her sides. Then he let go and walked away.

She followed him, watching in horror as he pulled open the front door and walked out without another word or glance for her. He was trying to do the right thing, the honorable thing, but how could she let him go? Who would teach him about God's love? She stood in the doorway, watching him go, and the cry was wrenched from the depths of her being. "Charlie!"

His body jerked as if he had just taken a bullet between the shoulder blades, but he kept walking. Hope closed the door and sank to her knees.

Chapter Thirteen

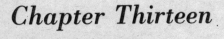

Almost a week had passed and Charles had not returned any of Hope's calls. By Friday night she admitted to herself that he never would. She went to bed early, testing her theory that if she was asleep, she couldn't cry.

She awakened at a quarter past two, the dampness on her pillow having conclusively disproved the theory.

She wiped her wet eyes with the back of one hand. This pain was even worse than losing Gramps. That goodbye had been bittersweet because her wise old friend had gone home to God. But there was no sweetness in losing Charles. Her grief at being parted from him was magnified by the horror of knowing that he was once again alone, lost in his private wilderness of doubt and confusion, far from God. Who would guide him now?

"I can't accept this, Lord," Hope said aloud. "I don't believe You want me to."

She switched on her lamp and reached for the slim volume of Wordsworth on her bedside table. With a thumb she absently traced the star-shaped coffee stain on the cover before opening the book to Charles's inscription: "For Hope, a better friend than I could ever deserve."

Yes, that was it. She hugged the open book to her heart. They were friends and he needed her more than ever. It didn't matter that he was unable to love her. With God's help she would make him understand.

She sat up and pushed her hair away from her face. This was Friday night, and he always worked Fridays. She would go to the hospital right now. She'd ask one of those nice nurses to tell Dr. Hartman she was waiting. Then she would camp out in his office until he gave up and came to see her.

Hopeful for the first time all week, she scrambled out of bed. She flung off her nightgown and tossed it at a chair before stepping into a pair of jeans, almost tumbling forwards in her haste. She pulled on a light cotton sweater, sliding her feet into her favorite loafers as she settled the ribbed bottom of the sweater over her hips.

In the bathroom she splashed warm water on her tear-stained face. "It's right," she said as she buried her face in a fragrant, fluffy towel. "I know it is. Lord, please make him understand."

She caught up a tote bag and hurriedly stuffed it with bottled water, granola bars, notebooks and pens. She didn't think she'd be able to concentrate on them, but she gathered up a couple of grammar books anyway. Even if he wasn't busy, he'd probably let her cool her heels for a while. Hope was determined to outlast him.

It had been raining steadily all evening, but now the storm was worsening. Bob whined shrilly as he paced the kitchen floor, his toenails making nervous little clicking noises on the vinyl. Hope refilled his water dish and gave him some food.

She kneeled in front of him and caught his head in her hands. "I'm going after him, Bobby," she said into the velvety brown eyes. ''Not because I'm a lovesick fool, but because he needs me.''

A thunderclap rattled the windows and Bob cowered. Hope took a minute to soothe him, then she went out, carefully locking the door behind her.

Halfway to the hospital she reduced her speed and switched her windshield wipers to ''high'' as the wind picked up and the furious rain lashed her car. She tensed and leaned forwards, white-knuckling the steering wheel as she peered into the deluge with a growing sense of unease. It was becoming increasingly difficult to see, so she began looking for a safe place to pull over.

A pair of headlights waggled crazily on the road in front of her. *Someone must be drunk,* she thought in alarm. She felt prickles on the back of her neck as the lights moved into her lane and bore down on her.

She took her foot off the gas, pressed hard on the brake and tried to turn out of the car's path. *This can't be happening,* she thought, but it *was,* and it seemed to be happening in slow motion.

There was a loud noise, then everything went eerily still.

Hope was surprised by the complete absence of sensation. She was adrift in a strange, dark world where she could hear, see, feel nothing at all. Her senses seemed to have shut down but her brain was working just fine. Concluding that she was critically injured, she gave herself to God.

Yes, Lord. All right, she prayed as the irresistible blackness reeled her in. *But I really would have liked to see him one more time.*

Something was on her face, covering her nose and mouth. Hope struggled, trying to get out from under it so she could breathe better.

"Try to be still," a woman said. "You've been in a car wreck."

Hope opened her eyes and looked straight into a pair of sympathetic brown ones.

"No, don't fight this—I'm just giving you a little oxygen," said the woman, readjusting the plastic cup over Hope's face. "We're taking you to the hospital. You'll be fine, don't worry, but I need you to be calm now."

What was wrong with her? Why did it hurt so much to breathe? She felt dizzy and she wanted to go back to sleep, but she had to make sure they were taking her to Charles. If she wasn't dead yet, perhaps it was because God was planning to grant her last wish. "Hospital," she said weakly. Her eyes begged the woman to understand. "Please, I need—"

"Yes, honey. We're taking you to the hospital right now."

"Lakeside," Hope demanded. Her voice wasn't strong enough, so she said it again. "Take me to…Lakeside Hospital." Her strength spent, she closed her eyes again. But every time she drew a breath she felt a fierce stabbing in her chest. She tried holding her breath, but that hurt just as much.

The woman spoke urgently and Hope heard crackly radio voices, but through the thick curtain of pain she was unable to make out what was being said.

She panicked, suddenly terrified that Charles might *not* be at the hospital tonight. But they would call him, wouldn't they? "Please," she begged, "I need Dr. Hartman." To her own ears Hope's desperate voice sounded miles away.

"What was that, honey?" The brown-eyed woman leaned closer and lifted the oxygen mask slightly.

Hope closed her eyes and summoned strength from every cell of her body. "Dr. Charles Hartman," she said clearly. "Tell him…I'm coming. My name is Hope. Please…tell Dr. Hartman."

The case was a stab wound, inflicted on a twenty-four-year-old marine during a barroom brawl. "He'll live to fight another day," Charles announced dryly as he finished suturing the man's lacerated liver.

Holding a mask to her face, a nurse stood just inside the doorway of the operating room. "Dr. Hartman? Excuse me, but don't you know someone called Hope?"

He didn't look up from his work. She'd been calling his home number, his cell number and his pager all week. Was she going to start calling the hospital now? In the middle of the night? He wondered briefly how she had managed to talk this particular nurse, a real hardnose, into interrupting him during surgery. Hope could charm the stripes off a tiger.

Talking to her tonight would only postpone the inevitable, but he longed to hear her gentle voice. Couldn't he give her a call after he finished here?

No. Under his mask his lips clamped tightly together. Hope needed to forget him, and she couldn't do that unless he kept his distance. That was the only thing he could do for her now, and he *would* do it, whatever it cost him.

"Doctor?" the nurse pressed.

"I know her," Charles replied tersely. "Take a message." He would never return the call.

The nurse hesitated. "Dr. Hartman, she's not on the phone. They're bringing her in to the ER."

His hands stilled but he didn't look up. "Tell me," he said in a strangled voice.

"Motor vehicle accident," the nurse said carefully. She said nothing more until he raised his eyes to hers. "Doctor, it's a Level One," she added gently.

Charles felt a thump inside him as his world was

violently tipped off its axis. "Level One" was the designation given to the most critical trauma cases. Hope was in serious trouble.

Reminding himself that he was still standing over a patient, Charles fought back flutters of panic as the nurse reported what she knew about Hope's condition. She ended with the information that Hope was expected to arrive in the ER within the next five minutes.

"Is Dr. Phillips in there?" Charles demanded.

"Yes, Doctor. They're ready for her."

"Okay. And I want Dr. Olmstead," he ordered.

"She's already on her way," the nurse said quietly.

Charles swallowed hard. "Tell Dr. Olmstead—just tell her Hope Evans is the best friend I have in the world. And…" He paused, dangerously close to losing his grip. He forced himself to breathe deeply as he glanced at the startled team around him. "If anyone in here prays, please do it now."

"Hope, can you hear me? Squeeze my hand."

Pain and confusion. Noise and bright lights. Why couldn't she wake up from this awful nightmare? She heard a low, agonized moan. Had that primitive, wounded-animal sound come from *her* throat?

"Hope, it's Charlie. Squeeze my hand." His voice floated closer, sounding more real except it was pitched a little too high.

What was that awful stabbing in her chest? *Lord, please help me catch my breath,* she prayed. *It hurts so much.*

"Come on, Hope. Give me a squeeze, will you?"

It seemed to matter an awful lot to him, so she squeezed.

"Good girl." He sounded enormously relieved. "I'm right here with you. Can you open your eyes for me?"

She could. "Charlie," she whispered gratefully.

"Right here," he said again. He leaned close and with a gentle thumb, nudged her left eye open a bit wider and shone a light into it. Repeating the process on her other eye, he asked an odd question. "Do you know where you are?"

His voice was thin and strange. He sounded frightened. The pain was incredible but Hope was determined to reassure him. "Relax, Doctor," she gasped, aiming for a flippant answer that would ease his mind. "My brain is…still…on the job."

Someone in the room chuckled and Hope heard Charles's immense relief as he replied, "That's very good to know, kid."

Her courage deserted her suddenly and she focused on his face. "Charlie, it hurts," she said in a pathetic, little-girl voice. "It hurts to breathe."

"I know," he said gently. "We're working on that."

She was being touched everywhere, jostled by several pairs of hands that were surprisingly ungentle. At least half a dozen bodies crowded around her, all coming and going like bees around a hive. Although she knew medical terms in four languages, these people were speaking a kind of shorthand she just couldn't follow.

And there was blood. It was everywhere, and it scared her. Where was it coming from?

Her clothes had been cut off and she was lying naked under the bright lights, in front of Charles and this swarm of jabbering strangers. That shocked her, but she tried to remember they were just doing their jobs. Still, she wondered whether she was blushing.

A woman with a musical Southern accent seemed to be directing the activity. She spoke often with Charles, but Hope didn't understand their exchanges.

Finally the honey-voiced Southerner addressed her.

"Hope, I'm Dr. Olmstead. I know you're in a lot of pain right now. You've got some broken ribs and a collapsed lung, for starters. But there's some internal bleeding that we need to check out right away. Do you understand? You need surgery, babe. Right now. In just a few minutes we're gonna take you in. Any objections?"

No, a question. Hope drew a painful breath. "Dr. Hartman?" He'd moved out of her line of sight and she didn't know whether he was still in the room.

Dr. Olmstead sounded amused. "I didn't invite him, darlin', but I suspect he's plannin' to crash the party."

"I'll be there." The beloved voice came from somewhere behind her head and Hope's eyes closed in relief. "I promise you, Hope. I'll be with you the whole time."

Hope opened her eyes and a ceiling of dingy-white acoustic tiles slowly came into focus. She was in the hospital, she remembered. She turned her head to the left and her heart sank when she saw the empty chair.

"Looking for me?" The deep voice, tender and amused, came from her right, so her head swiveled in that direction.

Sprawled in a chair that was jammed against her bed, Charles was so close she might easily have touched him. He sat facing her, using the edge of her bed as an armrest. He smiled gently. "The surgery went great. You're going to be just fine."

She fought hard, but her eyes wouldn't stay open. She felt him lean towards her, his warm fingertips lightly brushing her cheek. "Everything's all right, Hope. Go back to sleep."

She must have done that, because when she opened her eyes again she was in a different room. He was still beside her.

He studied her face for a moment and gave her a sympathetic look. "It hurts, doesn't it?"

Her chest and abdomen had united to form a solid wall of pain. "It hurts a lot," she said in a pinched whisper.

"I know," he soothed. "We'll kick up the pain meds, okay?" He reached for the intercom button just above her head and spoke briefly with a nurse.

Hope smiled drowsily as he stroked her hair. It felt beautiful to be touched that way. She wanted to tell him to forget the drugs and just keep caressing her, but it was too much trouble to talk. She was asleep before the nurse came in.

Alone in total darkness, Hope was falling. She cried out and a warm, strong hand closed around hers, catching her, arresting her descent. Gripping the hand tightly, she opened her eyes and looked around her in confusion.

"I'm here," Charles said. "It's all right. It was only a dream."

But it *wasn't* a dream, not really. "S-somebody hit me," she said, her eyes searching his face for confirmation.

"Yes. But you're safe now. You were having another nightmare."

She struggled to make sense of the images twirling like tornadoes in her head—horrible things and sweet things, all twisted together. Which were real and which were only dreams? "I remember being in the emergency room," she said at last. "You kept insisting that I squeeze your hand."

He ran his thumb back and forth across her knuckles. "As much as I like holding hands with you, that was just a doctor thing," he explained. "Part of a quickie neurological exam." He smiled. "You earned top marks for snapping at me and insisting that your brain was still on the job. The trauma team got a kick out of that.''

''You stayed with me,'' she recalled.

''Yes. I was your guardian angel, watching over you.''

She liked the sound of that. Pulling her hand from his, she attempted to shift a little in the bed. She was stopped by a white-hot spasm of pain. ''Charlie, what's wrong with me?'' she gasped. ''I hurt everywhere. And there's something odd about my left foot,'' she added in a worried tone.

Her hand was recaptured, engulfed in both of his as he looked straight into her eyes. ''Your left foot feels strange because there's a cast on it. Your chest and abdomen hurt because most of the ribs on your right side and a couple on your left are broken. Dr. Olmstead had to sew up your liver and your spleen. The incision is right here.'' He released her hand and pointed, his index finger describing a long line just above the sheet that covered her. ''And do you see this?''

Careful to preserve her modesty, he pulled down the sheet a little. He gently pushed aside the wide sleeve of her gown, revealing a plastic tube that appeared to be attached to her side, next to her right breast.

Her mouth went dry. ''That doesn't—oh, Charlie—that doesn't go *in* me, does it?'' she asked in a horrified whisper.

He spoke gently as he covered her again. ''All the way in, kid. To your chest cavity. It's for drainage, but you're almost clear now, so it'll come out soon.''

Drainage? Hope didn't want to think about what might have been leaking from her, and she was grateful when he didn't elaborate.

''Why don't I just tell you the rest later?'' he suggested as her eyelids drooped.

That woke her up. ''There's *more?*''

"Just a lot of little things. Like the fact that you have twenty stitches just above your left knee and you have an impressive black eye with—" he leaned close, inspecting her "—seven, eight...nine stitches just under your left eyebrow," he finished.

She studied his face. "Is that everything?"

"Well," he said slowly, averting his eyes. "There is something else...."

She gulped. "Tell me, Charlie."

He picked up her right hand and held it in front of her face. "Kid, I'm awfully sorry, but your manicure is ruined."

She tried to chuckle, but it hurt. She groaned instead.

Charles turned serious again, squeezing her hand to reclaim her attention. "Hope, you're going to be really uncomfortable," he warned. "And you'll see bruises and stitches everywhere, so don't be scared, okay? Everything's been fixed and you'll heal just fine, because you're young and strong."

As her eyes closed, she told herself it was well worth a broken body to be with him again. She pulled his hand to her face, rubbed her cheek against it and was suffused with peace.

"Hope," he said urgently. "I can't get Pastor Bill on the phone and I don't know how to get in touch with your family."

"I just want *you*, Charlie." She couldn't tell whether she had said the words aloud or merely thought them. Sleep beckoned to her, lapped at her like gentle waves, and she didn't resist.

Charles had finally reached Pastor Bill late on Saturday evening, but it wasn't until Sunday afternoon that the Evanses and all four of their sons had been contacted about Hope's accident.

Hope wasn't worried. Pastor Bill would take care of her family. He'd answer their questions and pray with them. She was concerned about Bob, though, until she learned Tom had paid a visit to the neighbors who always looked after Hope's pet when she was out of town. Even Bob was in good hands.

Grace Evans was preparing to leave Africa. Although it would take her a few days to get to Chicago, she was planning to stay with her daughter for at least a month.

On Monday evening Tom drove to Midway Airport to pick up Matthew, Hope's eldest brother, who was flying in from California.

"Your other three brothers wanted to come," Charles had told Hope that morning, "but I understand Matthew discouraged them. I'm glad he did—that many people would be a bit overwhelming."

Yes, her family was overwhelming, but in the most delightful way. If only Charles could see a gathering of her boisterous clan—how they laughed and loved!

"What time is it?" Hope asked Charles.

"I answered that question fifteen minutes ago," he responded with a grin. "Here." He removed his watch and handed it to her. "Now you can watch the second hand go around and around. Maybe it will put you to sleep."

"I know I'm acting like a six-year-old on Christmas Eve," Hope confessed, "but I haven't seen Matthew in over a year."

"Go to sleep," Charles urged. "I promise to wake you the minute he arrives."

Attempting to find a more comfortable position, Hope shifted in the bed. A vicious stab of pain made her catch her breath sharply. Aware that Charles was watching, she averted her face to hide the tears she couldn't stop.

He wasn't fooled. She felt his hand on her shoulder. "You don't have to be so tough. The injuries you've suffered would make a professional hockey player bawl like a baby.''

Her pain medication finally kicked in and she was able to doze a little. When she awakened, twilight was creeping into the room.

Charles put down the medical journal he'd been reading. He stood and stretched, then bent to touch his toes as Hope had seen him do once before. He moved to the window, his attention captured by the rising moon, which he pointed out to Hope. He stood still for several minutes, apparently lost in thought as he gazed at the moon.

From Hope's vantage point the window was like a mirror, clearly reflecting Charles's face. Her hungry eyes feasted on him as he finger-combed his hair. She watched him rub his hand over the stubble on his jaw and wondered what he was thinking. He looked infinitely weary.

In three days he hadn't left her alone for a moment unless a nurse was available to sit with her. Several times she had urged him to get some rest and then go back to his work, but he kept putting her off. She hated knowing it was guilt that kept him glued to her bedside, but she couldn't do anything about that. She was glad Matthew was coming because Charles might not feel so responsible for her now.

He came to sit beside her. "How is it, kid?"

"Not too bad," she fudged. She hated it that he worried so much. "You're awfully good to me, Charlie."

He turned anguished eyes on her. "How can you say that?" he demanded. "How can you still believe that? Hope, there is nothing good in me! *When* will you understand?"

Shocked into silence by his outburst, she watched as he tore himself from the chair and strode angrily back to the window. With his back to her, he raged, "I didn't figure it out until this morning. Of course I wondered why you had been out so late at night, but—'' He broke off, then he turned around, savagely accusing her. ''You were coming here, weren't you?'' Angrily he stabbed a finger towards the floor. ''You were coming *here,* at three o'clock in the morning. In a thunderstorm. Because I wouldn't return your calls. It's all my fault, isn't it?''

Annoyance helped Hope find her voice. ''That's ridiculous, Charlie. You can't blame yourself for—''

''Can't I? I blame myself for everything. All of it. I should never have let you get so close to me. I knew there was a danger to you, but I was selfish.'' He bowed his head, avoiding her eyes. ''I don't love you, Hope,'' he said bluntly. ''I feel affection for you, but I don't love you and I never will.'' His voice softened until it was barely audible. ''You have to forget any dreams you have about me. I'll never be able to make them come true.''

She shook her head emphatically. ''I don't have any dreams about you. I've never seen us getting married, if that's what you're afraid of.''

He said nothing.

''It's okay that you don't love me,'' she said steadily. ''I can live with that. In fact, it's better that way. So you see, nothing has to change.''

His hands gestured wildly and he made an explosive, exasperated noise in his throat. ''But everything *has* changed. And I *can't* live with it!''

Their gazes locked and time slowed to an agonizing crawl as their battle of wills was fought in utter silence. Hope was shocked and sickened by the naked despair she read in his eyes. Her heart almost failed, but Charles looked away first.

''You're not going to save me,'' he said at last. ''Why can't you just leave me alone?''

''Because I'm your friend. That's what I was coming to tell you.''

"Well, who doesn't know that?" he rasped. "You might have saved yourself that wild ride to the ER. But I'm *your* friend, Hope. That's why I can't just—" He stopped as a nurse entered the room.

As the woman looked from Charles's angry face to Hope's frightened one, her eyes widened until the full circles of her blue irises were visible. Obviously uncomfortable, she cleared her throat. "Let's check your blood pressure first," she suggested. A minute later she looked Charles in the eye and reported the numbers in a tone of gentle reproof. "I think we need to calm down in here," she remarked.

He said nothing, but turned to stare sullenly out the window as the nurse completed her tasks.

Just as the nurse left, Tom phoned from Midway to say that Matthew's flight was running over an hour late. Without looking at Hope, Charles relayed the news in a flat voice.

She clenched her teeth, fighting both physical pain and emotional agony. He wouldn't leave her tonight because he felt responsible for her. But he would go soon, probably when her mother arrived. And she'd never see him again.

Charles sighed heavily and slumped into the chair next to the bed. He didn't speak again and he didn't look at Hope, but he reached for her hand and held it tightly.

She had just reached the threshold of sleep when she felt Charles release her hand. She was dimly aware of the bedcovers being pulled over her shoulders, then her hair was smoothed away from her face and she heard his broken whisper. "I'm sorry, kid." She felt the light brush of his lips against her forehead. "Oh, Hope—I'm so sorry."

Even though drugs and exhaustion clouded her mind,

she didn't misunderstand. He wasn't taking back anything he had said. What he was sorry about was not being able to love her.

And that only made her love him more.

Chapter Fourteen

⤳❧

It was an amusing reversal of roles, Hope thought as she watched Charles sleep for a change.

His chair didn't look terribly comfortable for sitting, never mind sleeping in. With his left leg folded under him and his right thrown over one of the chair's wooden arms, Charles was twisted like a pretzel. His left elbow rested on the chair's other arm and his head was propped against his fisted hand. With his right arm he hugged a pillow to his chest, but Hope couldn't see how that was doing him any good.

He'd told her many times he could sleep standing up if he had to, and now she understood that was no idle boast. His deep, even breathing assured her that he slept soundly. She watched him for twenty minutes and he didn't move an eyelash.

Hope's eyes were drawn to a movement in the doorway, and she smiled a welcome to Matthew, her eldest brother. With a soft, strangled cry he rushed to her.

Matthew wasn't thinking. When Hope lifted her hands

to cup his face and kiss him, his arms went around her and he squeezed. She yelped like a kicked dog.

Charles was awake and on his feet in an instant, ready to do battle with the villain who was abusing Hope. From the far side of the bed he glowered at the intruder.

Shock registered on Matthew's face as he backed away. "Oh, Hope! Baby, I'm sorry!"

Hope couldn't breathe and she was actually seeing stars, but one look at Charles's stormy face forced a smile to her lips. "No, Charlie," she gasped. "Please don't kill him. This is Matthew!"

With obvious reluctance Charles offered his hand. "She's going to be fragile for a while," he said gruffly.

"Yes, of course." Matthew reached across the bed to shake hands. "I can't believe I was that stupid."

Charles's flashing eyes and tightly clamped lips said clearly that *he* couldn't believe it, either. He repositioned Hope's pillow and helped her to get settled again.

As Matthew removed his sport coat and draped it over a chair, Tom spoke from the doorway. "Honey, I'm going to take the old bear home with me for a while. I'll clean him up and give him a decent meal."

Hearing that did Hope a world of good. "And then you'll tuck him into bed?"

Tom shrugged. "I would if I thought for a moment that he might stay there. But you know he wouldn't. If I can get him away from here long enough to shower and shave, I'm going to call my mission a success."

Charles ignored the exchange. Still standing beside Hope's bed, he bent to tuck in her bare right foot, which had strayed from beneath the covers. "I'll be back in two hours," he promised, giving her toes a light squeeze. "Call me on my cell phone if you want anything." He nodded curtly to Matthew.

Matthew watched him go. "Whew!" he said in a low voice. "Your doctor friend is a little intense, isn't he?"

Hope wouldn't hear criticism of Charles, not even from her favorite brother. "You woke him up," she accused. "And unless things have changed, you're not exactly 'Mr. Sunshine' when *you* are awakened from a deep sleep."

He plopped into a chair and grinned at her. His dark curls tumbled onto his forehead, making him look more like an ornery seventeen-year-old than the responsible husband and father he was. "Things haven't changed, baby."

Charles needed to think about going back to work. Since Hope's accident he'd been calling in favors, but his absence was being felt downstairs. He didn't know how much longer he'd be able to stay away, yet how could he work when he was so tormented by guilt? He'd been responsible for breaking Hope's body as well as her heart.

That was probably why he was so fiercely protective of her now.

The endless parade of visitors grated on his nerves. Matthew's dawn-to-dusk presence was bad enough, but Pastor Bill and a couple of church friends had looked in, too. Claire brought a pretty robe one day and some glossy cooking magazines the next. Tom kept the room filled with flowers.

Hope appeared to be glad to see them all, but Charles thought nothing of throwing people out whenever she needed to rest. Between the constant pain and the recurring nightmares, she wasn't getting much sleep. He hated the way she'd sit bravely in her bed, dispensing sweetness to everyone who came in. Couldn't her friends see the weary lines around her eyes? Didn't they notice the way her smile wavered when her pain medication began to wear off? Too many people came too often and stayed too long.

Well, they probably couldn't help themselves any more than Charles could. Like moths to a porch light they came, hungry for her warmth. Who could resist Hope's charm? Even Granddad had fallen for her and Mother was probably next.

But she was finally asleep, and Charles was determined that she would receive no more visitors this afternoon.

Matthew was on his way to O'Hare Airport to pick up his and Hope's mother. If only Hope would sleep until they got here. Charles knew when she saw her mother she'd be too excited to rest anymore.

Careful not to disturb her, he propped his feet on the bottom of Hope's bed and leaned back in his chair. He reached for her half-finished cup of ginger ale. The stuff was awful, but there was sugar in it, and maybe that would fool his rumbling stomach into believing it was being fed. He could grab something to eat as soon as Grace Evans and Matthew arrived.

He turned on the television and watched a baseball game without the sound. When the Cubs made a brilliant double play he turned instinctively to Hope, wanting to share it with her, but she was still asleep.

A young, pretty nurse came in. Charles had never seen her before. ''Not now,'' he said tersely, waving his hand as if to shoo a pesky housefly.

She blinked at him. ''Excuse me, sir, but I have to—''

''Come back in an hour,'' he said quietly.

''But all I want is to—''

His eyes narrowed and his tone was softly menacing. ''You are not going to wake her now. Go tell your supervisor that Dr. Hartman says it's time for your break.''

The nurse's eyes grew round. Apparently, she'd heard the name. She retreated without another word.

Still asleep, Hope sighed and turned her head. Charles watched closely, ready to wake her at the first sign of a bad dream, but she didn't stir again.

It was understandable that she would have nightmares of the accident, but Charles felt her tortured sleep was his fault. He was consumed by guilt and he had no idea what he should do. He would do anything, anything at all to make it better for her. Perhaps he should talk to her mother or even Pastor Bill. They would know what was best for Hope.

A woman appeared in the doorway. She was short and trim, with dark hair and a sweet expression Charles knew very well. She gazed longingly at the sleeping Hope and her large gray eyes shimmered with tears.

Charles scrambled to his feet. "I believe I know who you are," he said softly.

"I know you, too." Grace Evans smiled as she walked towards him. "Thank you, Charles, for all you have done."

All he had done? If this woman had any inkling of what he had done to her sweet daughter, she would clobber him, not thank him, Charles reflected bitterly.

As Grace Evans's arms encircled his waist, something in him snapped. His eyes closed and he clung tightly to her for several long seconds before he dropped his arms and stepped back. "I'm sorry," he mumbled, deeply disturbed by the hunger he had just revealed.

She tilted her head to look up at him. "No. I think you really needed a hug, didn't you, Charles?"

He opened his mouth to deny it, but then he pressed his lips together and nodded dumbly, shocked by the discovery that he was starving for this kind of human contact.

"Matthew is parking the car," Grace explained. "He'll be up in a minute. Could we step outside and talk?"

Charles looked at Hope and gave his head a slow, solid shake. "I don't like to leave her," he said in a low voice. "She has nightmares. They're pretty bad."

Grace's eyes again brimmed with tears, but none fell. "It was awful, wasn't it?" she asked tremulously. "Please tell me about it, Charles."

He took her elbow and led her to the far side of the room. "It was a head-on collision," he said quietly. "Her seat belt broke and it was a miracle that—" He sucked in some air, fighting a growing tightness in his throat. "Anyway, she broke ten ribs, mostly on the right side, and her right lung collapsed. There was a huge tear in her liver, but that was fixable. Her spleen was pretty ripped up, but Dr. Olmstead managed to save most of it. She'll do fine."

He tried to speak dispassionately, but as he looked into Grace's watery eyes his control began to slip. His stomach lurched as he recalled the horror that had gripped him when he'd been told Hope was on her way to the ER.

Grace was waiting, and he continued in a voice that was not altogether steady. "We had a chest tube in her for a couple of days, but everything's good now. Her left foot is broken in three places and she has a number of cuts and bruises. She'll make a complete recovery, but she'll have some scars."

Grace had gone pale, but she was tough. "I understand."

"Her ribs will heal on their own," Charles said. "We can't bind them because that would interfere with her breathing. So every time she moves, it hurts. She rarely complains, but you can see in her face how much pain she's in.''

"Poor little thing," Grace lamented softly. "Oh, my baby!"

"Of course I couldn't operate on her," Charles said, "but I saw to it that she had the best care, and I stayed with her the whole time. Is there anything else you want to know?"

"What about the nightmares?"

He wanted to fall on his knees before this woman and confess he was to blame for Hope's accident, for her nightmares, for everything. "She remembers the wreck and she remembers being in the emergency room," he said. "She was in a great deal of pain and it was pretty scary. But I'm sure the nightmares will stop when you take her home."

Grace observed him keenly. "You look worn out," she commented. "Why don't you go home and get some rest?"

Home? He'd never thought of his apartment that way. He liked it, but it was little more than a place to hang his suits and his art collection.

Home. Involuntarily his gaze drifted to the young woman in the bed as he thought of a porch swing, a small dog and the aroma of apples and cinnamon. The modest house where Hope lived was the closest thing to home Charles had ever known.

Grace was still watching him. "Charles?" She reached up to give his shoulder a friendly pat. "Go home and sleep."

He forced himself to smile. "I'm a trauma surgeon, Grace. Sleeping isn't something we're trained to do."

When she smiled back, he was startled by the gleam of understanding in her kind eyes. Grace Evans had seen straight through him. She saw his guilt and his confusion, and somehow she knew how very sorry he was.

"I'm in trouble," Hope muttered. "Lord, help me."

She'd come far enough out of her drug-fog to start worrying. She chewed a fingernail as she stared out the window at a deep blue sky dotted with white cotton-ball clouds.

What was she going to do for a car? And how on earth was she going to pay her hospital bill? "It's going to be thousands of dollars," she whispered. "And I know my insurance won't cover all of it. Please show me what to do."

Charles entered the room carrying a large paper bag, and she was more than a little interested to know what it contained. The lunch trays had been passed out an hour ago, but they'd skipped Hope. When she complained to a nurse that she was starving, she'd been told simply that she was supposed to wait for Dr. Hartman.

"That's food, I hope?" she said, eyeing the bag greedily.

"Can't you smell it? Cream-of-asparagus soup. For sandwiches we have smoked turkey. The chicken salad is for your mom. Sorry I took so long. Traffic was awful."

It touched her that he'd gone all the way to her favorite deli to get her lunch. "Mom had a migraine so I sent her home. But thanks, Charlie. It's a beautiful day, isn't it?"

He put the food on her bedside table. "Then why were you frowning and biting your nails when I came in?"

She hesitated. "I have things on my mind."

He studied her face. "Yes." He opened a can of ginger ale and poured it over ice in a tall plastic cup. "Money things, I'll bet."

She sighed.

"Knock it off, Hope," he said impatiently. "You know I'll take care of the hospital bill." He set the cup in front of her and reached into the paper bag.

She watched as he unwrapped the sandwiches. "Charlie, I can't take money from you."

"Fine," he said airily. "Then *borrow* from me. You did once, you know. Fifty dollars, if I recall correctly. You paid it back promptly, with some delicious interest, I might add. I'm perfectly willing to do business with you again."

She looked at him soberly. "But it would take me years to pay you back. If you would even let me."

She took a drink of her ginger ale. He watched her, waiting for her to set the cup down before he spoke. His voice was low, serious. "Hope, you always insist that every good thing comes to you from God's hand. Is it so inconceivable that just this once He might use me as a conduit for His blessing?"

Hope shook her head in amazement. How did He *do* that? Not five minutes ago she had asked God to show her a way. It had just been offered to her—was she going to reject it? "I give up," she said simply.

"Good. I'm hungry. Just look at this beautiful soup," he said, removing the lid from a cup and handing her a spoon.

Hope awakened in the night. Her room was darker than usual, so she knew Charles had pulled the curtains and closed the door. She hoped that meant he was sleeping.

He wasn't. His hand found hers in the darkness. "I'm here. Do you need anything?"

"How did you know I was awake?"

"Your breathing is different."

Why was she surprised? He knew her, like nobody ever had. She laced her fingers through his. She knew *him,* too, and he was gripping her hand too tightly. That meant he was worried. "Charlie, what's wrong?"

She could barely see his face in the dim light, but she saw his head move back and forth. He cleared his throat. "I'm just thinking."

"About what?"

There was a long pause before he spoke. "About taking a job in San Diego."

She was suddenly wide-awake. "No," she said sadly, squeezing his hand. "You've already decided."

His silence confirmed it.

He had seemed preoccupied all evening, and now she knew why. He had already begun pulling back from her, preparing them both for what was to come. Her voice was gravelly. "How soon will you leave?"

"Three weeks."

She let go of his hand and tried to sit up, but she couldn't find the button to raise her bed. She fought to keep calm. "Is that really what you want?"

"No." He exhaled the word, stretching the single syllable to convey his frustration. "But it's what I'm going to do. I talked to your mother about it today. She agrees that—"

Outraged, Hope cut him off. "And the two of you decided this? What I want doesn't matter to you at all?" That sounded childish and selfish, but darn it, the man was an unbelievable blockhead and Hope's patience was at an end.

"Hope, what you need is more important to me than what you think you want. It's the right thing to do and you know it." A note of desperation crept into his voice. "Please don't make this harder than it already is."

She wanted to turn on the light, but she couldn't reach it. Again she struggled to sit up. Charles felt for the but-

ton and she heard the soft mechanical *whirr* as the bed
raised her almost to a sitting position.

She drew a shaky breath and let him feel the full force
of her anger. "You go ahead and run to San Diego, Charlie Hartman, and I'll be right behind you. I'll get a job
scrubbing floors in your hospital, and every time you turn
around, you'll trip over me. I won't *let* you run away."

Hope was gratified by his shocked silence, but her
breath was coming in gasps and her heaving chest ached.
Disregarding that, she went on. "For a genius doctor, you
can be breathtakingly stupid. You're terrified of hurting
me, Charlie, but you don't realize that what hurts me
more than anything is knowing how much you despise
yourself!"

The outburst had cost every particle of her strength and
her hot tears were due as much to physical pain as emotional distress.

"No more, Hope," he pleaded urgently. "Don't do
this." Moving to sit beside her on the bed, he put his
hands on her shoulders and leaned towards her. He laid
his cheek against hers and tried to quiet her sobs. "Please
don't."

"I can't help it," she cried pathetically. "It hurts."

"I know," he whispered.

He *didn't* know, and that fed her frustration. She shook
her head, pushing him away. "I don't—I don't m-mean
my chest."

Again he leaned his cheek against hers. "I know,
Hope. I know what you mean, and I'm so sorry. But
please be still now."

Entranced by his nearness and his warm, unsteady
breath against her ear, she grew calmer. Her left hand
was trapped under the sheet he sat on, but she lifted her
right hand to caress the soft hair on the back of his head.

When she touched him, he caught his breath sharply

and started to move away, but her fingers burrowed into his thick, wavy hair and she pulled him back. ''No!'' she commanded in a fierce whisper.

He relaxed suddenly, and a thrill of delight shot through Hope as his face nestled against the curve of her neck. Then she felt his kiss, just under her ear, so right, and he was still.

She was exhausted and her brain was spinning, but it was so lovely, listening to him breathe against her ear. She forgot everything else and concentrated on breathing with him.

When she awoke, it was daylight and he was gone. Her bed was still raised and she lay unmoving, remembering. As her chest rose and fell, a small, bright flash arrested her attention and she looked down. Against the shoulder of her blue satin nightshirt a small object glittered in the beam of sunlight that fell across the top of her bed.

It was his silver chain with the eagle. Hope was surprised that the sturdy chain had broken, but when she tried to pick it up she felt a tug that told her it was not broken at all. It was securely fastened around her neck.

She understood perfectly. She wasn't to have even the three weeks. He was gone already.

Chapter Fifteen

One week after her accident, Hope was well enough to leave the hospital. Her mother would take her home in the morning.

"Bob's going crazy without you," Grace said cheerfully. "He thinks you've abandoned him. I'm afraid he's going to jump all over you, so we'll have to be careful when we get you home. Here, let me do that. It can't be easy for you with those sore ribs."

Hope relinquished the brush she'd been trying to pull through her long hair. As her mother gently brushed out her tangles, Hope closed her eyes and tried to shut out the memory of how it had felt when Charles had done this for her, just yesterday morning.

Grace kept up her cheerful patter. "It's been a few years since I last did this. Remember how you used to cry when I combed the snarls out of your wet hair?" She chuckled. "I always wanted to cut it, but Daddy and the boys loved your long hair, didn't they? Oh! I forgot to tell you—Matthew called late last night. His flight arrived in L.A. twenty minutes *early,* if you can believe that. He really wanted to stay longer, but I guess the twins have been giving Megan fits and you know the baby is due any day now.''

Hope nodded, but she wasn't listening. All morning she'd been hoping it would turn out to be a terrible misunderstanding, but the message Charles had left around her neck was painfully clear: Don't waste your prayers on me. Let me go.

Grace ran a loving hand over her daughter's smooth hair and put down the brush. She looked into Hope's eyes and spoke seriously. ''Are you ready to talk about it?''

Hope turned her face away. How could she help feeling that her mother had betrayed her?

Grace sighed deeply. ''Sweetheart, he's a dear man, but there's no future for the two of you.''

Hope's hands clenched. ''You don't understand. I have never dreamed of marrying him. But he needs me, Mom. I can help him in ways that nobody else can.''

Grace put her hand on Hope's shoulder. ''Sweetheart,'' she said reasonably, ''you must realize it's not a good idea to—''

''You don't understand,'' Hope repeated, frustration making her fingernails dig into her palms. ''There is something in him that I recognize. Something that only I can see. I can't explain it, except to say that from the beginning I've had the strongest sense that God *sent* me to Charlie, to help him find his way.''

Grace was silent, obviously skeptical.

''Mom, Gramps believed it, too. He told me the night before he died.'' Hope's eyes misted as she remembered their last conversation.

''Come closer, sweetie-pie.'' Gramps placed his gnarled hand on top of her head and said a brief prayer, blessing her.

The lump in her throat made speech impossible. He

knew he was going home and he was telling her goodbye.
She wanted to say that she loved him, that she was grate-
ful to him, that she would always remember what he had
done for her. But he knew all that, and she would see
him again one day.

His hand moved from her head to her cheek, resting
there for a moment before he reached for her hand. "I
want to talk to you about Dr. Hartman. I believe God
has plans for that man, and you will figure in them. Never
stop praying for him, Hope. Things are very hard for him
and he needs you on his side."

Hope could no longer hold back her tears. "Oh,
please," she cried piteously. "I'm so tired. Mom, I can't
fight Charlie and you, too."

Her mother patted her arm. "I'm sorry, sweetheart. We
really shouldn't talk about this until you've had some
rest," she said. "I'm going downstairs for something to
eat. You try to sleep a little and we'll talk later."

Hope was too torn up to sleep. She leafed through a
thick cooking magazine but nothing in it interested her.
Frustration gnawed at her and she had to *do* something.
She rolled up the magazine, but as she drew back her
arm to fire her missile across the room, she was halted
by a spasm of pain. She gasped and dropped her arm,
still clutching the magazine as her eyes filled with tears.

"Careful, honey!" Tom stood in the doorway, concern
furrowing his brow. "Want me to throw that for you?"

Startled, she could only stare at him.

"I guess you're mad at Trey," he stated as he approached her bed.

She nodded, taken aback by the truth.

"Me, too." Tom took the magazine from her and
rolled it tighter. "What are we going for? His chair?"

Sucking her bottom lip, Hope nodded.

Tom moved back, wound up, lifted his right leg and

stepped into the pitch. The magazine hit the back of the chair with a resounding *thwack,* pushing the chair several inches across the floor.

Hope blinked at Tom and a tear rolled down her cheek. ''I didn't know you were a lefty,'' she said in a husky voice.

''Yeah. But I bat right-handed,'' he informed her. He started to say something else, but his mouth closed on the words and he merely watched her, his eyes darkening with compassion.

She moved her legs and patted the space she'd made for him on the bed. He sat next to her.

''I love you, Tom,'' she said softly.

He nodded, not looking at her. ''I love you right back, Hope.''

Her bottom lip quivered. ''He's gone, you know. He won't come to see me ever again.''

Tom's chin dropped to his chest. ''I know. This morning he told me he'd decided to take the San Diego job. I understand he won't be leaving for three weeks, but I guess he thought it would be easier to just…'' Tom didn't finish the sentence, didn't need to.

Pain ripped through Hope's chest as a sob escaped her. Tom sighed and carefully put an arm around her shoulders.

''Oh, Tom—what's wrong with him?'' she wailed. ''Why does he make himself so unhappy? Why won't he let us love him?'' Her chest ached and she no longer cared.

''Hope, I'm so sorry!'' The anguish in Tom's voice tore at her heart, so she pushed him away. He handed her some tissues and poured her a glass of water.

''No, *I'm* sorry,'' she said dully. ''I won't do that again.''

''Yes, you will,'' he corrected. ''And when you do,

I'll be right here. Just think of me as your great big hand-kerchief.''

She gave him a weak smile.

He patted her hand and rose from the bed. ''Try to rest now. I'll come back later, okay?''

At the door he turned. ''Hope? You won't forget him, will you?'' His eyes begged for her reassurance. ''What I mean is, you won't stop praying for him. Right?''

Fat tears rolled down her cheeks, but her voice was firm. ''As long as I'm breathing, Tom, I'll be praying for him.''

Charles needed to see a patient on the fourth floor, but when he got on the elevator he pressed ''three'' out of habit. He groaned softly, then pressed ''four'' and waited.

When the elevator opened on the third floor his body leaned forwards, wanting, but he set his jaw firmly and pressed the Close Door button. At the last second he saw Tom in the hall, pacing in front of the elevators. His hand shot out and the door reopened. He approached his brother. ''What's up, Tom? You look like thunder.''

''That's exactly how I feel,'' Tom growled.

Charles's mouth fell open. Tom was eternally, often even annoyingly, good-natured. What had gotten into him?

''You're not going in there,'' Tom said firmly. ''You're not to see her again, do you understand?''

''What's happened?'' Charles demanded, panic rising in him.

''I don't want you to see her,'' Tom repeated stub-bornly. ''Not today, not tomorrow, not ever. Clear enough?''

Charles gulped, stunned by his brother's angry defi-ance. Well, Hope couldn't ask for a better champion than faithful Tom. Charles had lost his brother's unquestioning devotion, but Hope had gained it, and he was glad. Perhaps Hope's friendship with Tom would ripen into something more. He would try to be glad about that, too.

Tom's eyes flashed fire. "You have no idea what you've done to that sweet girl!"

"I know exactly what I've done."

Tom gave his head an angry shake. "She didn't ask you for the moon, Trey," he spat. "She's not the kind to chase after you, begging you to marry her. All she wanted was for you to be her friend. Was that so impossible?"

More impossible than Tom would ever understand. Charles shook his head and stared at his shoes.

"I'm finished making excuses for you. You've nurtured your bitterness for so long, you've finally managed to turn yourself into an unfeeling monster!"

Charles nodded slowly, soberly. "I've always been an unfeeling monster," he said quietly. He looked up. "So you finally got a good look, did you, Tom?"

The elevator bell sounded behind them. A door opened and three people got off.

"Get out of here," Tom said evenly. "Leave her alone."

Without a word Charles turned and stepped onto the empty elevator. He pushed the button for the fourth floor, avoiding his brother's angry eyes as the door closed between them.

The elevator started, but it was going down, not up. As he touched the panel again, Charles saw what he had missed before—the button was lit for B2, the lowest floor of the hospital.

But I'm going even lower than that, he thought bitterly. *And I just can't seem to help myself.*

It was useless. Exhausted as he was, he wasn't going to sleep tonight. Charles sat on the side of his bed and stared into the darkness.

He'd never been able to refuse her anything. She could make him spit sunflower seeds and drink ginger ale. She could make him bite his tongue when he wanted to lash someone with it. He'd all but stopped swearing, even when she wasn't around to hear. He went to church and Bible study just to please her, and he'd even learned a verse of Scripture. But what she wanted now—for him to stick around, to act as if nothing had changed—was simply impossible.

She wanted him to be her friend. But he honestly didn't know whether his affection for her was strong enough to withstand his growing desire. All he knew was that by loving him she had dramatically increased her risk. Their friendship was impossible now because he was afraid he could make her want the same things he had begun to want.

A broken heart was something Hope could recover from, just as long as she had nothing to reproach herself for. Charles was willing to go to San Diego or to the moon to ensure that she would never know that kind of regret.

In the darkness he groped for his pants. He pulled them on and padded across the cold hardwood floor of his bedroom. He wrenched open the French doors and stepped onto his balcony.

The night air was cool and he shivered, taking fierce pleasure in the gooseflesh on his arms. He wished he could be even colder, that this small suffering would take his mind off the great one.

He dropped to the chaise lounge and put his hands behind his head, lying back to watch a full moon. There really was a man's face there, and it was a sad one. The trees below him whooshed softly in the night breeze, a lonely sound.

Hope. Her name used to comfort, but now it mocked him. Now he'd given up Hope, lost Hope. He wanted to cry, the way Tom had when Susan died. Stunned and silent, Charles had held his brother in his arms, knowing he could do nothing, say nothing to heal Tom. That realization had seared him with pain.

Now he felt it again, much worse than before. He was as angry as a man could be, but his rage was impotent, because it was directed at an unseen God.

Not long ago, he'd begged God to spare Hope the pain of loving a man who had a chunk of granite where his heart should be. But either God had no real power or He just didn't care about Hope Evans. Either way, there wasn't much to recommend him, Charles thought savagely.

Still, he had some questions.

What made Hope so sure of her God? She was an intelligent young woman, not easily fooled. One of the many things Charles admired about her was the way she filtered everything through that remarkable common sense of hers.

Yet she believed. And she believed Charles's salvation was even more important than whether he returned her love or not. Hope refused to let go because she was certain Charles was marked for God.

Could it be true?

"We can't prove God to you," she had said once. "But if you ask Him to, he will prove Himself."

"All right—I'm asking," Charles said aloud. He sat up suddenly, still gazing at the face in the moon, his fists tightly clenched at his sides. "I'm asking!" he shouted. His anguished plea splintered the quiet night, echoing across the bare floor of the empty bedroom behind him. "Please make me believe it!"

Somewhere in the distance he heard a police siren and a barking dog, but there was no other answer. He trembled more from fear now than from cold as a swiftly moving cloud covered the moon, blotting out its light.

It was raining hard on Saturday morning when Hope's mother arrived to take her home from the hospital. In her room, Hope sat in a wheelchair in front of the window. As the dark sky opened in another vicious summer storm, Hope turned a stricken face to her mother and insisted she couldn't possibly get into the rental car. Not in the rain.

It had been a miserable night. Twice she'd been awakened by the nightmare, and both times she'd cried herself to sleep because Charles wasn't there to comfort her. Now her chest heaved painfully and she was exhausted and frightened and heartsick. She tried to talk to her Heavenly Father, but her prayers were nothing more than silent screams of agony.

Hope realized her mother was beside herself with worry, but she couldn't stop trembling. Quiet tears coursed down her cheeks as she watched the rain beat against her window.

Grace took her daughter's hand. "You're so pale," she murmured distractedly. "It can't be right for them to send you home today." She hesitated, then seemed to make a decision. "I'm going to call Charles."

"He won't come," Hope said in a gravelly voice. "If you'll just give me a few minutes, Mom, I'll pull myself together."

What was she so afraid of, anyway? She'd already faced dying, she was intimately acquainted with intense physical pain and she would never again see the man she loved. What could possibly hurt her *now?* Cold fingers of bitterness wrapped around her heart and squeezed.

"Never mind, Mom," she said, lifting her chin. "Let's just go, right now. It doesn't matter anymore."

"Coffee, Dr. Hartman?"

Charles turned to Pastor Bill in irritation. "I'm not here for coffee," he said shortly.

"Then, Dr. Hartman…Charles," the pastor began, "please tell me what I can do for you."

Charles stopped pacing and stood before the window of the pastor's small study. Yellow sunlight squeezed through a break in the heavy clouds, making the raindrops that clung to the glass sparkle like diamonds. He thought of Hope's tears as he touched the window, tracing with one finger the wet trail of a falling jewel.

He loathed himself more with every breath he drew. After all she'd done for him, he had again turned his back on Hope.

But what else could he have done? He spun away from the window and flung himself into an armchair. As he met Pastor Bill's steady gaze, the anger drained from him as if a plug had been pulled. "I honestly don't know why I'm here," he confessed. "There was just nowhere else to go." His mouth twisted bitterly. "I guess Hope got me in the habit of coming to church."

Pastor Bill smiled. "A man could have worse habits," he suggested. "What's troubling you, Charles?"

"I've hurt her," he said steadily.

"Yes," said the pastor. He looked genuinely sorry. "I thought you would, in the end. I tried to warn her."

Charles swallowed hard. "Is there anything I can do? To make it easier for her? Her God has failed her and I just—"

"What makes you think God has failed Hope?"

Charles shuddered. "He didn't protect her from me. And I asked Him to."

Pastor Bill's eyebrows lifted slightly. "Did you? Why?"

"I have no heart," Charles said dully. "I can't return her love. And there's something more. Something she doesn't know. I'm dangerous to her now because I want—" He drew a breath, let it out, looked the man in the eye and told him the truth. "I want what she can't give."

Pastor Bill didn't look at all shocked.

"I thought it would be best to leave her alone," Charles continued. "But she's so miserable."

Pastor Bill gave him a dismissive shrug. "Well, there's really nothing you can do about that now, is there?"

Charles stared at the floor. "I knew what I was doing," he said brokenly. "I knew she was tenderhearted and I knew what it would mean for her if she came to love me. I knew the risk and I took it because I was selfish."

He pressed his fingers to his temples in an effort to stop the throbbing inside his head. But his chest hurt, too, and his throat burned. Guilt overwhelmed him, causing physical pain.

After a long silence the pastor spoke briskly. "Well, now that you've got that off your chest, why don't you go on home?"

Charles stared.

From a cup on his desk Pastor Bill removed a pencil and examined it. "You can do nothing for Hope," he said bluntly. "So unless there's something else you'd like to discuss…"

Charles eyed him suspiciously. "Such as?"

Pastor Bill held the pencil at both ends, absently flexing it by pushing with his thumbs. "Oh, I don't know," he said a little too casually. "Maybe you'd like to tell me what it is that's got you so paralyzed with fear?'' He looked into Charles's eyes and deliberately snapped the pencil.

Charles flinched.

"Exactly," said Pastor Bill.

Charles leaned his head against the back of his chair and closed his eyes. "There's a struggle in me," he said baldly. "It has something to do with God and it scares me."

"Ah," said the pastor. "Yes. It *is* frightening. I felt that struggle myself, nearly forty years ago, and I've seen many men face it since then. Why don't you just let go, Charles?"

The answer came without hesitation. "Because I will fall." As soon as the words were out, Charles realized how horribly true they were. He looked down, suddenly aware of his death grip on the arms of the chair.

All his life he'd been clinging desperately to the edge of some terrifying precipice, but he was just too tired to hold on any longer. What was the point, anyway? Mere survival was not enough for him anymore.

"Yes," Pastor Bill Barnes said gravely. He nodded for emphasis. "If you let go, you will definitely fall." His vinyl swivel chair squeaked a protest as he rose from it. He moved away from the desk, coming to stand just behind Charles, where he rested heavy hands on the doctor's slumped shoulders.

"But God will catch you, Charles. Why don't you just let go?"

Chapter Sixteen

Home at last, Hope was settled on the living room sofa with soft pillows and a handmade quilt. Tom's latest floral tribute, a lovely bouquet of pink roses and fragrant white lilies, graced the coffee table in front of her. Under the canopy of flowers lay a box of Hope's favorite chocolates, left by Matthew for her homecoming, and an untouched cup of peppermint tea.

When the rain ended, Grace opened the living room windows. The fresh, damp breeze tickled the lace curtains, making the late-morning sunlight dance across the bare pine floor and up the wall. Numbly watching the intricate and ever-changing patterns of light and shadow, Hope reflected that Charles had told her it would take at least six weeks for her broken body to heal.

He hadn't said a thing about her heart.

The telephone rang. Fresh waves of grief washed over Hope as she remembered that he wouldn't call—not today or ever. She closed her eyes and two tears slipped out. Surely someday, she thought miserably, she would run out of tears.

She took her sorrow and confusion to the One who knew both her heart and Charles's. *If You want me to let him go, Lord, You're going to have to show me how to do it. I'm so frightened for him that I just want to hold him tighter. I thought—and Gramps thought—that he was to be one of Yours....*

"Sweetheart, it's Pastor Bill."

Hope opened her eyes and saw her mother standing in front of her with the cordless phone. She took the phone and spoke into it. "It's nice of you to call," she said listlessly.

"I have some news," the pastor said. "It's very *good* news, but it's going to shock you a little. Are you ready for it?"

Her eyes widened. "Yes," she said faintly. "What is it?"

"Hope, Dr. Hartman came to see me this morning."

"Charlie?" She could find no other words for her amazement.

"Yes." The pastor's voice trembled with eagerness. "It's wonderful news, Hope—everything's all right with Charles. He was ready, finally, and he gave in to God."

Hope's face crumpled. "Charlie?" she whispered. "Oh!" The pain in her chest was nothing to her now. Her profound relief could be expressed only by sobbing, so she did that.

Clearly alarmed, Grace took the telephone from her. "Bill, what's happened?" she demanded. She listened for a moment, murmured something into the phone and hung up. "Oh, Hope!" she said incredulously. "It's wonderful!" Her voice shook with excitement. "He said Charles is on his way here. I'll wait to let him in and then I'll take Bob for a nice long walk, okay?"

Hope was still too moved to speak, so her mother took her hand and offered a prayer of awed thanks. She said a quick "amen" as they heard Charles's car in the drive-way. "I'll tell him to come right in," Grace said. "And I'll see you later."

As her mother left, Hope again bowed her head. *It's okay that he doesn't love me. What I couldn't bear was his not loving You. Thank you for this wonderful gift. But, Lord, don't let him go to San Diego. He needs to be close to Tom and he needs to reconcile with his family. Don't let him be afraid that I'll cling to him. I won't pester him anymore. I'll be content now that he's safe.*

The front door opened and Hope looked up to see the answer to her prayers. He wore jeans and a white dress shirt with rolled-up sleeves. He was unshaven, and from the state of his hair, she guessed he'd pushed his fingers through it a time or two. But he had never looked more handsome.

"Hello, kid," he said softly. "May I come in?"

She gave him a tremulous smile.

He stepped inside and closed the door, but he didn't approach her. Biting his lower lip, he looked like a ner-vous schoolboy in a principal's office. "I'm not heart-less," he said in a low voice.

She shook her head, not trusting her voice.

"You've known that all along," he stated.

She nodded.

He licked his lips. "That's why you wouldn't let me go."

It required a tremendous effort for Hope to speak past the enormous knot in her throat. "You had come so far," she managed. "I was afraid you would slip back, out of reach, and be lost forever. How could I let you go?"

He slid his hands into his pockets and stared at the floor. "But that stubborn loyalty cost you dearly, didn't it? Hope, 'thank you' sounds ridiculously inadequate," he said huskily.

No, it was plenty good enough for her. Her heart overflowed with gratitude and she was afraid she was about to cry again, so she said nothing at all.

"You stuck by me," he said, his voice not quite steady, "but I abandoned you twice." He looked up, meeting her eyes, and she was astonished to see his were shining with unshed tears.

He swallowed so hard she could hear it across the room. "Hope, I swear to you, whatever happens, I'll never turn my back on you again. Unless…you don't want me now?" He winced like a man expecting to receive a blow.

It took Hope a moment to understand why he was so nervous: he was afraid she didn't love him anymore. But why on earth would he be worried about that, when he didn't—

Or *did* he?

A delicious tingle spread through her body as she looked into his worried eyes and saw something so impossibly wonderful that she'd never even allowed herself to dream about it.

She dared to ask. "Do you love me, Charlie?"

Wide-eyed, he nodded. "Is that…all right with you?" Without waiting for an answer, he rushed on. "Because if it isn't, I'll understand. I don't deserve it, after everything, and I wouldn't blame you for changing your mind. I just want you to be happy, Hope, and—"

"Charlie…" She began a protest, but was unable to halt the raging river of words that flowed from him.

"—I'll do anything you say. Just tell me what you want. Please tell me what to do now."

And he called *her* a chatterbox, she thought in amusement. She arched an eyebrow at him. "Are you finished?"

He hung his head. "No, there's more," he said. "I

have to tell you how sorry I am. For everything. I hope you can forgive me for hurting you. And I want to thank you for showing me the way to God.'' He looked up. ''That's all. Should I leave now?''

''No. You should come over here and kiss me.''

His amazement showed plainly on his face. ''But…you can't love me,'' he objected.

She lifted her chin, defying him. ''Oh? Is there a law against it?''

His relief was almost comical as the breath he had been holding came out in an audible rush. ''There probably ought to be,'' he admitted as he approached the sofa and carefully lowered himself to sit next to her.

Hope shivered deliciously as his long, graceful fingers touched her left earlobe, then lightly traced the line of her jaw before exploring her sensitive lips in a way that made coherent thought impossible.

She closed her eyes, waiting for his kiss. When she felt his warm breath against her face, flutters of delight raced up her spine. But nothing *else* happened. What was going on? Why wasn't she being kissed breathless?

She opened her eyes. Yes, he was still there, just two inches away. ''What are you doing?'' she whispered.

''Taking my time,'' he murmured. ''Savoring the moment.''

She was incredulous. ''Well, stop it!''

He did. Without further delay his mouth settled right where she wanted it. If she had been able to think at all, she would have agreed that it was worth waiting for.

A minute later she pushed her forehead against his neck and sighed. *Just let the world stop here,* she thought. Nothing could ever be more perfect than this moment.

And then the world *did* stop. It came to a crashing halt as Charles spoke in her ear and ruined everything.

"You have to marry me," he said urgently. "You just have to."

Hope's heart pounded, wild with frustration. Couldn't he have held her a little longer, kissed her again? Did it have to end so soon? "I can't marry you," she said miserably.

He leaned away from her and looked into her eyes. *"What?"*

Her hands fell to her lap, where they twisted and fought. "I can't," she said woodenly, afraid to look at him. "I've told you before."

"But you love me."

"Yes," she agreed sadly. "But I can't get married. Please don't ask me again." She gave a quick, tiny shake of her head and stared at the hands in her lap. "I'm sorry," she whispered.

He sighed deeply and pressed her head against his shoulder.

"Please, Charlie," she choked. "I just need—"

"Shhh," he interrupted, stroking her hair. His voice was infinitely gentle. "I know you, Hope. I know what you need."

He held her silently, and as she grew calmer she became aware of the steady thudding of his heart. She flattened her palm against his warm, solid chest, drawing strength from him as she allowed herself to remember the night Trevor Daniels had broken her heart....

She'd waited until her parents were asleep, then she'd gotten out of bed and removed the torn yellow dress from its hiding place on her closet shelf. She'd stuffed it into a paper bag and had sneaked out to the garage.

She buried the bag in the middle of a full trash can, then tiptoed back to her room and quietly cried herself to sleep. She would never wear yellow again.

At breakfast she explained the bruise on her cheek by

*saying she'd been hit with a basketball in phys-ed class.
That was partially true—she'd actually been hit on the
side of the head, but nobody at school would remember
that. The bruises on her upper arms were easy to hide
under long sleeves.*

And only God could see the bruises on her heart.

*Three weeks later, Trevor was dead. Supported by her
father's arm, Hope had walked on unsteady legs towards
the casket. Taking a deep breath, she'd peered into the
casket, assuring herself that he was really gone.*

And that he could never hurt her again....

Hope shivered and Charles put his hand under her chin,
lifting her face to study it. He drew a long breath, holding
it for a couple of seconds before he asked, in a voice
thick with emotion, "Did a man hurt you?"

She nodded, and with the movement of her head two
tears fell. Charles watched their slow progress down her
cheeks. "Tell me what happened," he urged.

She trembled violently. "I can't," she whispered,
knowing that by *not* telling, she had just explained everything. She sucked her bottom lip in a futile attempt to
stop the quivering of her chin.

He reached for her hand. His voice was all tenderness.
"Who was it, Hope?"

She took a ragged breath. "My b-boyfriend. Trevor."

"When?"

She wiped her cheeks with the back of her free hand.
"Just before my s-seventeenth birthday."

"You never told anyone, did you?"

Almost imperceptibly, she shook her head.

"Why not?"

Her anger flared, and she turned it on him. "How
could I? It was all my fault! How could I tell my father
that I—"

"No!" he said forcefully, making her heart jump. "It

is *never* the woman's fault. Nobody deserves it, Hope. Not ever.''

''But it…must have been my fault,'' she said brokenly, although she was less certain now. ''Because I…'' she faltered.

''Why?'' he spoke harshly. ''Because of the way you let him kiss you? Some provocative thing you said? You might have been unwise, but nothing could excuse what he did to you.''

''But you don't understand!'' she cried bitterly. ''I let him in the house when nobody was home. It was against the rules, but I thought it would be exciting to be alone with him and—''

''So you made an error in judgment,'' Charles interrupted, reaching for her other hand. ''You disobeyed your parents. But Hope, that's *all* you were guilty of.'' He raised both of her hands to his mouth and kissed them. ''It wasn't your fault.''

For the first time she began to believe it. She watched in wonder as Charles closed his eyes and pressed his mouth hard against the hands he held. ''It wasn't my fault,'' she echoed softly, tasting the words for the first time. She shook her head. ''But he died, Charlie. He got drunk and ran his car into a tree. And I wasn't even sorry! I had been afraid that he would hurt me again, so after he was gone I felt…safe.''

''That's understandable,'' Charles soothed. She withdrew a hand to wipe her wet cheek, but he still held the other one to his mouth. He spoke against it and his words were muffled. ''Let it go, Hope. Don't let it matter anymore.''

He let go of her hand and carefully wrapped his arms around her. ''Hope, I love you,'' he murmured in her ear. ''You're a beautiful woman, inside and out. Please say you'll do me the honor of becoming my wife. I promise to give you all the tenderness you deserve. I'll make you forget everything that—''

She pushed him away. "But he hurt me!" she whimpered, dropping more tears. "He was angry because he thought I was teasing him. He hit me and…and then…it was so *awful!*"

Charles kissed the tears from her hot, damp cheeks. "I'll never hurt you, Hope. I love you."

She sighed and leaned against him. "I want to marry you, Charlie. But I'm afraid, and I can't help it."

"I know," he said. "So I'll just stick around until you stop being afraid. I'll wait a year, two years…whatever you want. I swear I'll do whatever it takes to make you happy."

She raised her face to him and his kiss was unbelievably sweet. It was warm and comforting, healing. When she looked into his soft eyes, she understood that he really *would* wait, as long as she needed him to.

She leaned her forehead against his chin. "Oh, Charlie, we're a ridiculous pair, aren't we? The man who could never fall in love and the woman who would never marry!"

He kissed her ear. "Well, I've definitely fallen in love. So the only question is—are you going to get married?"

His mouth was still against her ear, so Hope knew he was holding his breath again. She wondered how long he could do it, but this was probably not the kindest time to experiment. She'd have the rest of her life to learn that about him, wouldn't she?

"Yes," she whispered. "I'm going to get married."

He sucked in a breath and let it out in a sigh, warm and shivery against her ear. "Oh, God—thank You," he breathed.

She pushed him away a little. "As for the rest, Charlie—I need some time."

"Of course you do," he agreed. "I won't pretend that I'm not eager. But I want you to know this—your acquiescence is never going to be enough for me. I won't marry you until I believe you want it as much as I do."

She was coming closer with every heartbeat.

He kissed her temple. "I should go now."

She wound her arms tightly around his neck, oblivious to the pain the movement caused her. "No, not yet!"

"Hope," he said reasonably, "you're exhausted." He brushed her hair away from her face. "I want you to rest for a while. Please? I'll come back later. But right now I have to call the hospital and I want to see Tom."

A fresh surge of joy overpowered her as she thought of Tom. He would be ecstatic over this news.

Charles smiled tenderly. "Will you pray with me?"

She trembled in his arms. "I'm too excited to think of anything to say!"

Still careful of her ribs, he moved closer, whispering against her hair. "Well, couldn't we just tell Him that?"

Charles meant to pay attention, he really did. He was a brand-new Christian and here he was in church, hearing a sermon meant to instruct him in living a godly life.

His eyes were fixed on a water spot on the ceiling of the small sanctuary. *Surely you understand that I can't concentrate on a sermon when my heart is doing these cartwheels,* he said to his God. *First You thaw my heart and draw me to You, then you give me the woman I love more than my own life. And You have captured my brother's heart, as well! Who am I that You would do all this for me? I'm afraid I will burst from the joy of it!*

Hope leaned her head against his shoulder and sighed. The service was only half over, but she was already tired.

She'd come home from the hospital just yesterday, and Charles had strongly advised her to skip church this morning. He understood what it meant to her, going to church with him and Tom and her mother, but it was still a bad idea. Then he'd seen the disappointment in those lovely sapphire eyes and he'd given in. Had he ever been able to say no to Hope?

Yes. In fact he had done it twice. But yesterday afternoon she had commanded him never to think about that again, so those times didn't count.

She'd wanted to sit in the comfortable padded pew, so Charles had parked her wheelchair and scooted her in between her mother and himself. He was glad of that now because when he slipped his arm around her, she moved closer to his side and rested her hand just above his knee. He wondered briefly whether it was proper to sit so close in church, but Hope's mother had seen the move and was smiling indulgently.

He whispered in Hope's ear. "I can't concentrate on the sermon at all."

"I can't, either!" she shot back.

His eyes strayed to her mouth as she spoke and he was immediately sorry he'd looked. He turned his head and caught his bottom lip sharply between his teeth. Here he was in church, supposedly listening to a sermon, and all he could think about was covering that luscious pink mouth with his own.

The Sunday bulletin slipped out of Hope's open Bible and floated to the floor. Tom leaned forwards and picked it up, handing it back to Charles with a smile. "I'm so happy," he whispered. "For all three of us. And for Susan."

Charles nodded, blinking moisture from his eyes as he stared at the bulletin he grasped between his fingers and thumb. Something in bold print caught his eye. "Flowers have been placed on the altar today by the children of our late brother John Seltzer, in honor of his birthday."

Susan wasn't the only resident of heaven Charles was eager to see again. He looked forwards to seeing Gramps because he had a question for the man: *How did you know?*

"I think we'd better skip Sunday school," Charles said to Hope as the church service ended.

"Yes," she agreed, sounding as exhausted as she looked.

They took her home, and after Grace helped her undress and get into bed, Charles went in to wish her sweet dreams. When he leaned down to kiss her lightly, she favored him with a sleepy smile. His heart lurched and he wondered how he'd managed to make himself believe for so long that he didn't love her.

Her eyes closed but he couldn't bring himself to turn away from her. He shrugged out of his coat and yanked off his tie, carelessly tossing both at the rocking chair by the window. Then he slipped off his shoes and eased himself onto the bed.

Sitting with his back against the headboard, he adjusted pillows until Hope was in a comfortable position and he could put his arm under her head. She barely opened her eyes, but she made a soft sound of contentment and snuggled close. When her breathing was deep and regular Charles leaned his head back, absently watching the slow-moving ceiling fan as he gave thanks to God.

Grace looked in. Her eyebrows went up a little, but she smiled. Charles spoke softly. "I'm not budging, Grace. If you insist on chaperoning, pull up a chair."

Her smile widened. "Oh, I think I can trust you."

Yes, she could trust him. He would die before he'd ever hurt Hope again. He would wait for her, and even if their wedding day never came, he would have no grounds for complaint. Because he didn't deserve her, never *could* deserve her. That she loved him was pure grace—an unmerited gift. Like the salvation God had granted him, it was completely unearned, absolutely undeserved. But, oh! It was so gratefully received!

He spent almost two hours in prayer and meditation. He needed to make a number of changes in his life, he knew. There were so many things he wanted to do differently now, for God and for Hope. He couldn't wait to get started.

She stirred in his arms and her eyelashes fluttered. She gave a small sigh of pure pleasure. "Am I dreaming?"

He offered to pinch her.

She yawned. "I'd rather have a kiss, if you don't mind."

He didn't mind a bit.

Her hands cupped his face for a moment before her fingers wandered into his hair. "I want to marry you, Charlie," she said against his mouth. "Next month, okay?"

No. He was prepared to wait for her, however long it took. He would show her how gentle he could be, how patient. He would make her understand that she was worth waiting for. "I thought we agreed that you needed some time," he countered.

"Oh, I've had enough time."

"Yes, a whole day." He laced his words with gentle sarcasm.

She snuggled closer. "Did I kiss you just now?"

"Um…" He pretended to think about it. "Yes. I seem to recall something along those lines."

With one finger she traced his bottom lip. "Was it nice?"

She had to be kidding. A kiss like that was worth dying for. "You *know* it was nice," he murmured.

"Did my kiss seem at all ambivalent?"

He didn't see where this was going. "Not to me, it didn't. You appeared to be extremely interested in what you were doing." He fingered a lock of her dark hair. "Just what are you trying to say?"

She tilted her head back and gave him a long, steady look. "I'm not afraid of you, Charlie," she said, her bright blue eyes shining with confidence. "Not the tiniest bit."

He noted that her gaze didn't falter. "There's no reason for you to be afraid," he said, dropping a butterfly-soft kiss on the tip of her nose. "I am a Charlie, after all."

"A Charlie among Charlies," she corrected. "Do you believe it now?"

He buried his face in her soft, fragrant hair. "Hope, I'll believe anything you tell me to."

Chapter Seventeen

"What kind of wedding do you want?" Charles asked Hope as they swayed gently on the porch swing. She pursed her lips and stared at him, considering.

She sat sideways with a large cushion behind her back. Charles held a pillow on his lap, her broken foot resting on top of it. Her right foot was flat against the seat of thè swing, and Charles was using her raised knee as an armrest. They'd been sitting like that for half an hour, both of them too comfortable to move.

It was early Sunday evening and more dark clouds were moving in, dropping the temperature. When a fresh breeze ruffled Hope's hair, she shivered and Charles yelled, "Hey, Mom! Bring us a quilt, will you?"

"Coming," Grace Evans sang cheerily. A moment later she arrived with the quilt and arranged it over Hope. "Will there be anything else, Your Majesties?"

Charles smiled up at her. "No, I think we're perfectly content, thanks."

Hope smiled dreamily. She *was* perfectly content. She closed her eyes and once again gave silent thanks to God.

"So, what kind of wedding?" Charles asked after Grace had gone back inside. "If you really want to be married next month we'd better start making some decisions. And will you have any objection to my paying for it?"

"None at all," she said slyly. "Just as long as you're willing to make the same deal we did for my evening gown."

"That was nothing. Let's make it a little more interesting, shall we?"

Hope loved this game. "*How* interesting, exactly?"

"You tell me."

She gave him a wicked grin. "Charlie, you know I'm going to milk you for every penny I can get to send to mission organizations. So why don't you just tell me what you can afford?"

The light in his eyes died suddenly and was replaced by his old wary look.

"Charlie, what is it?" she asked urgently. A nameless fear tightened her throat.

He hesitated. "I never actually spelled it out for you, but I thought…" He shook his head. "Hope, I have a *lot* of money," he said carefully.

Of course he had a lot of money. He was a brilliant surgeon who probably pulled down more green stuff in a single year than she would see in—well, a whole *lot* of years.

Not only that, but his family was loaded. He would come into a bundle someday, and although she knew without a doubt he'd disregard his parents' wishes and split that inheritance with Tom, there would still be enough money to scare the socks off Hope, judging solely by that monster house the Hartmans lived in. "I know you have money."

"No, you don't," he argued. "You don't know that I inherited a considerable fortune from my aunt."

Of course Tom had mentioned that inheritance, but Hope had assumed it was just a nice little nest egg. Now she began to worry. "You don't mean you're rich like your parents?" She shook her head as if that might convince him.

"Actually, I have quite a bit more than my parents do," he apologized. "Tom made me buy technology stocks years ago, then he got me out again before that balloon burst. As I told you, he's a fiscal genius."

Awestruck, Hope searched Charles's face for some sign that he was kidding. She found none. Her heart fluttered wildly and she raised her hand to her forehead. Her vision began to blur, so she closed her eyes.

She'd never really thought about his money. She knew he was "rich," but to her that simply meant he never had to balance his checkbook or ask the price of anything.

This wasn't rich. This was something else entirely. Something frightening. How could she ever live in his world? In her mind she viewed a slide show of terrifying images: monster houses with elaborate security systems. Long limousines and heavy diamond necklaces and endless, mindless champagne-guzzling at charity galas. And bodyguards for the children.

She opened her eyes and was startled by the haunted look in his. He spoke softly, sadly. "Oh, Hope. Have we overcome the other obstacles just to get hung up on money?"

When she didn't answer, he raked his fingers through his hair and looked away from her. "Why does it worry you? I'm the same man I was five minutes ago."

"But I never guessed you were that…rich." She almost choked on the word.

"Please, Hope," he said in a low voice. "Don't let the money make a difference to you. Why should it change anything?"

It would change *everything*. Didn't he see that? It would change *her,* and she didn't think she'd like the new, rich Hope. Maybe Charles wouldn't, either.

But God had done so much to bring them together. Couldn't she trust Him for this, too? "All right," she said firmly. "It will take some getting used to, that's all."

His head rolled back and he stared at the porch ceiling. "You had me scared for a minute. But after everything I've put you through, I could never blame you for turning your back on me."

Compassion squeezed Hope's heart. Did he honestly imagine she could turn her back on him? Hadn't she proved her devotion?

A flash of insight told her deep wounds like his would not heal overnight, although the process had definitely begun. The doubts and fears he'd harbored all his life would require love and patience to dispel. But Hope had both. "Charlie, I won't turn my back on you," she promised. "Not ever."

Being careful of the cast on her foot, he moved closer. He kissed her so tenderly, she felt as if all the life had been drawn out of her body and replaced with his.

"To backtrack a little," he said cautiously, "I was planning to make some substantial gifts in celebration of our marriage. Tom's researching a few mission organizations for me, but maybe you have some suggestions?"

Things were coming into sharper focus now. She ought to have known Charles would have better ideas than diamond necklaces and mindless champagne-guzzling. "That's wonderful, Charlie!" she said. "But I'll bet you give away a lot of money, don't you?"

"Well, I—"

"Charlie!" she interrupted. "It was *you*, wasn't it?
You gave the last three hundred thousand to the building
fund!"

He hurried to explain. "I only did it because I wanted
to see your eyes shine when Pastor Bill announced the
money had come in."

"But you missed it! You were in Mexico when he
announced it."

He touched her nose with his finger. "And did your
eyes shine?"

"Probably. I was deeply moved."

"Well, I actually gave only two hundred and ninety-
nine thousand, nine hundred and fifty-eight dollars. That
left a difference of—"

"Forty-two dollars!" Hope squealed. "So we did it
together! Oh, thank you." She sighed. "What else have
you been doing behind my back, I wonder?"

"Before we get married we'll have some frank discussions about money," he promised. "But right now I'd
rather kiss you."

She gazed into his calm eyes and shook her head helplessly. "I love you, Charlie." Catching the faintest whiff
of his spicy aftershave, she leaned closer to enjoy his
scent. Nose-to-nose with him, she looked into his eyes
and saw green flecked with gold, miniature Impressionist
paintings. She told him that and he chuckled.

"You must be in love, kid."

"Oh, I am! Didn't I say that just a minute ago?"

"I'm forgetful," he lied. "Better tell me again."

She wasn't in the mood to verbalize, so she showed
him, instead.

"Wow," said Charles after a few moments. He cleared
his throat and stared at her. "Hope, that was..." He
shook his head quickly. "We'd better get back to making
wedding plans."

"If you insist," she said under her breath.

"I think I'd *better* insist," he muttered. He cleared his throat again. "Where was I? Oh, yes—as for the guest list, there won't be too many on my side. My parents and grandfather, of course, although I'll be surprised if my parents come. We'll pray about that, shall we?"

Hope leaned against him and nodded. "Isn't God wonderful?"

"Yes. And I am profoundly grateful that He sent you to me." Charles pushed her hair away from her neck, making a bare place to kiss. Then he whispered in her ear. "Thank you for smashing my taillight."

"It was my pleasure, Dr. Hartman."

On Monday evening a new ring sparkled on Hope's left hand. As Charles and her mother cleaned up the dinner dishes, Hope sat at the kitchen table, absently twirling a lock of hair around her right index finger as she admired the twinkling blue stone on the third finger of her other hand.

Late that afternoon Charles had pushed her wheelchair into a private room in a jewelry store where an obsequious salesman tried to interest them in diamonds just a couple of sizes smaller than golf balls. Noticing Hope's increasing discomfort, Charles had asked the salesman to excuse them for a few moments.

When the man left, Charles turned to Hope. "What do you want, love?" he inquired softly, his marvelous hazel eyes full of tender concern. "Just tell me," he urged, stroking her arm.

She didn't know anything about diamonds. She didn't know how to choose one. "I don't like all these big, flashy things," she said, "and I—"

"It's okay," he soothed, tucking a strand of her dark hair behind her ear. "Don't worry about what anyone else expects. You don't have to get the most expensive thing in the store just because you can. Do you see anything you like?''

She did. She pointed to a ring in the glass case before them. It was an oval-shaped blue stone with a triangle of diamonds on either side in a simple gold mount. ''I think that blue one is beautiful, and it's not so big that I'd be embarrassed to wear it. It's a sapphire, isn't it? Would that be all right?''

''It's lovely,'' he had agreed. ''Just the color of your eyes.''

Now Hope smiled at the ring on her finger. It was beautiful without being showy. Perhaps it wasn't the traffic-stopping sparkler people would expect a rich man's fiancée to wear, but Hope loved it.

Sneaking up behind her, Charles leaned down to nibble her ear. She tilted her head to one side so he could kiss her neck.

As he did she held up her hand and turned it, watching in delight as the six tiny diamonds flashed fire and the sapphire winked at her. ''It's pretty, isn't it?''

Charles made a soft sound of agreement and she felt a delicious flutter of happiness in her chest. ''You're not even looking at it,'' she accused.

''You go ahead and admire your little treasure,'' he said complacently. ''I've got mine in my arms.''

She sat perfectly still, thrilled by the sound of his breath against her ear. It tickled her that he was a dedicated neck-nuzzler. She never would have guessed that testy Dr. Hartman, of all people, would turn out to be so affectionate. She told him that and he laughed.

''I never was before,'' he asserted. ''You did it to me.''

It was time for him to leave for the hospital, so he

kissed her one last time. "Give it back, will you, love?" he murmured. "I've missed having it."

She didn't need to ask what he meant. She reached under the neckband of her T-shirt and grasped the braided silver chain. She pulled it over her head, then slipped it over his.

To help her handle the wedding expenses, Charles gave Hope a credit card and saw to it that her anemic checking account received a massive infusion of cash. She wasn't yet able to drive, but they'd been looking at new cars for her. They finally decided that she should have Charles's car, which felt safe and familiar to her. He would buy a new car for himself.

It was exciting to have money for everything she wanted, but Hope was still apprehensive about marrying such a rich man. She confided to her mother that she was worried about becoming a different person after she was married.

Her practical mother set her straight. "Sweetheart, you will face trials and temptations that I can't begin to imagine," said Grace Evans. "Just keep your eyes on the Lord. And you can look to your husband for an example. Charles may not have been brought up in a Christian home, but somehow he has managed to acquire some very solid values. He doesn't live extravagantly, even though he could. That says a lot about his character."

Fingering her lovely sapphire ring, Hope nodded thoughtfully.

Grace leaned forwards and patted her daughter's knee. "Don't you see? You're worried about living in what you call 'his world,' but, sweetheart, he's not asking you to. Charles isn't interested in glitz and glamour."

It was true. Charles didn't have an extravagant bone in his body. They weren't planning a three-month world tour for their honeymoon—they were simply going to spend three days alone at his apartment. Then he'd go back to work and she'd finish her master's thesis and in a couple of months, they'd take two weeks off and go somewhere fun.

And they weren't going to live in a mansion, either. Charles had asked her to think about whether she wanted to build a new house or buy one with some history. She realized now that what he had in mind was not a monument to his vast wealth, but a real family home. Somewhere to hang a porch swing.

In the three weeks since they'd become engaged, he had not presented her with a Greek island or an emerald necklace. His gifts had been flowers and books of poetry. Yesterday he'd brought her a CD of romantic classical music. He'd even written her a love letter; late one night at the hospital he'd filled seven pages of a prescription tablet with professions of his undying devotion.

"As the wife of a very rich man you'll have a unique set of challenges and responsibilities," her mother continued. "But I'm confident you'll bring honor to your husband and to God. Of course, Daddy and I will be praying for you. Trust God for everything, just as you have been taught."

Overcome with gratitude, Hope leaned her head against her mother's shoulder. "If only Charlie could have had parents like mine," she said wistfully. "Mom, they don't love him, not like you and Daddy love your children. It's so horribly sad."

Grace stroked her daughter's arm and spoke with a tenderness that soothed Hope's aching heart. "I know, sweetheart. But God gave Charles exactly what he needed to make him the dear man he is today. Don't you ever doubt that."

Chapter Eighteen

Hope's heels clicked noisily over the hardwood floor before going silent as she stepped onto an enormous Oriental carpet. In the middle of the room she stopped, resting her hands on her hips as she surveyed her husband's apartment.

It was not, as she had once imagined it would be, impossibly huge and extravagantly furnished. It was spacious, but not overwhelming. There was some lovely antique furniture and there were a dozen very good paintings; but for the most part the apartment had a Spartan feel. It cried out for a few homey touches, a plant here and perhaps a curtain there, but Hope liked it.

"It's just like you, Charlie," she said over her shoulder. "Quietly valuable."

He was behind her, chuckling softly as his arms encircled her waist and pulled her against him.

"It's odd that you never brought me here," she commented.

She felt him shrug against her. "You never asked to

see it," he said. "And I always preferred to be at your house."

Hope twisted slightly, looking up at him. "So, do you have a castle somewhere?"

"No. I've never had a house, but I want one now." He kissed her ear. "I want so many things now."

She covered his hands with hers and leaned her head back until it was cradled against his shoulder. "Tell me what you want, Charlie. Tell me everything that you want."

He was silent for a moment, then he drew a deep breath. "I want to rake leaves in our own backyard. I want to see Bob curled up by our fireplace and I want to smell apple tarts baking on rainy Saturday afternoons. I want to wake up to your smile every morning. I want several noisy little people who will call me 'Dad' and beg me to read storybooks and take them to ball games."

He turned her around to face him. Leaning his forehead against hers, he went on. "I want to rethink my position at the hospital and drastically cut my hours so I can be a real family man. I want to go to church every Sunday and learn how to please God. I want to see what you look like with silver hair and laugh lines. And when we're very, very old, I want to die knowing that walking through life together has brought us both closer to God."

He kissed her, long and slow, and when his mouth abandoned hers she moaned an incoherent protest and tried to entice it back. He leaned away from her, teasing her, his rich chuckle triggering a tiny explosion of delight deep inside her chest.

"Your turn, Hope." His low voice flowed over her like warm water as he caught her hands in his. "What do *you* want?"

What did she want? She wanted to die in his arms. How could he kiss her like…like *that*…and then imagine she would be capable of coherent speech? "Kissing," she blurted. "What I want is more kissing."

He raised her left hand to his lips, his warm eyes mesmerizing her as his mouth touched the two rings on her third finger. "Anything you say, Mrs. Hartman," he said complacently.

Several minutes later Hope unknotted his bow tie and tugged on the ends, pulling his head down until his nose pressed hard against hers. She looked straight into his eyes, giggling when she found it impossible to focus at such close range. "Did you like our wedding, Charlie?"

"I loved our wedding," he said. "It was perfectly sweet in every way. And I'm so glad my parents came."

It had been something of a surprise. Old Dr. Hartman had been looking forwards to the wedding, but right up to the last minute Hope had been afraid Charles's parents wouldn't come. Then Mrs. Hartman had rapped softly on the door of Hope's dressing room, bringing a gift—an exquisite pearl necklace that had belonged to Charles's great-grandmother, the beloved bride for whom the Hartman house had been built in 1917.

"Of course I'm delighted, but I wanted to wear *your* wedding pearls," Hope confided to her mother after Mrs. Hartman left them.

"No reason why you can't," Grace replied. She removed her own pearls from their velvet pouch and wound them around Hope's wrist, fastening the clasp to make a lovely bracelet.

So the Lord had worked everything out, and, holding tight to her father's strong arm so she wouldn't float away, Hope drifted happily down the aisle to take her place beside Charles.

The windows of the picturesque chapel had been thrown open to welcome the glorious September evening, and amid a hundred flickering candles and the incredibly sweet fragrance of gardenias, Charles and Hope were married.

Now as she stood in the safe circle of her husband's arms Hope silently thanked God for the thousandth time.

"By the way," Charles said, "did you see how well Tom and Claire were getting along? I believe he finally asked her out."

"He did," Hope said eagerly. "Dinner on Tuesday. Oh, Charlie, wouldn't it be great if—"

She was silenced with a soft kiss. "Let's just wait and see," he suggested. "I'd rather concentrate on our romance right now."

She didn't object.

"Such a lovely gown," he murmured, leaning away from her to appreciate the luscious white silk. "And so very fetchingly rumpled."

He kissed her again, then his hands were in her hair, his long fingers gently probing for the pins that held the graceful twists Claire had so painstakingly arranged. "This is pretty," he said. "I like all the white flowers in your dark hair. But I've been waiting all evening to do this."

He pulled a gardenia loose and touched her nose with it. Hope's eyes closed automatically as she inhaled the flower's heady scent. Charles dragged the cool, velvety blossom across her lips, over her chin, down her neck before opening his hand and letting the gardenia fall with a whispery plop to the floor.

More flowers and pins followed, raining softly all around Hope until her hair fell free, tumbling to her shoulders. Charles watched in openmouthed fascination, then he wove his fingers through her dark locks and pulled her close. "Hope..." he breathed softly, kissing both corners of her smile. He pressed his cheek against hers and spoke in her ear. "I love your name. It suits you perfectly."

She stood absolutely still, scarcely even breathing as she thrilled to the exquisite tenderness of the voice in her ear.

"Hope..." he said again. "You're like a warm burst of sunshine after a winter storm." He moved back a little to look into her eyes. "I was bitter and cold and my heart was so shrunken, I didn't even know I had one. But you took my hand and led me home. How can I ever thank God for sending you?"

With one finger she lazily traced the curve of his ear. "Well, the donations to the missionary society and the building fund made a nice start. And the checks you wrote this morning were even better," she said. She gave him an impish grin. "But I hear they could use some Bibles in Russia and my father was telling me the other day about some plans they have to build a clinic in—"

"Go ahead, Hope. Give it all away if you can." Sliding his hands out of her hair to cup her face, he slowly shook his head as if he just couldn't believe the treasure he held. "And when the last penny is gone, I will look into your sweet face and swear that I am still a very, very rich man."

* * * * *

Dear Reader,

It's a great feeling when you get to the last page of a romance novel and think, "Aw, isn't love sweet?" I hope you got a little goose bump when Charles and Hope were finally united in marriage.

But I hope for more than that. I hope when you close this book you'll take a few minutes to reflect on the power of true friendship, the virtue of steadfast loyalty, the value of selfless devotion. More than anything, I pray this story will bend your heart a little closer to God.

Yes, love is sweet. And God's love is the sweetest of all.

By the way, this is my first book. If you have enjoyed reading it and would like to give me a thrill, please stop by on the Web at www.BrendaCoulter.com and beg me to write more. You can also write to me c/o Steeple Hill Books at 233 Broadway, New York, NY 10279.

By His grace,

Brenda Coulter